HONG KONG BELONGERS

Simon Barnes is an award-winning sports journalist (*The Times, The Spectator*) and author of *Rogue Lion Safaris* and *Horsesweat and Tears*, as well as several books on wildlife and conservation. He lives in Suffolk.

SIMON BARNES

Hong Kong Belongers

HarperCollins*Publishers*

HarperCollins*Publishers*
77–85 Fulham Palace Road,
Hammersmith, London W6 8JB

A Paperback Original 1999
1 3 5 7 9 8 6 4 2

A catalogue record for this book
is available from the British Library

ISBN 0 00 651195 3

The extract on p. 234 from the poem 'Two Laments'
is reprinted from *Chinese Poems* translated by Arthur Waley
(Unwin Paperbacks, 1989, p. 30), courtesy of the Arthur Waley Estate.

Set in Sabon by
Rowland Phototypesetting Ltd,
Bury St Edmunds, Suffolk

Printed and bound in Great Britain by
Caledonian International Book Manufacturing Ltd, Glasgow

For Al and Les, with thanks,
and for CLW, with eternal gratitude (again)

PART I

CHRISTMAS

The past is another country: an aggressive, imperial power seeking constantly to invade and overwhelm the peace-loving present. Death is part of its nuclear arsenal, the midnight telephone a favourite tactic.

And so they were launched across space and through time, worries about the present – their daughters' ability to cope with a stay at their neighbours', the animals that were their livelihood – meeting in pitched battle with the unresolvable anxieties of the past.

Alan Fairs looked at his wife, marooned in a troubled doze at the window seat, about her neck the thin gold chain he had given her yesterday: her Christmas present, a Christmas not untouched by the shadow. He thought of the dolphin she had given him: carved on bone by an Eskimo, she said, a handsome little thing. She always gave him a dolphin, a tribute to the Christmas Day when they had met, a day not without its shadow.

He had twenty of these dolphins now, for she had marked their initial meeting with the first of these serial gifts. And now flying back: back in time, back to their meeting place, back to Hong Kong, back to Tung Lung, back to the past and its various moments of horror and shame: naked women; projectile vomiting; death by water – suddenly he found himself laughing silently. Laughing as the aeroplane grumbled on north and west to their destination, laughing at naked women and projectile vomiting, laughing at his own shame, laughing at Charles, who, wiping tears from his eyes, tears of laughter and agony, had said to him: 'Sweet Jesus, what an indescribably sordid scene.'

Madness.

9

He saw without willing it, and with quite extraordinary clarity, the body of Karen Song. Sitting on his, or in fact his wife's, cushions, drinking tea, both of them quite naked. He saw her reach for the tea, jasmine tea she had made herself, for he, also naked, was quite unable to do so. It was her voice that he had heard on the midnight telephone, half-cockney and wholly Chinese. Karen Song as was: Karen James now, of course, Karen James for nearly twenty years. He had never told James of their naked night: had never dared. The shame was too great.

The telephone had splintered the silence. That had once been a favourite phrase of Alan's, for it was what James Bond's telephone did when M needed him. And for once it was more or less appropriate: the silent night shattered by the insistent bell. And by about the fifteenth ring, Alan had made it across the warmth of the Christmas night, a sarong tied about his waist. He held the receiver like a weapon. But it was not M, with a summons to take on Smersh and Spectre: it was Karen Song, a call to take on an enemy more fearful than either. Sorry to wake you, she said. Got the time difference muddled, thought it worked the other way for New Zealand. That's all right, Karen, good to hear your voice again. And sorry, Alan, but I've got bad news to bring you . . .

And, thirty-six hours later, he and his wife were roaring towards the jaws of the past.

'How did he die?' she asked as he held her, her face, lit only by the night from the open window, looking almost as it did that Christmas twenty years previously. In tears then, too, of course.

'More or less of a slight chill,' Alan said, 'from what Karen told me. He'd not been well for a few weeks, but nothing serious. That's how it seemed, anyway. Series of colds and flu and coughs. Just took to his bed, she said. And sort of faded away.'

'He died of a broken heart,' she said. 'I always wondered how Dad was going to cope with 1997. Now I know.'

She had discussed the matter, a trifle obsessively, over the course of Christmas Day and Boxing Day, as people with a sudden grief must. She talked of 1997, and how Hong Kong's return to Chinese hands was the final invalidation of the dead man's troubled life. Alan had objected that the handover did not take place for another six months, but she said that it had clearly been impossible for him to live into a calendar year that bore that ominous number: 1997: it was the rejection of himself by the people he had called his people.

Noble savages! Alan remembered the dead man's orations on the subject, and the trouble the phrase had once made for him. My people are noble savages, Alan. And then he had given Alan the keys to a new life, a new freedom, and one he had never thought to end, settling into his Chinese village, an aggressive imperial power himself, and embarked on a course of delighted folly which he believed no 1997 could ever end.

'What did you *do* out there?'

A question his neighbour Brett had asked him. They had gone to Brett's for Christmas lunch, the usual barbie beside the pool. Alan, who never minded an excuse not to drink, had offered to be the abstemious one and to bring the horses in that evening, while his family stayed on. Brett, neighbourly and perhaps wanting a break from his own party, had driven him the few minutes between their next-door places. He watched Alan's calm, quiet handling of the beasts. Afterwards, he had accepted a beer, and listened to Alan's tale of sudden death and his wife's need to return to Hong Kong for the funeral.

'Are you going?'

'Wish I could. Can't afford the fare.'

Brett snapped his fingers, a normally irritating habit of his. 'Tell you what. I wanted to do a Hong Kong piece in the paper, 1997 and all that. Why don't you go out there and write it? Can't afford expenses, but I'll pay for the piece, and that should cover most of your costs.'

Brett was editor of the local daily newspaper; Alan did two days a week chief-subbing the Sunday edition. It was an unusual arrangement that allowed Alan to spend most of his time with the horses.

'That's a kind thought, Brett.'

'What did you do out there?'

'Now you've got me.' But he talked a little about it: the year of madness, the island of folly.

'Don't you miss it? The thrill of the mysterious East and all that?'

Alan gestured to the extensive fields, the line of horses, heads nodding over the doors. 'Try meeting the payments on this lot,' he said. 'That can get pretty thrilling.'

'I thought it was a pretty good living you made.'

'Nope. Not really much of a livelihood. Not a bad life, though.'

Brett, not being English, took a moment to realise that this was understatement. 'Yeah, I see. Your own spread.'

'Our own island.'

Hardly drunk at all, Alan Fairs raised his glass to wish a happy Christmas to the junk that was puttering gently into the harbour. 'Happy Christmas, junk,' he said softly, glorying in his solitude.

The junk bore no batwing sail, but that would have been too self-righteously picturesque. It was enough that the boat was shaped like a Spanish galleon, and that it swung its high square backside away from him. It was enough that the island of Tung Lung rose up behind it: its high and pointy hills. Until today, Alan had assumed that such hills were a graphic convention, a precious affectation of the painters of Chinese scrolls. Now he could see that it was a question of pedantic accuracy.

'I am sitting here, drinking beer in a Chinese scroll,' he said to himself. He drank a little more, for the glory of the thought.

He had journeyed here from the island of madness, or Hong Kong. In less than an hour he had passed from the great harbour and its endless castles of glass, to this other place, this toy harbour, its jolly bouncing boats and steep little hills crammed with elven dwellings.

He had resolved to turn down all Christmas invitations in search of a proud self-sufficiency. In the event, no invitations had come, but this had ceased to cast a shadow over his day. He had lunched, beerily, alone and in perfectly Chinese splendour, at a restaurant on the far side of the island of Tung Lung. He had handled both chopsticks and the occasion with some élan, he thought. Afterwards, he had walked, somewhat dizzily, over the spine of the island, up the pointy hills and down the other side, until he had reached the island's second village. Here, he would soon be catching a ferry home – home! – to the island of madness, and his rather hateful flat in the Mid-Levels.

But he was in no hurry to make this retreat, for here on Tung Lung he felt like a conqueror. A red and white butterfly, the size of a bat, flapped about by his feet before dipping down to where the Christmas bounty of flowers bloomed out of sight. At a table beside him two young Chinese men played cards with cries of triumph and dismay, unmoved by the exoticism of their home. One man, grey-haired – unusual in the Chinese who dye their hair an iridescent black at the first hint of time's passage – sat in regal dignity, served Coca-Cola by the fat proprietor with understated deference. A scent of dead and dying fish was wafted towards them in little spurts, on occasional gusts of wind.

Alan turned his attention to the boats in the little harbour. The junk had moored at the small jetty on the far side, half a dozen more motor-junks were tied up together in the middle beside a cluster of portly sampans, on one of which a man in a black shirt worked with absorption. And alongside that, a strange craft, apparently two plastic canoes linked by a trampoline, the whole thing an offensive shade of yellow. Alan speculated on an unseaworthy experiment, lashed together by some eccentric, dashing Chinese youth from the village. Yet again he sipped, savouring warm air, chill beer, the little harbour, his glorious Christmas self-sufficiency: above all the sense of distance from Hong Kong. By making this brief journey to this outlying island, he felt he had achieved some kind of tenuous control. He placed his left ankle on his right knee, a very subtle form of self-celebration. It was the James Bond Position: Bond had once been photographed thus, in 'the sort of position only an Englishman would adopt'. Alan, on a dangerous mission overseas, was in control and, unshaken, was drinking San Miguel beer.

Smirking a little at this fancy, he became aware of a steady procession taking place behind him. He turned in his chair, looking back to the café from which he had bought his beer. Between him and the tubby young giant of a proprietor, who was lounging against the wall of his establishment, a tidal flow of people moved with single-minded determination along the larger jetty. Alan inspected them with fascination: island-dwellers moving out to Hong Kong for the evening; Hong Kongers returning home after a too-brief day of exile. Many seemed young, school-children, most of them clutching ferocious double-pointed spears three feet in length. Alan pondered their use without coming to any firm conclusion: perhaps Hong Kongers carried them as protection against the wild Tung Lung natives. Among these returning exiles, little motorised carts buzzed about dangerously, trolleys powered by loud Rotavator engines, guided with languid gestures by the young men who clasped the long, elegant handle-bars with the pomp of Hell's Angels. The people shoved hard, but without active malice.

A dismal hoot sounded from across the waters, and Alan turned to see the ferry approaching: dingy; white; two-storeyed. It bore on its funnel the letters HYF, for Hong Kong and Yauma-tei Ferry Company. This, according to his plans, was the boat that was to take him home, returning exile himself. He watched with disfavour as the boat came to a halt by the simple means of ramming the jetty wholeheartedly. It then performed a series of infinitely fussy forward and backward movements, with snarl-ing engine and repeated distant blasts of the whistle. It took an astonishing length of time. Then all at once the tide turned: the incoming wash of islanders returning home. Home: again the word pricked at Alan's heart.

He watched a stream of girls, dazzling nymphs all. Stragglers pushed their way undazzled against the flow. Others, family parties in their finery, walked cheerily, noisily back onto their island. They had, Alan guessed, been spending the day holi-daying, shopping, eating in Hong Kong, for in Hong Kong noth-ing closed, ever, not for Christmas nor for anything else. Alan raised his glass, intending to drain it in a final brave swallow, to run to the ferry, last one aboard, just as the gangplank was pulled away. But with the swallow half done, he lowered his glass. A weak defiance had seized him. Thus do our lives change for ever.

The ferry hooted once more, reproachfully, and began its effortful journey back to the island of madness. Leaving Alan on the island of Tung Lung. It was warm, and anyway he had on the back of his chair his bad jacket, an unfortunate purchase in purple tweed. And he had money, money enough for another beer, at any rate. He would watch the sun go down from this scrap of a café, from this table on the edge of the toy harbour, watch the sun go down behind his Chinese scroll.

It was then that the impossible happened. Ambling, strolling at his ease, in marked contrast to the babbling crowds that had preceded him, not so much a stroller as a *flâneur*, tall – an inch or two over six foot – clad in a suit of unnatural perfection but worn with a studied insouciance, a gweilo. A round-eye, a European, a foreign devil, and anyway, quite clearly an Englishman. There was a slim attaché case in his hand, a garment bag over his shoulder. By his side walked a Chinese boy, pushing a trolley on which stood two suitcases of imposing size and solidity. The gweilo – Alan already thought in the Hong Kong idiom – was smiling faintly to himself.

He turned into the café and, in a voice of unexpected harshness, shouted out a few words of Cantonese. The fat proprietor came out to meet him. The two shook hands and discoursed with some warmth. Then the gweilo turned away, laughing, throwing out some quip that made the proprietor laugh in turn. Still smiling to himself, he walked to the tables by the harbour. It was then that he noticed Alan. 'Good afternoon,' he said, all trace of coarseness gone from his voice.

'Hello,' Alan said. He saw with some surprise that the newcomer was a little younger than himself; for all that, his ease of manner and his maturity of expression left Alan rather intimidated. In this moment of awkwardness, he wished very much that he had caught the ferry that was now turning away to the north.

The man stopped at the adjoining table, a move nicely calculated to avoid any accusation of unfriendliness without seeming to force friendliness upon him. It was a moment of perfect Englishness. Before sitting, he hung his garment bag from a branch of the banyan tree that shaded their tables. He did so with an air of quiet delight, as if the tree had grown in that shape especially for his convenience, and he couldn't help feeling flattered by the attention. He then sat, unbuttoned the collar of his shirt

16

of virginal whiteness, and unknotted his tie. This he rolled around his fingers and slipped into the pocket of his jacket.

The proprietor approached him with a glass and a dewed bottle, and received courteous thanks in Cantonese. Then, with very careful attention, the gweilo poured liquid gold into tilted glass. He placed bottle and glass on the table, not drinking, savouring their beauty.

'Visiting the island?' he asked.

'Came out for lunch. Can't bear to go home.'

'My dear chap. Stay for ever. Beer?'

'Thank you.'

He filled Alan's glass with the same care with which he had filled his own. 'Well,' he said. 'Happy Christmas.'

'Happy Christmas.'

They drank.

'I'm André Standing.' This announcement took Alan by surprise. It was simply not English, neither the name nor the bare fact of its announcement. After the business of the man's choosing of his seat, Alan had expected to be playing by English rules. André, clearly, was English, yet not English. Alan played his own name in return; André asked: 'On holiday?'

'In a manner of speaking. I've just started work at the *Hong Kong Times*. We all got Christmas Day off, by a miracle, so I thought I'd spend it on Tung Lung.'

'Get on all right with old Simpson?' This unexpected dropping of his editor's name was disquieting.

'Only met him the once. Seems all right. Rather a change of pace after Fleet Street.' Alan was seeking to impress in his turn. 'What about yourself? What brings you out here?'

'My dear chap. I live here, you see.'

Alan was riven through the heart with envy. 'What do you do?'

'Well, I'm sort of an entrepreneur, really. Bit of import/export. Do a fair bit in your line too; I've been known to sell advertising space for the odd magazine. Take my card.' He pincered two fingers into his breast pocket and produced it. It was nicely engraved, a statement of class.

'Merchant,' Alan read.

'That seems to cover it, on the whole.'

'Very stylish.'

'Well, very Hong Kong, really. Or very Asia – I'm just back this minute, actually. Been in Seoul, South Korea, you know. Just for a few days, but did some very sweet business.'

'What sort of thing?'

'Oh, the usual stuff, you know. I'm interested in the pharmaceutical trade.'

'Oh.' Alan drank, from nervousness. André, observing this, called out again in Cantonese; the fat proprietor returned with two new bottles. He seemed greatly exhilarated, and clapped André on the shoulder several times. The two exchanged a series of surprisingly excited remarks, all in Cantonese, and then the proprietor withdrew, beaming. André, too, seemed tremendously bucked by the exchange.

'Good old Tung Lung,' he said, pouring his beer.

'It will make my flat in the Mid-Levels seem doubly poky tonight,' Alan said.

'Yes,' André said. 'I love it here. Don't suppose I'll ever move away. Most Europeans are just staying in Hong Kong for a while. How long have you been in Hong Kong? Standard Hong Kong question. But here on Tung Lung, I'm home. I have a nice flat, a nice boat, nice friends, a nice life. Nice Chinese girl – well, some days she's nice enough. But all thanks to this island here. Who cares if Ng's well runs dry and you have no water for a week? This is Tung Lung, and it simply doesn't matter.'

'Mm, yes, I envy you.' Alan thought all this was rather overdoing it, sympathetic though the message was. But then André, lowering his voice in a rather stagy manner, came down to it. 'In fact, I may be able to fix you up with a flat on Tung Lung. Do you like the sound of that?'

So that was what they had been talking about. 'My God. I'd adore it. But –'

'That's settled, then.'

'But what time does the last ferry leave Hong Kong in the evening?'

'Oh, late enough. Ten thirty.'

A thud of despair. 'No good. I'm a downtable sub; I don't finish work till eleven thirty. Three times a fortnight, I do a late turn, finish at three.'

'Oh really. I say, what a terrible bore. You're the sort of chap who'd do well here. Resign at once, come and join us out here.'

'Wonderful thought.'

'No, really, you can do it: moonlight flit on the job and the flat, take up residence here, start merchant-venturing about the place. I've got a row of contacts in your line of work. You'd be up to your eyes in business in no time. How about it?'

'André – I wish I could. But it's not possible right now.'

'Ah well. You're still new here, aren't you? You're not close enough to the edge yet. But you'll get there soon enough. I promise you that.'

Alan sat on the ferry drinking his beer. André had insisted on buying him a can for the journey. They had shaken hands warmly by the café, and then André had turned inland, attaché case in one hand, garment bag over his shoulder. Had he forgotten his suitcases? But perhaps he had arranged for someone to do the portering for him. That sounded André's style.

Alan looked back, the faint lights of Tung Lung fading behind him. Ah well. He would take his Boxing Day dinner at the Country Club with Bill and Wally, the other two Englishmen on the subs' desk. That is, if Wally was back from his trip to Bangkok. They had, in their way, been very decent to him. The question of the Country Club had come up on Alan's first day at the *Hong Kong Times*.

'But do you think they'll let him in, Bill, in that shirt?'

'I'll have a little word with the doorman.'

The occasion was the sub-editors' evening break. Alan accepted their invitation, flattered and a little flustered. Bill disrobed himself of his cardigan, which was baggy and leather buttoned; Wally removed his own generous maroon sweat shirt. Alan, who had not known to arm himself against the boreal chills of the *Times*'s air conditioning, merely stood. The wet warmth of Hong Kong greeted them as they left the building.

They led Alan not to the opulent doorway he had feared, but to a small grocery store a couple of hundred yards from the newspaper offices. Its owner, a wispy-bearded and gold-toothed ancient who looked like Lao-tzu, greeted them. Then, very spryly, he rolled a great wooden cartwheel from its resting place against the wall and unfolded from it four legs: at once it was revealed as a table. He next unfolded three stools; then, as the final touch of elegance, he placed a roll of lavatory paper on the table. He asked, in Cantonese that Alan could follow even then, if all three required San Lig, meaning San Mig, meaning San Miguel, the beer of Hong Kong. They did.

Cans served, Bill and Wally each helped himself to a sheet of lavatory paper and commenced the energetic cleaning of the can top. Alan, eyeing their every movement like a hobbledehoy at a banquet, followed them a beat behind. Satisfied, they pulled the ringpulls from their cans, tossed them lightly into the gutter and drank. 'Thank Christ,' Wally said. 'Why do we live here, God fuck it?'

Wally always wore a safari suit: trousers that matched in colour an epauletted, patch-pocketed, quasi-military garment that was neither jacket nor shirt. Alan was to learn that he had three of them, and that he wore them each for two days at a time. One was salmon pink, one pistachio green, the third pale dogshit. They were safe and conservative Hong Kong clothes. Wally was a slight man with a belly that travestied pregnancy.

'Got my flight fixed up for Christmas,' he said. 'A whole lovely bloody week in Bangkok. Thank Christ.'

'What does one do in Bangkok?'

'In Bangkok one gets fucking well fucked.'

Bill was quieter, bitterer. Wally spoke with a flamboyant, almost a romantic pessimism; in Bill, as time passed, Alan wondered if he would not sense despair.

'Why do we live here, God fuck it?' Wally asked again.

'Anywhere.'

'Soon be dead, anyway, thank Christ.'

'Downtable sub on the *Purgatory and Hell Gazette*,' Bill said. He was, Alan was to learn, a man of quite extraordinary professional competence. That afternoon, challenged by Wally, he had named the last three prime ministers of Belgium.

Alan knew sub-editing skills when he found them. He had done his time on local newspapers, subbed in Fleet Street and had contemplated seeking permanent employment within its fastness. But the combination of the end of a love affair and of his training prompted him to seek jobs abroad: Robert Simpson had offered him, sight unseen, a job on the *Hong Kong Times* on three months' trial. Thus the great adventure had begun.

Wally knew his job too, though he attacked it with the same savagery he brought to conversation. He called Soviet dissidents 'fucking troublemakers'; the Pope was always 'Popeye'; stories about the local police gave him especial delight. 'Listen to this: "A bullet was removed from his left kidney." Good on yer, PC Wong. Shot the bastard while he was running away, didn't he? "The suspect remains in critical condition." Course he does. They took the poor fucker to Queen Elizabeth Hospital; no one gets out of that kip alive.'

Alan did not reply. Well, he told himself, Hong Kong was what you asked for; Hong Kong is what you have got.

'Ah Christ, why do we live here, God fuck it?' Wally asked, taking another mighty pull from his beer.

'How long have you lived here, Wally?'

'Twelve years, Christ help me. I must be mad. Been a Hong Kong Belonger for five years now.'

'Belonger?'

'After seven years you can apply for Belonger status,' Bill said. 'Did it myself a couple of years back. Regularises the visa situation, means you can vote in municipal elections. Not that anyone ever does. Just an administrative convenience.'

'It's the day they throw away the fucking key,' Wally said.

That first expedition to the Country Club had been an initiation. Soon Alan was flinging his ringpull into the gutter without a backward glance, dining merrily and nightly on three cans of San Lig or Mig and a packet of peanuts. Remarkably good peanuts, which he would hull abstractedly, broadcasting the shattered halves into the street.

'What were you rowing with Johnny Ram about?' Bill had asked him on their last day at work, the night before Christmas Eve. There had been a slight, unseasonal chill in the air, and they had retained their air-conditioning-beating overgarments. Alan had bought himself a rather sporty top with a hood to wear in the office.

'Letters page,' Alan said. 'Unbelievable stuff. I suggested to Johnny that we really ought to leave it out. He was of a different opinion.'

'Opinion? Johnny? Do me a favour,' Wally said. 'Johnny doesn't have opinions. Other people have opinions, other people being Simpson. Know how the letters page is run? Simpson skims the letters that come in and scribbles instructions on 'em. Then he passes them to Johnny and Johnny does what he's told. What you were doing was asking him to walk into Simpson's office and say, Simpson, you silly bastard, this letter is bollocks.'

'Look at it this way,' Bill said. 'Can you imagine Moses going back up Mount Sinai with the tablets and saying, look, Jehovah, you silly bastard, can't you see that this commandment about coveting your neighbour's ox is bollocks? What was in the letter anyway?'

'Some lunatic from one of the outlying islands. He said that the people who lived there were noble savages. I thought that was a bit stiff.'

'So you subbed out the word "noble"?' Wally said.

'I said that no self-respecting newspaper would print such rubbish. I made him quite cross.'

'Nevertheless, you made a valid point about the *Hong Kong Times*,' Bill said. 'What did you do?'

'Par-marked it. Put "Noble Savage" in the headline, why not?'

'The boy learns wisdom,' said Wally.

'I think I know the old bugger you mean,' Bill said. 'Always writing to the paper. One of those. Lived here since the fall of Shanghai. Dedicated man.'

'They should send PC Wong over to his island to sort him out,' Wally said. 'Couple of slugs in the kidneys then over to the QE Hospital for the coup de grâce.'

Alan rose and purchased three more beers. They all tore, wiped, threw. Alan saw a sleek and graceful rat cross the street a few yards off, but knew enough not to pass comment. 'Johnny really was rather cross,' he said. 'He doesn't bear grudges, does he?'

'I'd like to fuck Eileen Sung,' Wally said. 'Did you see her in the newsroom this evening? That arse of hers in those red trousers. Jesus.'

'He won't complain to Simpson about Simpson's choice of staff,' Bill said. 'He won't go out of his way to help you, but he won't go out of his way to harm you. Either way it would be rocking the boat, and that is against everything that Johnny understands.'

'Don't rock the boat,' Wally said. 'They ought to print that on the front of the *Hong Kong Times*. Put it on the masthead, a bloody great banner supported by Simpson at one end and PC Wong on the other.'

'I get worried every now and then,' Alan said. 'I'd be in serious trouble if I lost the job.'

'Christ, you won't lose it,' Bill said. 'You can sub. Besides, no one gets fired.'

'What do you think this is?' Wally asked. 'A newspaper or something?'

'Just keep your head down,' Bill said. 'The one thing Simpson doesn't like is trouble. Promoted a step beyond his competence, just like Johnny Ram. Perfect way of making yes-men. What Johnny is to Simpson, Simpson is to the chairman. And the chairman is in the same situation *vis-à-vis* the board of Hong Kong Estates. And Hong Kong Estates owns the newspaper, as they own everything else around here. So – don't rock the boat.'

'I've had a change of heart about Eileen Sung,' Wally said. 'I'd like to bugger her.'

On Boxing Day Alan sat before another harbour with another bottle before him. The sun was going down and his legs were weary. This was because he had walked most of the length of Hong Kong Island. He had walked from the offices of the *Hong Kong Times* to Central, and there, turning right at the Great Orient Hotel, he had passed on to the Star Ferry Pier. He had then climbed a flight of steps that took him to Blake Pier. He had walked its length in order to contemplate the harbour, as a dismal ceremony of farewell, but he had found a dreadfully sordid café. So he took a seat, ordered a beer.

He had made his walk because walking keeps despair at bay. He had walked through Quarry Bay, North Point, Causeway Bay, Wanchai and Central, managing scarcely to think at all. Now, beer before him and the light beginning to fade, he inspected the boat-jams of Hong Kong harbour. Tangled together were various craft of the Star Ferry, the Jordan Road Ferry that carried motor cars, the ferries to Lantau, Cheung Chau, Lamma, Tung Lung, Po Toi. Alan watched, cut off from the world of purpose.

It was not the row about the Noble Savages letter that had got him the sack. It was the Gestapo. A few days before Christmas, Alan had subbed the report of a speech made by the chairman of the South China Bank, Sir Peter Browne, to the Rotary Club of Hong Kong. About three paragraphs from the end, the speaker had referred to the Hong Kong police and their 'Gestapo tactics'. Pleased, Alan had seized on this, promoted it to the first paragraph, fitted the story around it, and used the word 'Gestapo' in a headline that had fitted to the last character. Nice, he had told himself at the time, bloody *nice*.

There had been a note on Alan's desk when he returned to work on Boxing Day afternoon. Written on pink card, in fountain pen. See me. R. S. But Mr Simpson, what I did is just standard practice in Fleet Street. Mr Fairs, you do not seem to realise that we are not in Fleet Street. We are in Hong Kong. I happen to believe that a newspaper has a responsibility to the community. You clearly fail to appreciate that. It is my belief that you never will. Your professional standards, of which you make so much, are not ours.

Alan said thank Christ for that, and marched out slamming the door. No he didn't. He sat on Blake Pier wishing he had. Instead, he had begged for a last chance, thinking of rent, debt, the distance from home. Pride had gone. Simpson asked if he would vacate the building. Now, please.

And so the great Hong Kong walk; the great Hong Kong adventure in ruins. He turned and looked bitterly at the tallest of the tall buildings on the waterfront, the one with round windows which, Wally had informed him, was known to the Chinese as the House of a Thousand Arseholes. Along the length of the pier, teenage Chinese couples embraced unrestrainedly, Blake Pier being a good deal more private than their homes.

What would he say when he got home? Didn't work out. Couldn't get on with the place. Journalistic standards appalling. Walked out of the job after six weeks, matter of self-respect. And they would all say in the pub after he had gone – all those who would never dare to make such a journey themselves – well, he couldn't take it, could he, scuttling back home with his tail between his legs. Shall we give him a couple of shifts anyway? Oh, come on, hardly the type, is he?

Below, a motor-junk approached the pier, its seesawing deck loaded with large waste-paper baskets full of vegetables; choisum and pak-choi. He heard a voice chanting out some request or order – everything in Cantonese sounded like an order – concluding the sentence with a long *aaa* clearly audible above the grumble of the engine. Master that sound and you have mastered street Cantonese. The junk's captain, if it were he and junks had captains, stood stocky and strong in a white singlet as the deck danced beneath him. He shouted again at a man hidden from view, perhaps on the lower level of the pier. Another merchant, no doubt. Buying cheap and selling dear: passage for choisum and pak-choi; passage too, perhaps, for more exciting cargoes, for brandy and American cigarettes, bears' paws, tigers' penises, pharmaceuticals. Or people. Perhaps even now a crop-haired, frightened boy crouched beneath the dancing deck, sick with both fright and motion, escaping from China to this promised land. In the morning he would make his run for freedom. The land of opportunity. The junk tucked snugly into the pier and was lost from view.

Alan ordered more beer and gave himself up to self-pity. He felt it was expected of him. But even as he did so, cursing Simpson, his luck, the woman who had left him in England, he knew that he was only going through the motions. He did not, in his dismay, permit that thought to come to the surface, but it lay beneath, awaiting its moment. Yes. Tie already rolled and in his pocket, strolling at his ease, a *flâneur*, through the unmalicious shoving of his fellow islanders. Stopping to buy a beer from the fat proprietor. And Alan knew that he could activate that destiny: in a single moment he could do it. The café would have a telephone, and no objection would be made to his using it, calls being free. André, I've been thinking over what you were saying yesterday . . .

Alan drank his beer and watched the light fade and the lights of the buildings and the advertisements come on one by one. At last in darkness he walked back to the Mid-Levels and took the lift to his flat on the fifteenth floor.

How early could you have a drink? This was not a question to be dismissed lightly. He had dined the previous night off a six-pack of San Mig and a packet of peanuts, and had played patience until the beer was finished. One o'clock was all right, surely? Well, twelve. The pubs opened in England on Sunday at twelve. On weekdays they opened at eleven, and this was a weekday. He did a deal with himself: a beer after he had spoken to the editor of the *China Gazette*. This was the competition, if such it could be called, to the *Times*, a newspaper that expressed the spirit of opposition by seeking to outdo its rival in fuddy-duddyness. Alan bravely rang the number. The editor would be in at two.

By five past two, Alan had finished the second beer of the day. The first didn't count and the second was necessary. He had learnt that no vacancy of any kind existed on the *China Gazette*. He had run the gamut of Hong Kong newspapers.

The telephone splintered the silence. It was Bill. 'Bad luck, lad, I know, yes, Simpson's a bad man. Look, I don't know what your plans are, but there's a friend of mine who produces a shitty little magazine that circulates free to businessmen. Sells editorial space, that kind of carry-on. It's not exactly journalism, but nor is working for the *Times* is it? Know anything about business?'

'No.'

'That's all right, nor does Reg. I know he's looking for an assistant, by which he means someone to do the dirty jobs while he goes to the bar and to Bangkok and so on. Want his number?'

It took Alan a couple of tries to say thank you, yes please. Then, after Bill had rung off, he dialled the number without giving himself a moment to think.

'Top-hole,' said Reg unexpectedly. 'Excellent. Let's discuss it right away. Beer after work, you know the Two Brewers in Lockhart Road?'

Alan spent the afternoon playing patience, an attempt, not as effective as walking, at keeping both hope and despair at bay. Then he took a taxi to the heart of Wanchai, and walked along Lockhart Road, a narrow gully above which hung an endless procession of Damoclean neon signs: Crazy Horse, New American Restaurant, Ocean Bar, Seven Seas Bar. Alan walked, striving to give no more than a casual glance at the photographs, outside the topless bars, of glorious ping-pong ball breasts.

The Two Brewers stood between a tattoo parlour and a restaurant decorated with the wind-dried corpses of chickens. To open the door was to pass, as through the looking-glass, into the Home Counties. The sort of dingy pub you find by the railway station. There, beer and a copy of *Hong Kong Business* on the bar before him, in safari suit (electric blue) and behind a small paunch, Reg. Two strange white tufts of hair sprang from his head, behind his ears. They looked like powder puffs. Reg looked like a saloon-bar golfer, half a pint of cooking and a Scotch egg please, landlord. Odd to think that his favoured, apparently unashamed, leisure pursuit was not golf but whoring.

'So you're a friend of Bill's, what a good sort he is, terrible shame of course but there you are, that's Hong Kong. But he knows his job and he says you're OK, and that's good enough for me. Worked at the *Times* myself, of course, years ago, never could get on with Simpson, set up on my own and here we are.'

Reg was not a man to deal with any subject briefly, but several beers later, hands were shaken on a decision. Alan was to work for Reg five afternoons a week for two thousand dollars a month. 'Flexible as you like, old chap, so long as we get the work done. I need a dogsbody, to tell you the truth, and some of the work will be an awful grind. But if you can put up with that, I'm more than happy to have you on board.'

Alan could. He was invited to start the following Monday. Did he need an advance?

Back on the fifteenth floor, head slightly fuzzy after his interview with Reg, Alan stood at his window with the telephone in his hand. He could see the harbour between the two buildings that rose up in front of him, the moving lights of the shipping, the still lights of Kowloon on the far side. He grasped the instrument like a weapon, Bond setting an assignment in motion. 'Hello. This is Alan Fairs, remember we met –'

'Alan, my dear. How perfectly splendid. Are you coming out to see us again? How is the *Hong Kong Times*?'

Alan did not feel it necessary to hide things from André. 'Rather why I'm calling you. I've just been sacked.'

'I *knew* you were the right sort for us. I have an instinct. But my dear old thing, how perfectly rotten all the same. Being sacked always depresses me for hours. But, Alan, could it really be that you are coming to join our glorious community on Tung Lung?'

'Is the flat still free?'

'Yours for seven hundred bucks a month.'

'Done.'

'Naturally you must sign some bits of paper and shake hands with your new landlord. Let me see. Tomorrow I can make the four thirty ferry home from Central. Why not catch it too?'

Home. 'All right.'

'And your life in Hong Kong can begin.'

It was now four thirty-five. The ferry hooted and growled restlessly, and then moved fussily away from the jetty. André had clearly missed it. Alan would have to wait to see if he arrived on the following ferry. Well, he would do so at the café beneath the banyan tree, drinking beer served to him by the fat proprietor. No hardship. Or perhaps André wouldn't be there at all. The whole deal was about to fall through. Perhaps André was not the infinitely plausible person he seemed, but a fey, untrustworthy rogue. Alan felt a pang of fear at this thought. Future Hong Kong life was feasible only in terms of Tung Lung rent.

Then, like a miracle, André's head appeared at Alan's feet, rapidly rising in the stairwell. The rest of him followed: another beautiful suit, another beautiful smile of greeting.

'I thought you'd missed it.'

'Not me. I don't miss ferries. But come, we must sit at the *back*.'

He led the way to the last bench, the only one that was open to the world. A sprightly wind whipped in off the harbour; André smiled quietly to himself as he felt it against his face. He sat, removed his tie, wound it around his hand and slipped it into his jacket pocket. Then he placed his attaché case on his knees, caused it to open with a double detonation and produced from it two cans of San Mig. Cold, naturally. They opened, drank.

'So, my dear, how does it march?'

Alan explained a little. André listened with interest. The connection with *HK Business News* amused him. 'Done some work for old Reg myself, in my time. Usual standby, selling advertising space, selling editorial space, too, if it comes to that. No false pride, old Reg. Made rather a little killing, actually, in Singapore.'

'Really? Oh well, I'll pass on your regards.'

'Wouldn't do that, my dear. Had a bit of a falling-out. The killing wasn't actually for him, you see. But shall I tell you an important fact? In this town, the one thing you never run out of is clients.'

'Mags, you mean?'

'Well, I meant it more generally, actually, but it is certainly true of magazines. One mag folds, another two spring up. Same in every other business. Drives some people crazy. But we who keep light on our feet rather like it that way.'

Alan, more interested in his own affairs than in André's summary of Hong Kong life, returned doggedly to the subject closest to his heart. 'Do they take copy from outsiders, then?'

'My dear, you are living in a freelance's paradise. You'll make a great living, have loads of fun. Get some travel under your belt, get around Asia a bit. That's the thing. Why not start your own magazine? I'll sell the advertising space, editorial space too. We'll make a fortune.'

It was not until the ferry cut its speed and made its laborious approach to the Tung Lung ferry pier that André turned to the business in hand. 'I've pretty well settled everything with your new landlord. We'll go straight up and see him, if that's all right with you. He's got a lease all ready.'

'Chinese guy?' It seemed worth asking.

'Lord, no. Well, born in Shanghai, but the son of Baptist missionaries. All English blood, but rather Chinese in some ways. *Plus catholique*, in fact. Name of John Kingston, lived on Tung Lung for about twenty years. Unusual chap. You'll like him.'

Alan looked out over the surrounding land, the awaking

mountains. It was as if he had received a light blow on the chest: the smallest tap, little more than the brushing of Oddjob's finger, but a touch performed with such acute, well-nigh surgical skill that it was enough, for one half-second, to suspend the processes of life. I am to live behind this toy harbour, before this green mountain. I am to live in a Chinese scroll.

'Ready for a climb?' André asked. 'You're going to live in the highest house in the village.'

André led the way past the café and the banyan tree, and past a tiny, almost a doll's house, branch of the South China Bank. Beside it stood a fly-thronged collection of wide, flat, woven baskets, from which arose the scent of the death of a thousand sea beasts: the ambient odour of Tung Lung. 'Shrimp-paste factory,' André said airily. 'One of Chuen-suk's money-spinners. Here's where we start to climb.' They turned left off the main path and concrete steps rose up before them. Though winter and the temperature barely turning past 70 degrees, Alan felt sweat burst from him. After a while, begging a halt, he asked, mouth-breathing fiercely: 'How many more?'

'About halfway. You'll soon be used to it. Look on it as Nob Hill. Worth climbing 176 steps for. Catch the breeze in the summer, which is pretty good news, on the whole.'

Alan looked around him. A shower of inky blooms hung over a mesh fence; before it danced a butterfly, orange, black-veined. It looked like a stained-glass window. 'Onwards,' André said. 'Onwards and upwards.'

More leg-weary than he had been since his epic walk from Quarry Bay to Central, Alan reached the top. A narrow concrete path led onward, mercifully now along the level. 'We use Calor Gas for cooking,' André said. He seemed unaffected by the climb. 'For an extra five dollars they deliver it. Best deal on the island. Two old ladies do it.' Alan didn't actually believe this. André led him to another flight of stairs, no more than a dozen steps. Straight ahead stood a huge pair of iron gates, beautifully ornamented and painted green. They were flanked by two bulging-eyed, door-guarding lions. Through the chain-link fence on either side, Alan could see a shaded green garden, and set within it three separate, small but majestic houses. 'Old man Ng's place,' André said. 'Richest man on the island.' He turned his back on this vista of expensive living, and gestured to another dwelling. He announced, not without pride: 'Here we are.'

The lemon-yellow house stood head and shoulders above those around it. Two houses, in fact. Semi-detached. How odd. Two front doors, a shared front yard, a garden of concrete. 'My place,' André said, pointing to the left middle floor. 'Charles lives next door to me – you'll meet him soon enough, a great man in his way. You're underneath me; the flat next door to you isn't finished yet. Yours was only finished last week. King has the entire top floor; he knocked it through, done a neat conversion job. So he has the roof, and he's made a nice little garden up there.'

Alan peered through the seven-foot-high mesh of the fence to what would soon be his home. He followed André round to the back of the building. Another door, and more stairs to climb. Halfway was a door, on which had been stuck a colour photograph of a sailing boat leaving behind it a long creamy wake. It also bore the legend 'Cool Cool Cool!'

'That's me,' André said. 'But let's find King.' Up another flight of steps; there André knocked jauntily on a door. It opened. 'Hello, King, here's your new man. Pretty smart of me to find him, I think you'll agree. Alan Fairs, John Kingston.'

John Kingston stepped onto the landing to meet them. He was tall, with a massive chest, and he moved with a strange deliberation, rather like a troll. It was as if his aim were to frighten, though not very severely, an audience of uncritical children. He fixed Alan with a challenging eye and said, basso profundo: 'Welcome to the real Hong Kong.'

Alan took the proffered hand; received an expected bone-crushing. 'Er, thank you.'

'The people are real here. Do you feel a sense of privilege in being here? Do you feel that already?'

'Well, I do as a matter of fact,' Alan said, half ingratiating, half honest.

'The people here are real.'

'Yes.'

'I call them noble savages.'

Alan felt momentarily at a loss. This would have been the case even without the dizzying sensation of the wheel turning full circle. He found himself babbling: 'Great, yes, sure, I'm glad about that, because I haven't met anybody noble in Hong Kong yet, apart from André, of course.'

Kingston received this in long, serious silence. After a while, he said: 'Noble savages.'

André was suddenly beside him, pushing a beer into his hand. 'Beer. Have a beer, King. I found it in your fridge.'

'Thank you, André,' Kingston said. 'You are indeed a generous man.' Kingston said this as solemnly as he had spoken of noble savages. Alan was having a little trouble with his sense of perspective. 'Now. Alan. Come. Before anything else occurs, you must inspect your flat.'

'All right. Though I am sure it will be perfect.' Even a concrete shell would be perfect in such a setting. King led a beer-clutching procession back down the stairs and round the outside of the building. A gate, of metal bars, spike-topped and unlocked, guarded the way into the concrete garden. Kingston walked through, opened the door to the flat, and announced, 'Seven hundred square feet,' though whether in apology or boast Alan could not tell.

It was a concrete shell. It was perfect. The walls had been lightly painted with whitish paint. Four tiny rooms led off the main area. Two were bedrooms, one containing an actual bed, double, with a thin foam mattress. Alan walked around the flat. This did not take a great deal of time. A kitchen, with a Calor Gas stove on a tiled concrete shelf. A bathroom with a shower in it. 'Water is sometimes a problem on Tung Lung, my friend,' King said. 'We use the Ng well here, of course. If it runs dry, we have permission to use the standpipe below the last flight of steps. That is connected to Chuen-suk's well, and that never runs dry.' And the concrete apron before the house, half of it shaded by the balcony above. On the far side of his fence, another tumble of the purple stuff; was it bougainvillaea? And a jumble of houses marching down the hillside before him, and beyond them the harbour of Tung Lung and beyond that the South China Sea. He turned inland, to a flat-bottomed valley floored with a chessboard of green fields. Allotments, really. Alan could just make out a man working on his little square of green, two watering cans suspended from a yoke that rested on his shoulders. He wore a pointed hat; he too lived in a Chinese scroll. Alan found that he could smell the sea.

'I love it. If you'll have me, I'll take it.'

'Yours for seven hundred dollars.'

'Done.'

'Then let us sign the lease. How are you off for furniture? I can sell you some electric fans, chairs and so on.'

'Thanks. Though I'm a bit strapped for cash just now. At least, I will be once I've paid you a deposit.'

'Pay me later, then. No hurry. I may be a landlord, but I am a landlord with a human face.'

'A noble landlord,' Alan said idiotically.

Kingston greeted this with a great hohoho, like the demon king. 'I can see that this is going to be a very happy community,' he announced. 'A great future stretches before us.'

They returned to Kingston's flat. After the bare expanse of the downstairs flat, the contrast was apparent. Kingston's style of decoration was disconcertingly – Alan groped for a word – *permanent*. There was even a large photograph of a family group. This had been printed onto canvas, to make it look like a painting. It showed a pretty woman with an elaborate, slightly dated hairstyle, a pigtailed girl, a boy who looked like the illustration on the fruit gums packet. Kingston stood at the rear of the group, beaming in satisfaction.

Alan signed his lease, wrote a cheque for $1,400, deposit and first month's rent, and received a second bone-crushing in recognition of the completion of a deal. 'I'll move in tomorrow or the next day,' Alan said. 'Just as soon as I have fixed up things with the landlord of my Mid-Levels place.'

'What's he got to do with it?' André asked. 'Does he owe you money?'

'I think I owe him, actually.'

'Then surely the only thing to do is to lug your stuff into a taxi and get the hell out? He'll never trace you to Tung Lung.'

Alan could not help but think about this. Such a manoeuvre would, he reckoned, save him about $2,500. The thought went, and he was sorry to see it go. 'André – can I be utterly frank with you? I don't have the nerve.'

André looked for a moment deeply saddened, as if by a friend's unwitting blasphemy. 'My dear, it's hardly the right way to begin your career as a freebooter.'

'André, I was brought up to be honest – more or less, anyway. It's a handicap. But keep faith with me; I'm sure I shall rise above it in time.'

Alan stood at the centre of a kind of refugees' camp. Six vast striped plastic bags formed a circle around him: the contents of his flat in Mid-Levels. He had in his pocket a cheque for $1,000, returned deposit on the furniture.

The loading and unloading of the taxi had been accomplished, not without superhuman exertions. The carrying of the bags, two by two through the little gate beside the ferry turnstile, normally used for the passage of vegetables, had brought out resources Alan did not know he possessed. But the next stage, the carriage of bags to the ferry, seemed impossible. He could not even begin to think about the 176 steps.

The ferry arrived, and eventually opened its doors to admit new passengers. Alan made his first effort, and carried two bags on board. He fought his way back against the unstemmable tide of passengers to collect two more, in a state of blind frazzlement. He had just reached his encampment when he heard a voice call: 'New neighbour!'

An impression of suit, size and extraordinary freshness of face. Alan was not quite in the mood for being bothered, but managed a flustered greeting.

'Your gear?' the stranger demanded.

'Yes, I –'

'Hold,' he said sternly. He handed Alan a briefcase and a pink carrier bag. Then he squatted, and addressed the four bags rather formally. He inserted his arms through all the handles, straightened his back, and seized his own forearms in a grip of steel. He inhaled and exhaled through his nose, very noisily, about half a dozen times. Then he stood. Miraculously, the bags rose with him. He marched inexorably to the boat, benignly shoving passengers from his path with every step, tendons standing out from his neck like steel hawsers, breath roaring from his nose. Alan followed bearing his presumed neighbour's briefcase, his own shoulder-bag full of valuable items, and the pink carrier bag. Condensation had formed, though not to his surprise, on its surface. With every appearance of relish, the neighbour lowered his preposterous load to the floor, back still perfectly straight.

'Thank you,' Alan said inadequately.

The neighbour rose with slow grace from his squat, and rotated his shoulders just once, so that the shoulder blades almost touched. Then he made a strange, rather papal gesture to the stairs that led to the top deck of the boat and a smile of rather unearthly beauty lit his face. 'Beer!' he said. Then he turned and absolutely sprinted up the stairs.

Alan followed more sedately, arriving on the top to find his neighbour sitting on the very back seat, both arms outstretched along its back in a crucifixion position. Alan passed him his two bags. The briefcase was placed on the floor, but from the carrier bag he produced two cans of San Miguel, passing one to Alan. Alan thanked him and reached for the ringpull. The neighbour at once placed a huge paw over Alan's hand. 'Wait!' he said. 'Not until the ferry moves.'

He sat quite silent, after this, his own unopened can in his hand and a rather solemn expression on his face. Alan watched as the stragglers came aboard. The day was chill, and most people wore jackets on top of shirts. They crowded together towards the front, enclosed section of the boat, from love of crowds, from dislike of air. There was a clatter from below as the gangplank was raised. The engine roared, and the ferry pulled away with the usual exchange of referees' whistles. Alan's neighbour, roused from a species of trance, smiled his beatific smile, tore the ringpull from his can, tossed it over his shoulder into the wash of the screw behind them and then positively threw the can into his face. Alan watched, fascinated, as his throat worked convulsively, like a pump. At last, he lowered the can, and smiled again.

'Hello, new neighbour. I'm Charles Browne, the man upstairs. Browne with an E.'

Alan said his own name, and they shook hands. The clasp was gentle, unKingston-like.

'You are going to like Tung Lung,' Charles said.

'Have you lived here long?'

'Tung Lung? Or Hong Kong?'

'Both, I suppose.'

'Hong Kong, all my life, or twenty years. Tung Lung, ever since I went to the bad, or about two years. Here's how!' He raised his can once again and drank with the same primeval ferocity as before. He tossed the can, presumably now empty, over the back of the boat. He took another from his pink bag and opened it. 'Your beer all right?'

'Yes, great, thanks.'

'I mean, you do drink?'

'Of course.'

'I mean, not a single beer and that's it for me thanks, I've got a busy day tomorrow.'

'No.'

'In fact,' Charles said, more or less beseechingly, 'you drink quite a lot.'

'Well –'

'And get drunk and throw up and go to bed and it spins and get up next morning feeling shithouse and then have a drink to feel better.'

There was an expression of touching eagerness on Charles's face. Alan could not bear to disappoint him. 'Oh yes.'

'Well then. Time for another beer, isn't it?'

Alan made a quite heroic effort. He lifted his can, half full, and finished it in a series of frantic swallows. Tears pricked the back of his eyes and he wondered for a second if the shock of the chill and the bubbles would effect an instant purgation, even as he wiped his mouth with feigned relish. He threw his can overboard and took the new one.

'Good man!' Charles said, with restrained violence.

Alan opened his new can and consigned its ringpull to the deep. He took a semireluctant sip. 'Are there many Browne-with-an-Es in Hong Kong?' he asked. 'I came across that name once or twice when I was working for the *Hong Kong Times*.'

'Course you came across the name. My old man owns the bloody place.'

'What bloody place?'

'Hong Kong, of course.'

'He can't actually own all of it, can he? I expect you're having me on.'

'Well, sucks to you, because he does. More or less, anyway. My old man happens to be the chairman of the South China Bank.'

Once again, the wheel spun full circle before him. 'Golly,' Alan said. 'That's quite a grown-up job, really.'

There was a split-second pause, during which Alan thought he might have caused serious offence. Then Charles threw back his head and gave a dramatic howl of laughter. 'Grown-up!' he said. 'My old man's got a grown-up job!' He laughed out of all proportion to the merits of Alan's remark, rocking forward, resting his forehead on his beercan, finally emerging, wiping his eyes. 'So that's what's wrong with the bastard,' he said. 'He's got a grown-up job!'

'I had a grown-up job last week,' Alan said. 'But I got fired.'

'Is that why they sacked you?' Charles asked. 'They discovered you weren't a grown-up?'

'That must be it.'

'André hasn't got a grown-up job,' Charles said. 'I don't think

King has one either. He acts as if he has one, but I think he's only pretending.'

'What about you?'

'Oh, me? I've got a grown-up job. I have a very grown-up job indeed. But shall I tell you how I handle it?' He turned with sudden elephantine staginess to Alan, and whispered hoarsely and penetratingly: '*I do it very, very badly.*'

It was impossible to tell how serious he was, or even if he was serious at all. 'Is that a good idea?' Alan asked.

The response startled him, because it came as a bellow, one that turned the heads of the passengers ranged before them, all engaged till then in noisy conversations of their own. 'Course it's not! It's a bloody appalling idea. They give me hell. Browne, you bastard, they tell me, you're not shaping up. Do the job properly or we'll sack you and then you'll be sorry. We'd sack you today if it wasn't for the fact that your old man owns Hong Kong.'

'Jolly good,' Alan said.

'What do you mean, jolly good? Don't talk wet, it's bloody awful.' Charles started laughing again. He wiped his eyes briefly, and eased up his laughter a little. 'Now. Listen to me. I have a plan. It's a good plan, so pay attention. The ferry stops. We get off it. We take your bags to Ah-Chuen's. That's the café by the harbour run by the fat bastard. We drink beer. Then we take the bags up to your flat. Then we have a beer at my place. Then we go down again and have supper, say, a bucket of shit at Ah-Chuen's. Then, we sit about drinking beer. How does that sound in general terms?'

'It sounds perfection itself.'

'And we'll roll the dice a bit, of course. You play yah-tze?'

'No. I'm not terribly good at games, cards and so forth. Always lose at poker and stuff, never seem to have a card.'

Charles held up a hand in a stately gesture of reproach. 'Have no fear, neighbour. Yah-tze requires no skill, no thought, no mind. It's almost impossible to lose much money at it, because it is the longest, most boring game in the world. That's why we love it; that's why we play it all the time. You need never fret about life when the five dice roll across the table.'

'Then I long to learn,' Alan said.

Charles tossed his second can into the sea and produced a third, opening it with calm certainty. 'Then here's to us. Here's to Tung Lung. Health, wealth and long life.' With his can he caught Alan's own a glancing blow. And drank.

PART II
SPRING

The telephone splintered the silence. Alan ceased typing and got up from his desk, a massive metal thing rather like M's. King had supplied it to him on indefinite loan. He passed through to the main room of his flat. The telephone stood on a smallish table by the window. Alan seized it. 'Hello?' he said, looking approvingly at the South China Sea. He could see the triple-decker ferry moving out towards Cheung Chau, also a small craft near the shore from which a pair of noble savages did the rounds of their fish traps.

'Colin Webb, *Business PanAsia*.'

'Oh, hello –' was it too early in the relationship to say Colin? – 'there.'

'Thanks for coming in last week, Alan. Sorry not to get back to you before, but you know how it is.'

'No worries, Colin.'

'I was looking over your list, some smart ideas. I particularly like the eccentric businessman. I'd like you to go ahead on that one.'

Pleasure flowed through Alan. Here he was, being commissioned to write a story for the top business magazine in Hong Kong, and yet he was watching a sampan and wearing a sarong. A sarong? Well, why not? The temperature was in the eighties and air conditioning was for non-island-dwelling wimps.

He put the phone down and adjusted the sarong. He hadn't quite got the folding right yet, it tended to slip without warning. André, who had donated the sarong to Alan – it was bright red and copiously flowered – said he had spent half a lifetime watching the sarong-clad women of various Asian nations in the eternally disappointed hope of seeing the sarong slip unexpectedly from their golden bodies. Alan wore the sarong as his island work uniform, with a khaki army surplus shirt worn unbuttoned above it.

It was time – no, it wasn't time for a beer, don't be stupid, it was time for another cup of coffee to celebrate the glories of the commission. Let's see, two thousand words at sixty cents each was, well, more than a thousand anyway, well, it was $1,200, wasn't it? And there was the story on the trams for *Hong Kong Life*. And the story about the Peak for the Hong Kong Airlines magazine *Josun!* And there was the regular work, the subbing and rewriting for Reg at *HK Biz*. And it was all going to add up to, well, er, definitely more than he would have made had he been working for the *Hong Kong Times*. My God, a milestone had been passed. A triumph. Surely that was worth – no, it wasn't. It was barely eleven o'clock. He filled the kettle and put it on his two-ring stove. It leapt into life at the merest touch of a match, and so it should have done. He had purchased a new cylinder of Calor Gas the previous day. He had paid an additional five dollars so that the cylinder might be carried up the 176 steps to his door. The task was accomplished by a pair of ancient women who suspended the cylinder from beneath a bamboo pole for portage.

The kettle boiled and Alan poured boiling water onto brown powder, adding a splash from a carton of UHT milk. He must get round to making proper coffee. But anyway, a proper coffee break was in order.

He took the mug of brown liquid to the door, which stood open as usual. Outside, in his concrete garden, he had set out a few plastic chairs and a table. To one side an inflated airbed lay perishing slowly in the sun. He sat on one chair, placed his feet on another. From the village below, he heard the sound of power tools in operation. Building, always building. But even from his seated position, he could see the chessboard field below. A slight figure, in jeans rolled to her knees, was working one of the patches. Was it the beautiful schoolgirl that André had introduced as Priscilla? He would marry Priscilla and live for ever on choisum and pak-choi and beer. But he was winning, was he not?

Voices rose suddenly in the Ng estate below and beyond his flat: the Ng clan had several ancient women about the place, and a number of unexplained females of all ages – whether retainers, meddling half-retired servants or poor relations, Alan did not know. One of these, the youngest but by no means young, a woman of some character, with a certain faded beauty, he knew was called Chai. They were given to energetic quarrelling, of which the only word Alan could understand was 'Aiyaaaah!' This, he thought, could mean anything at all save the possibility that it was the speaker's own fault.

Which reminded him. He finished his coffee and went inside to call Reg, grabbing just in time at his sarong. 'Looking good, old boy. Cleared up a hell of a lot yesterday. Good of you to stay late. It will be off to the typesetters any minute now. No, no, no, I'll lock up, don't dream of coming in. Not even sure about tomorrow. Let's talk after I've gone through the post. Call me about ten.'

'Thanks, Reg.'

'No, no, thank *you*, old boy. Never known what it's like to be ahead of myself before.'

After a few more gratifying amiabilities, they rang off. How splendid. The way was clear for the first step in the piece on the eccentric businessman. Alan took a perfunctory wash beneath the dribbling showerhead; it's like little boys pissing on you, Charles had said. Surely the Ng well wasn't running dry again.

Alan dressed in cotton jeans, twenty bucks the pair in the place behind the tramstop in Wanchai, and an almost respectable shirt. Combed his hair, removed the loose hairs from the teeth without looking to see how many. Did that show how relaxed he was, or how worried? He put on a pair of black cotton kung-fu slippers bought from China Products, and left the flat. Closed the door behind him, as a security measure, but did not lock it. He did not even know where the key was. Hadn't seen it for weeks.

He walked around the side of the house and climbed the stairs.

As he walked past Cool Cool Cool!, he tapped the poster, as was now his superstitious habit. This was to remind him that never, no matter how drunk, would he again venture out into the South China Sea with André and his ghastly boat. He climbed the last flight, and knocked on the door. King's voice called out in Cantonese bass, presumably bidding him welcome. So Alan let himself in.

King was sitting on one of the sofas; opposite him, the far side of a low glass table, a Chinese man. 'Ah, my young friend. You know Mr Ng, of course. And Ah-Hei.'

'Of course.' Mr Ng, possessor of that most wonderful of Cantonese surnames, was a man he saw regularly, and nodded to. As well as the estate next door, he owned Ng's restaurant, down in the village, where Alan ate two or three times a week with his island companions, any time they felt like aiming above the traditional bucket of shit at Ah-Chuen's. It was a place decorated with the single-mindedness that all Chinese prefer when it comes to eating: no frivolous distractions. The principal decoration was a series of tanks containing still-swimming dinners. Mr Ng himself was another aspect of décor: he was invariably to be found, sitting on a high stool behind a desk, clacking at an abacus and calligraphing mysterious signs into a huge ledger. Business was business and food was food, and Ng's restaurant was a temple. Ah-Hei was another aspect of décor. He had a shimmering black mane of hair, and looked like the hero of a martial arts film. This was because he was a martial arts hero: a real one. He was a genuine kung-fu adept. Charles said he had once seen Ah-Hei deal with a tableful of belligerent Chinese revellers: 'Fastest thing on two legs I have ever seen. Looks stupid on the movies. But that bastard is real.'

Mr Ng had smartened himself up for this visit to King. He wore a clean white shirt instead of his usual dirty white singlet. Even so, his outfit probably cost even less than twenty dollars; Alan guessed that he could put his hands in the pocket of his China Products trousers and pull out enough cash to buy a Mercedes. He smiled at Alan; one large and unmissable gold tooth. 'You like my restaurant.'

It was not a question. 'Oh yes, very much. Nice place.'

'You drink much beer in my restaurant.'

Nor was that. Praise, admiration, or perhaps a neutral accept-ance of the differences between races. It was all profit, anyway, and boozing gweilos hardly made more noise than feasting Chinese. 'Nice place,' Alan said lamely.

'Ve'y nice place.'

Alan turned to King. 'Er, something I want to discuss with you, but it'll keep.'

'A moment, my friend.' He and Mr Ng then embarked on a conversation in Cantonese with much guffawing from Mr Ng. No, he really *would* start to learn the language properly. Buy a book. Buy a tape. No, fall in love with a beautiful Cantonese girl. Alan examined King's family photograph, idly speculating on the sexual potential of the pigtailed daughter. Perhaps she was now grown up, beautiful, available, ready to fall in love with him at first sight, to tumble into his bed in a wild whim of passion. King and Mr Ng shook hands, not without warmth. Then Mr Ng turned to Alan, and bestowed on him a final bless-ing from his golden mouth.

'You come to my restaurant tonight, drink much beer, hahaha.'

'Hahaha,' agreed Alan. Ah-Hei got to his feet, still without offering a word, and walked cat-footed after his master.

'You moving into the restaurant business, then, King?' Alan asked, when they were alone.

'Ng is an old friend of mine. We have done business together for many a year. His restaurant is only one of his interests. He owns the well, for example. Water is power on Tung Lung, Alan. Ng is also in property; he owns this place, among many others. He sub-lets much of the market-gardening land in the valley. He has a share in most of the fishing boats.'

'And he owns the shrimp-paste factory outright, doesn't he?'

'No, that is Chuen-suk.' Alan remembered the silver-haired Coca-Cola drinker at the waterfront café. 'Chuen-suk and Ng are big rivals. Chuen-suk has the better well, and that means greater power. But my partner, Ng, is the more enterprising man, with more diverse interests. A big man, Alan, a big man on Tung Lung.'

'Oh,' Alan said. 'I didn't realise you were in partnership.'

'In some aspects. In property, a little, but mainly we work together on import-export.'

Oh. 'Actually, it was business that I wanted to talk to you, King.'

'What else does anyone ever want to talk about in this town?' This was brought out with a rhetorical flourish, as if it were something of a *mot*. Alan laughed, remembering from somewhere a line about it being almost as good being a hypocrite as a liar: the same warm feeling inside. And, allowing the smile to remain on his face, he made his proposal: suggesting that King be the subject of a 'portrait' in *Business PanAsia*. He had not expected difficulty, relying on King's habitual readiness to oblige. But he was surprised by King's flattered delight. Alan felt a comfortable frisson of the journalist's endless source of power: the promise, or threat, of publication.

'Tremendous, Alan. I'd be happy to be a "portrait". When would you like the ordeal to commence?'

'Right now, if by any chance you are free.'

'For you, Alan, I am always free.' So Alan ran downstairs to fetch a notebook, and returned to find King at the fridge liberating a pair of cans. 'Would the roof be a suitable place for this inquisition?'

'Admirable.' So they climbed the island's final flight of stairs. Table and chairs stood beneath a canopy of vine; other plants grew around in heavy glazed pots, decorated with Chinese characters or bamboo leaves. Below them the harbour, the fields to one side. Priscilla, if it were she, had gone. At sea, the twelve o'clock ferry was heading towards its berth. Alan could see the flow of people moving towards the jetty through the narrow streets, the wheeled motor-carts vying for the leading positions for loading and unloading.

'To business, my friend. Shoot. As they say.'

'Well, er, what is your main line of business?'

It was a question that gave deep delight. King smiled to himself for a long time, looking out across the sea, for all that there were no noble savages in sight. At last he replied, 'Love, Alan. Love.'

Alan wrote 'love' in his notebook.

'Now I can see that I have surprised you. Business is supposed to be a matter of oppositions. Enmity and hatred. But that is not how I work, my friend. I say this: there is only one sort of good business, and that is when both parties walk away as winners.'

King spoke as if listening to him speaking at length was an experience all serious people should undergo at some stage in their lives. He started, fulsomely, with his childhood in Shanghai, the Baptist school run by his father. 'I learnt love in English, Mandarin, Cantonese and Hokkien.'

His father had died shortly after the fall of Shanghai and their enforced move to Hong Kong. 'Of a broken heart, Alan. I was sixteen, and never went to school again. There was nothing anyone could teach me.'

By the age of twenty-four, he was a millionaire. 'Import-export. Contacts with China, always contacts with China. Hong Kong was ever the financial pore through which the Chinese dragon breathed.' Alan hesitated over the shorthand outline for dragon.

The enmity of his partner, who was involved in the Triads – 'for the love of God don't print that, Alan' – had seen King reduced to nothing. But by the age of thirty he had built up a second fortune. 'Like Hong Kong itself, I diversified into manu-facturing. Plastics. The joy of plastics, Alan.' He bought a house on the Peak, married a beautiful Australian woman. 'On the wall downstairs, the two women of my life: Monica, my lovely wife; Jacinta, my lovely daughter.' For a second Alan wondered if King had read his mind as he'd mused over the pigtailed photograph. 'You see them pictured below with the man destined to become my business partner and, ultimately, should we be saved, my boss. My son, Byron.'

'Nice names,' Alan said. After all, you had to say something.

'They are all, alas, in UK,' King said. 'A matter of education. God, Alan, I miss them. Every day of my life, I miss them. A temporary thing. We remain a devoted family. I love my wife, and shall I tell you something else? I still *fancy* my wife. Twenty years we've been married, and when she was last here we were like two teenagers in love. Taking baths together. A honeymoon.'

'And the kids?'

'Fine children, Alan. Jacinta is now nineteen, and no longer in pigtails. Beautiful, wilful, headstrong, intelligent. Byron is sixteen, though most people take him for twenty-one. A remarkable boy who makes his father very happy. But where was I, Alan, in this history lesson?'

'Living in millionaires' row on the Peak.'

'I merged my business with a larger concern. Things hotted up. I was on the move constantly: Singapore, KL, Bangkok, Manila, Jakarta, Taiwan. Busy beyond belief, stressed beyond belief, powerful beyond belief, rich beyond belief. And then one day, do you know what I said?'

'Tell me.'

'I said "fuck it". I walked into a board meeting one morning, and told them all. I said "fuck it".'

'And how did they respond?'

'They begged me to stay. Naturally. But I said "fuck it", and I meant it from the bottom of my heart. And so what do you think I did?'

'You moved out to Tung Lung and founded a business based on the principle of love.'

'My friend, you are very wise. And do you know what, Alan? I prosper. I really do.'

The beauty she possessed was so perfect, so profound, that it constricted Alan's breathing. With a vast effort of will that did him great credit, he found a voice, and asked if he might be admitted to the editor of *Business PanAsia*. She performed this small miracle for him, and bestowed on him the gift of a smile. Love beat him lightly about the head and neck.

Colin Webb greeted him, and then insisted on reading, while Alan watched in fidgeting silence, every one of the two thousand words he had written.

'Virry nice, Alan. Virry, virry nice.' You could hardly tell that he was Australian. 'I had a feeling this piece was going to be nice. So I was planning to ask you to write something else for me.' Soon, Alan was accepting a commission for a cover piece. Hong Kong as manufacturing base: the shift to quality. 'Talk to a lot of people, Alan. Put a lot of work in. I want three thousand words, and I'll pay seventy-five cents a word for this one.'

Alan, much made up by this, decided to speak to the receptionist on the way out. Hello, you're very beautiful. You're rather tall for a Chinese girl, aren't you? I suppose marriage is out of the question? My God, he was a genius. 'Hello, er, I wonder if you could tell me the best place to find a taxi around here.'

A white blouse opening in a narrow V. Hair a raven's wing, iridescent black, falling straight and simple to her lovely shoulders. My God, this really was love. 'Best place is in front of Fragrant Harbour Hotel. On the waterfront, you know?'

'Won't the hall porter be cross?'

'You give him a dollar, he won't be cross.'

Alan made a creditable attempt at a winning smile. 'I'm still new here. Don't know all the dodges.'

'How long have you been in Hong Kong?' The great conversational gambit of the territory.

'Maybe six months.'

'You like?'

'Very good.'

And suddenly, her face was illuminated with delight – almost, Alan thought, with love.

'Sophie, my dear, how beautiful you are looking today. Alan, what a pleasant surprise. Dean, I believe you are employing the finest journalist in Hong Kong, and I am quite certain that you have the most beautiful receptionist.'

The receptionist spoke one word. 'André.'

André was standing by the reception desk, one hand in a pocket, with a man, severely rather than elegantly suited, who had the finicky-tough air of a Mormon proselytiser. 'Dean, have you met Alan Fairs, the journalist? No? Alan, this is your publisher, Dean Holdsworth.'

'Glad to know you, Alan,' Dean said, in flawless American. 'You're doing the June portrait, right? Look forward to reading it.' This was a very creditable feat of memory. He shook Alan's hand with every appearance of warmth. 'André, if I might have a further moment?'

'By all means, Dean, by all means. Alan, if you care to wait, we might share a taxi.'

'All right.'

André followed Dean into his office. Alan did not have to rack his brain for a new conversational gambit. Sophie was now ready, in fact eager, for conversation.

'You know André?' she asked.

'Neighbour of mine.'

Her eyes grew a little bigger. Were they rounder than was usual for a Chinese girl? Or had he never looked quite as closely before? 'You live on Tung Lung?' she asked reverently.

'Yes.'

'Very beautiful.'

'Yes.' A beat later, he decided that he had missed an opportunity.

'I like to live there one day.'

Alan could think of no rejoinder that did not indicate absolutely helpless desire. They talked a little of the ferry service, and whether or not the restaurant on the far side of the island, where Alan had eaten his Christmas lunch, was better than Ng's. Then a door opened and jovial voices rang out in the corridor.

'Well, André, all I can say now is have a good trip.'

'Consider the target already met, Dean. Consider it obliterated.'

Dean continued to escort André to the door, evidently a mark of considerable favour. 'Great, André. Just great. Send my regards to the Great Orient.'

'I shall indeed. Sophie, thanks, as ever, for everything. Goodbye, Dean. I shall call you to touch base on arrival. I have all the documents. Goodbye.' They shook hands, not without warmth, and Dean wished him good luck as he returned to his office.

'Alan. Excellent. So good of you to wait. I shall buy you a drink. Not dead set on catching the six thirty, are you? Then perhaps I shall buy you two drinks.'

'Excellent thought. Two Brewers?'

A slightly pained expression passed across André's face. 'I think not. The Harbourmaster's Bar, do you know it? Rather a favourite spot of mine.'

André led the way out onto the crazy pavements of Causeway Bay. It was impossible to walk two abreast as the tall buildings simultaneously debouched their million inmates onto the streets. André led the way: the crowd seemed to part before him, only to reform itself in front of Alan. André did not check his pace for anyone, not even for the road, picking his way fastidiously through the lorries, trams, buses, taxis and private cars. A man who jay-walked through life. They passed the usual collection of street stalls, all selling clothes of remarkable newness and high quality; to each André gave an all-embracing glance that took in both merchandise and price. He was never off duty. He passed onto Lockhart Road, but to Alan's surprise kept on, past this street of a thousand bars, ignoring the claims of a man selling fishballs from a vat of boiling oil to a small group of enthusiasts starved after two or three solid hours without food. Here Alan was able to move alongside. 'Not in Lockhart Road, this place of yours?'

'My dear old thing. No, it's in the Fragrant Harbour Hotel.'

Alan at once felt his clothes, a fairly respectable outfit as recently as this morning, grow ancient and ragged about him. Jacketless in the sticky April warmth, a yellow shirt, rather too many buttons undone at the front, and the sleeves rolled past the elbows. No tie, of course, not even one in his bag. And this object, hanging from his shoulder and containing too many papers to yield to the zip, lacked the cool precision of André's attaché case.

The Fragrant Harbour Hotel stood, as Sophie had justly

pointed out, on the waterfront, a precipitous many-windowed cliff. A Sikh, bearded and turbaned, guarded the entrance in top boots and a species of guardsman's jacket. He saluted André as they walked past him: 'Good evening, sir.'

'Good evening, Mr Singh, thank you so much.'

He led the way across the marbled lobby to the lifts. Alan, hit by the sudden chill of the air conditioning, rolled down his sleeves and did up a few buttons. The lift panel bore thirty-four buttons, plus a thirty-fifth labelled Harbourmaster's Bar. This André hit, and they were fired courteously skyward while André gave a brief summary of the nature of *Business PanAsia*, its strengths and weaknesses, and the problems it created for itself by its refusal to countenance paid editorial. Then the doors slid open.

Thirty-five floors high, they seemed to have descended to the depths of the sea. The room was murky and green with mysterious enigmatic lights. Towards them gliding or swimming rather than walking the normal way, a woman, an angel fish, perhaps. Her face was painted with a beauty that was formal rather than erotic. Yes, there was a tank of fish, a huge tank, its denizens to be admired rather than eaten. 'Good evening, Mr Standing.'

'Good evening, Helen.' She was clad in a wonderful way, a high mandarin collar on a floor-length dress of green silk. There was something odd about the garment but Alan couldn't quite, as it were, put his finger on it. 'And would you be so good as to take my bag? Thank you so much.'

'Lilac will look after you, Mr Standing. Customary table?' And she gave a sudden instruction, harsh after her honeyed English, to a woman who materialised beside her, smiling almost as beautifully as Sophie had been earlier. As Lilac stepped forward, Alan realised with a glorious start that her dress was split from floor to hip.

She led them to a table in the corner, by the floor-to-ceiling window from which they could see the harbour, Kowloon, the hills of the Nine Dragons beyond the buildings. Alan could see at least one thousand boats; a jet attempted to defy gravity jinking its way through the far buildings to touch down at Kai

Tak. 'I think in view of the occasion, I'll have a Singapore Sling,' André said. 'I seriously advise you to do the same.'

Alan was quite definitely beginning to panic. Even a beer would be beyond his funds. This was hideous. He would have to run.

'On me, my dear. On me. I'm celebrating, you see.'

'Well. Thanks.'

André turned again to Lilac and gave the order, with a glittering exchange of smiles. He caught Alan looking, with rather provincial fascination, at the lower half of Lilac's costume. 'Did you know that the tailoring of a cheongsam is so complicated that they take a measurement from nipple to nipple?'

Alan was fractionally recovering his nerve. 'I feel happier for knowing that,' he said.

Lilac brought the drinks. She had to take extremely small steps in order not to fall over. Every stride threatened to expose the entire length of her, from sculpted ankle to journey's end, and every dozen or so strides this actually happened, but for no more than a nanosecond: it took all Alan's concentration to catch the moment as it flew. The drinks she brought were longish and pinkish, and tasted as if the barman had started at one end of the bar and worked his away along, pouring as he went.

'Good,' said André. 'They look after one, don't they?'

Alan looked down at the puny craft crisscrossing the harbour. 'It's rather like being taken to the high place by the devil and shown all the kingdoms of the world,' he said. 'By the way, André, what are we celebrating?'

'Oh, I am going to do a spot of selling for Dean. Wants me to sell some advertising space to airlines, hotels and stuff for *Business PanAsia*, round up some specialist stuff for *Cargo News* and *Asian Shipping*. But he's planning a Singapore special issue for the autumn, and I'm to try and get a few ads for that. The fact of the matter is that Dean is sending me to Singapore for a fortnight, and putting me up at the Great Orient, nice pub, and it's all the most frightfully good news because I don't expect it will take more than a week to get Dean's stuff sorted out, and earn my commission. I've got some awfully good contacts there.

So for the rest of the time – well, you know me, Alan. I can always find things to do.'

André started to expound on Singapore, and how it differed from Hong Kong and from KL and various other Asian cities. This became a dissertation on Southeast Asia.

Lilac brought more drinks in response to André's languid summons. 'Might pop over the causeway while I'm there. I know a rather nice girl in Johor Baharu. Might be time to get as far north as KL. Met some interesting people there, nothing came of it, but they said to look them up next time. But you see the principle, don't you, Alan? Dean gives me a free flight and base, and, as it were, a guaranteed minimum for the trip. But my real profit won't come from selling advertising space.'

'Where then?' Alan, feeling the ambush of the Singapore Sling, was moved to forthrightness.

'I specialise, my dear, in omnifariousness. Chap in Denpasar once told me that. One more? And then perhaps some dinner? In the hotel? On me?'

They dined, then, in some splendour. Alan wore a tie for the occasion, for André produced a spare one from his attaché case. He retired to the gents to put it on: a Chinese ancient watched the knotting process with great concentration, as if he were to be asked questions about it afterwards. Alan joined André, who was already at the table and by now utterly magnificent.

'Fish, yes, they do it rather well here. We are, as you note, not too far from the sea.' He ordered sole véronique with a polished French accent and sent back the white wine as imperfectly chilled. Alan wondered rather incoherently if the ordering of the fish was to make possible the ordering of the white and its subsequent rejection.

'Well, it's in the blood, you see, as you can no doubt tell from the name, bloody silly name to have in Hong Kong, or anywhere else in Asia for that matter. I have to spell it exactly one hundred times per day. Girls can never say it in bed. I don't think I have ever made love to a girl who called me by my name. I am always On-jay, or worse, On-lay.'

'Karen calls you André. I've heard her.'

'She does, bless her. It's her chief attraction, really.'

André insisted on Armagnac with the coffee. 'Did you ever meet Pearl? Nice girl, works in a travel agency. I rather think she was before your time. She used to come out and see me on Tung Lung now and then. There was something of a kerfuffle when Karen paid me a surprise visit.' He started laughing a little. 'On a clear day you can still hear the echo. Sophie's a nice kid, isn't she?'

'Who? Oh, the receptionist at *Business PanAsia*. God yes, gorgeous.'

'I quite agree. An ex of mine, as you may have guessed.'

'Lucky fellow.'

André put his head to one side and regarded Alan kindly. 'We really must get you fixed up with a nice Chinese girl. You won't want to look at a Western woman after a bit.' He called for the bill and settled it with a lordly flourish of the credit card. The Sikh doorman showed them into a taxi and received five dollars for doing so. André gave the driver hectoring instructions in Cantonese.

'Oh God, is that the time?'

'Certainly. Be calm. Allow nothing to trouble your mind. The ten thirty ferry is never less than ten minutes late.' The taxi pulled up outside a small shop in Lockhart Road; André left the car. He returned a moment or so later carrying, inevitably, a pink carrier bag filled with beer.

'Oh Jesus, we'll have to spend the night in town.'

'Not a bit of it. You worry too much. Fai-dee, fai-dee, aaa!' This last to the driver, who fai-deed as best he could. They reached the ferry pier after a sick-making slalom along Connaught Road. André negligently dropped a ten-dollar bill for the six-dollar ride, and strolled towards the ferry. Alan, heaving his bag to his shoulder and rescuing a sheaf of papers with a mad grab, scuttled after him. The gangplank was raised the instant they stepped on board the ferry. The time was ten forty-two.

'See what I mean?'

'Oh God.'

'Have a beer.'

57

'André, you are an appalling person.' By this stage, Alan had begun to giggle foolishly. 'I can't begin to keep up with you. Not the beer. I mean, the chances you take.'

'I take no chances, my dear. I take the trouble to learn the odds. There is a difference, you know.' They reached their seat at the back of the ferry as the boat pulled away from the pier. They sat; opened their cans in unison.

'Perhaps so. But I couldn't do it.'

'That, my dear, is why you are a journalist and I am a merchant venturer.' They both laughed a good deal at this, but then André was suddenly and rather dramatically transfixed by seriousness. 'Listen, Alan. Last year, I was down the tube for about thirty grand. Three companies were after me for money I no longer had – never did have, to tell the truth. I went to Bangkok, a few hours before the storm broke. Had five grand up front, in cash, from someone who wanted something I could get in Thailand. I did a deal – one deal. I was gone for a week. It was a rather sordid trip, actually, had to pay for my hotel, and thought I'd better keep my head down, so I stayed at the Malaysia – back-packer's place, terrible old dump. Anyway, I was back in Hong Kong a week later with all debts paid and twenty grand to the good on top of that.'

'Christ,' Alan said respectfully. 'A miracle.'

'But it isn't, you see. You tell me you've just written two thousand words on King.'

'Very true. The business of love and his total faithfulness to his wife.'

'Laid that one on you, did he? Didn't tell you about shagging Chai, then?'

'I thought she just came to clean up his flat.'

'Oh, Alan. My dear Alan.'

'Hong Kong will never return to China,' Alan said, repeating King's words in King's voice. 'You might as well expect the UK to have a female prime minister. These two things are simply impossible.'

André laughed at this impersonation. 'But where was I? Ah yes. Well, I couldn't write two thousand words about King or anybody else. But if you want two thousand bucks, then I'll raise it in no time. Or lose it in no time, but it doesn't really worry me, because I know I'll be able to make it up some other way. It's my experience that most people only have one talent. Yours is journalism. Mine is money.'

'The other night you said the same thing, but that your one talent in life was sailing.'

André began to laugh again. 'So it bloody well is. I can sail the arse off anyone.'

'You'd be first in any capsizing race.'

'I do regret that, Alan, I really do. But you have to get close to the wind, you know. I thought you'd like it.'

Alan winced at the memory. 'It wasn't the closeness to the wind I minded. It was the closeness to the water.'

'Well again, Alan, as I say, it's not about taking chances, it's about knowing the odds. I don't capsize in races, when I'm playing different percentages.'

'Charles wouldn't let you capsize in a race.'

'He does take it seriously, doesn't he? Bit of a sobersides when it comes to sailing, old Charles. But no, in a race, I like to win, and so does Charles. You can capsize at home any time you want.'

'If there's a moral in that, I lost it somewhere. Give me another beer.'

The ferry at last arrived at Tung Lung. Laughing, zigzagging a little, very happy with each other, they essayed the 176 steps. At one point, Alan fell up a few of them, but André hauled him to his feet.

'Alan. Something to help you sleep?'

'A wise precaution, André.'

No light shone from the house. They entered André's flat, which always surprised Alan by its austerity. There was not a picture on the wall, save a single poster of a catamaran in full sail towing a water-skier. The only furniture was a set of folding tables and chairs from China Products. A ghetto blaster the size of a suitcase provided music when required, which was often. André disappeared into his bedroom, and reappeared with a plastic bag. Delving into its contents, he began to roll a joint. Pure grass, no mixing with tobacco.

'Hey,' said Alan. 'It's illegal, that stuff.'

'What are laws?'

'The crystallised prejudices of the masses.'

'Karl Marx?'

'Goldfinger, actually.'

'I like it.'

'Isn't that stuff hard to get here?'

André did not reply, completing his work with great attention to the fine detail. He then lit the joint, bringing the flame to its tip three times to ensure a perfectly even burn. He drew twice before passing to Alan, and then spoke smokefully: 'Not if you know what you are doing, my dear, like so many other things in life.'

Alan laughed loudly at this, then realised, with mild embarrassment, that there was no call to do so. 'Expensive, I suppose.'

André took the offered joint. 'Alan, I am going to show you something beautiful. It is so beautiful, so *perfect* that I really ought to keep it a secret. But I am going to show it to you, because I know you are a good chap and you won't blab.' André returned the joint and went again to his bedroom. He came back, his steps weaving just slightly, and passed Alan an aerosol can, retaking the joint. 'Get a load,' he said, 'of this little baby.'

Alan coughed. 'Deodorant,' he said. 'Grass is cheap to those who don't have smelly armpits.'

They both laughed a good deal at this.

'No. Look at it. I mean, look at it.'

It was a well-known make. Alan shook it: he felt the soft rattle of fluid. He removed the top: a nozzle, just as you would expect. 'Try it,' André said, stubbing out the joint with maniacal care. Alan squirted a little onto the back of his hand. He smelt it. It smelt like deodorant.

'So what?'

'Unscrew the top.'

Alan did so. Absolutely nothing happened, precisely as you would expect.

'Now watch me.' André took the can from Alan and gave it a gentle twist in the opposite direction. 'Try it now.'

Alan took the can once more. He began to twist *clockwise*. After a great amount of turning, the thing came apart. In his right hand he held the nozzle and a tiny reservoir of deodorant, perhaps an inch deep. In his left a canister, hollow but not empty. Alan pulled out a plastic bag containing a densely packed mass of dried and shredded green leaves. He hefted it in his hand: perhaps a quarter-pound.

'Magic!' André said. 'The bugger's on a left-hand thread. Isn't that beautiful? Isn't that the most perfect thing you have ever seen in all your fucking life?' And André laughed and laughed; laughed till he wept.

But electronics, Alan bade his keys, *is only the tip of the iceberg.* Was that grammar? *Other industries have also been swept along on what has become a tidal wave of quality. In the field of optics, for example* . . . Where the hell were those quotes from the bloke at Zoffel?

Alan stood, adjusted his sarong with decorous haste. A ferry had just arrived; he had heard without registering its self-welcoming hoot. A young Chinese man in a very pale grey suit passed his door, presumably to visit the Ngs. He walked with springy certainty, sparing no glance for the humble dwelling on his left and its humble, sarong-clad master. A couple of minutes later, moving on careworn, velvet-slippered feet, shuffled the chief of the Ng tribe of redoubtable women. Behind her walked another woman, ancient as she, carrying the bags, pink carriers, filled not with beer but with, Alan knew, morning-plucked vegetables and morning-slaughtered meat. Alan longed to visit their establishment, where of them all, only King was permitted to pass. From its depths, two Dobermans bayed, occasionally flinging themselves at the gate in orgiastic hatred of a passer-by. It was a place of monumental self-certainty, entered only by the numberless tribe of the Ngs, with their endless supplies of babies and ancients.

And then walking uncertainly in the wake of the two black-clad ladies, a quite extraordinary figure: a boy, in his teens, though it was hard to read age in the smoothness of a Chinese face. And dressed in a species of hussar uniform: very tight pale khaki trousers that did up underneath his feet; an electric-blue jacket covered in gold frogging, with thick and elaborate epaulettes. On his head, at a foolish angle, a pillbox hat, improbably small and secured by a golden strap. He was carrying in his hands a silver ice-bucket that contained what was obviously, from its gold foil crown, a bottle of champagne. For God's sake, Alan thought. Who is Ng trying to impress now?

The boy advanced as far the great green gates and paused, uncertainly. He looked doubtfully at King's yellow house, and the plastic tables and chairs in Alan's concrete garden. Then he passed through the permanently open spiked gate that separated the concrete garden from the world and called out in Cantonese at Alan's open door.

Alan, more curious than obliging, went to his door to speak to him. 'Hello. Are you lost?' The pillbox hat bore the golden legend 'Great Orient Hotel'.

'Mr Fairs?'

It was a remark that made Alan feel terribly dizzy. 'That's me, yes. What's up?'

The page-boy allowed himself a small smirk of triumph. He produced a white envelope, and passed it to Alan. He was wearing white gloves. Alan opened the envelope and took out the single sheet it contained. This bore the Great Orient crest, the words 'Great Orient', and below it, 'Hong Kong'. Two words had been handwritten below: 'Santé! André'. Not André's handwriting, but the style was his all right. Alan wondered who was paying, and then stopped wondering. All the same, how was André going to get this one past the accountants at *Business PanAsia*?

'You'd better come in.'

Grinning to himself, the page-boy entered. His eyes flickered round the room, pricing everything, observing the empty beer cans, unwashed dishes, the pile of newspapers and magazines.

'Where shall I put this, sir?'

There was no obvious place, for there was no proper table. The small one with the telephone would not do. There were no chairs, either: the room was furnished with half a dozen extremely large cushions, loaned to him by King. 'They were a whim of Jacinta's on a visit some three years ago, my friend. Return them to me when she makes another visit, but not before.'

The cushions made an L-shape around a long, low table. Alan had actually bought this, with money, from Stanley Market: an insubstantial-looking thing made from rattan, and imported from Malaysia. 'Er, yes, on the little table there.'

The page-boy shot another look at Alan, the drooping sarong, the flapping unbuttoned khaki shirt. Quite without expression, he squatted on the tiles of the floor and deftly began to fidget with the bottle.

'Why are you opening it?'

'Instruction.'

It was then that Alan realised that he would have to hand over some kind of tip. No pockets in the sarong, but surely some money in last night's trousers. Or had he lost it all to Charles at dice? Surely not. Or had he spent it all at Ah-Chuen's? Had he paid? Had anybody paid? And where were the trousers? He hadn't slept in them, that was something.

He went into his bedroom; really must do something about all this, still at least the page-boy can't see. His trousers lay before him, folded with pedantic neatness on the floor. How more than odd. Had he done that? Still, never mind that now. He picked them up: a pair of dice fell to the floor. He rescued them, one rolling on its corners across the floor. Six. Lucky? But no rattle of coins. He groped the pockets: a few loose and rumpled notes. Christ, ten dollars? Well, better hand it over.

The page-boy, absorbing the ten dollars without pain, withdrew, taking the silver bucket but leaving behind the now open bottle. God, he must have looked wonderful on the ferry, among all the old ladies and straw baskets, all returning from market where they had been selling the produce of the chessboard fields and of the sunken fish-traps, sitting there in his uniform, clutching his silver bucket, picking his way along the jetty past the great stink of Chuen-suk's shrimp-paste factory.

Then all at once Alan saw why André had arranged all this. It was the thought of the uniformed page mingling with the noble savages of Tung Lung, *at his behest*. André had used money, not his own, as a form of surrealism. Wealth, vicarious wealth, used in a fashion that recalled the man who took a lobster for a walk on a lead. The joke gained in subtlety from the fact that André would not actually see the event himself. Arranging it was enough. It was a perfect blend of power and absurdity. Alan suddenly saw André as a spoiled intellectual; as a poet manqué.

So much for conceptual art; what to do with the actual bottle? Only one option, really, the bottle being open. But a whole bottle before lunch? With only a couple of slices of toast and Marmite to soak it up? Grinning, Alan seized the bottle and ran around the back, climbing up to King's place, rapping jovially on the door, preparing a dramatic entrance. No reply. Unusual, that. Oh well. The afternoon of subbing at Reg's was not really a champagne prospect, but what choice did he have?

He washed the toothpaste from his only glass, and set about the task. A good job the page-boy had not demanded to pour the champagne. But look here, really, he ought to get the next ferry.

Alan walked into his bathroom, abandoning the sarong as he did so. He spun the tap of the shower and stood beneath its rose. Nothing happened. He cursed, with resignation rather than fury, and regained his sarong. He took up a red plastic bucket, and carried it along the path and down the dozen steps. He walked back with the bucket, with Chuen-suk's water slopping onto the sun-heated concrete. He gave himself a vigorous and too-cold splashing and then dressed, drinking chilled nectar as he did so. He finally set off down the hill, holding an opened beer can which brimmed, not with beer but champagne. Alan had rinsed it with some care before filling it with Veuve Clicquot.

He subbed the afternoon away with an ever-waxing headache, but that went away with his first beer on the ferry home.

Alan spent a quiet evening drinking with King and Charles, rolling the dice, King discoursing at length on island politics, and the latest inflection of the rivalry between Ng and Chuen-suk.

The following morning, scarcely hung over at all, Alan continued with 'The Shift to Quality'. He had found the quotes about optical glass. He had the first draft finished by noon, and celebrated this – three thousand words required celebration – in the day's first beer. On Fridays it was acceptable to have a beer a little earlier than usual, especially if you had written so many words.

Once again, the passing of passengers as the twelve o'clock ferry disgorged. The Top Dame from next door shuffled past his gate, with her bearer as ever shuffling a pace behind with the pink beerless bags. And then, ridiculously, once again the page-boy. Oh really. Once was surreal. Twice was a bad joke.

Alan thought to himself: '*Y*b**nna mat!*' This necessarily silent exclamation came from *From Russia With Love*: an expression so obscene it could not be written out even in transliterated Russian. The situation, Alan thought, demanded this response.

The page-boy bore no ice-bucket this time, no champagne. Instead, he was almost invisible under a Birnam Wood of flowers. Well, this can't be for me. And of course, he was wrong. The page-boy turned in through the gateway – he had to turn sideways to get through with his burden – and once again, Alan met him at the door.

'Good morning, Mr Fairs.'

'Hello again. Surely these aren't for me.' Alan felt the treacherous sarong make a threatening movement, but he was too quick for it.

'Yes, Mr Fairs. I have a letter for you, Mr Fairs.'

Alan opened the white envelope. It was a longer epistle this time. It was from André all right, though again, not his handwriting.

Hello my dear, hope you enjoyed the fizz. Look, could you do me a favour and pass these flowers on? I arranged to have a couple of young ladies come out and visit me, separately of course, and rather expected to be back in time. However, things have got rather interesting out here, and I may be a little time, as they say. Please entertain these ladies in any way you think appropriate, but for Christ's sake don't tell either one about the other. See you when I'm back, whenever that is. Yours aye, André.

Alan found another ten dollars for the page-boy, who went smirking off down the 176 steps. He then put the flowers, still in their cellophane, into his washbasin, which he filled up with water red-bucketed in from the Chuen-suk standpipe. Two bouquets. Why didn't he telephone? Why these messages by hand of bearer? Surely it was not beyond the wit of man to telephone these girls and put them off? Unanswerable questions. Was this André being surreal again? Or what? Time for a shower, anyway, and to get into town, and *damn* it, there was still no water. A small light illuminated in his brain. Well, why not? Make some profit from the irritation.

The telephone splintered the silence. 'Alan, old chap. Can you do me a favour?'

'Anything for you, Reg.'

'I'm out of town for a few days. Had a trip come up at short notice. So, don't come in this afternoon.'

'That's a favour?'

'Well, thing is, I wondered if you could come into town first thing tomorrow morning. I know it's Saturday, I know it's a lot to ask. But could you meet me here and man the office after I'm gone, wait for the printer, give him all the stuff when he arrives? Then lock up and so forth?'

'Not a problem, Reg, so long as the ferry timetable fits your aeroplane schedule. Where are you off to?'

'Oh, you know, usual spot.'

'Have a lovely time. How early do you want me?'

'How early can you make it?'

'The earliest ferry I can get is the six fifty, so I'll be at the office not much after seven forty-five.'

'Perfect. Alan, you're a great support to me.'

'Any time, Reg. Oh, you know we still haven't got anything for the 'Last Word' column? I thought I could knock out a piece on the endless water politics out here on Tung Lung. Two tinpot taipans fighting it out over the well water.'

'Nice idea, Alan. You go for it. Just put it in with the rest of the copy, and that's the last of my worries sorted out.'

But in fact Alan spent the afternoon putting together the second draft of 'The Shift to Quality', thinking more about women than glass or electronics. He wouldn't mind a shift to quality himself. Or a shift to quantity, for that matter. 'I love my wife,' Reg had said in one post-work session at the Two Brewers. 'But you know, physically, I just need . . . well, a man has physical needs.' Reg explained this as if he had invented the concept himself. What did he tell his wife? Business trip, darling. I love you, I'll miss you. Did she know or suspect the nature of the business? Did she turn a blind eye? Did she have a handsome young Chinese lover, perhaps a female one? André had said that Chinese women were rather partial to that sort of thing: 'It's something about the Asian type of beauty, you know, Alan. After you've made love to an Asian girl, well, everything else, you know . . . I mean, an Asian girl is a perfect scale model of a real woman.'

Alan, who had not made love to an Asian girl then, and still had not for that matter, nodded understandingly. He typed on and thought of André, and what he was up to in Singapore. Or who. What golden beauty was getting the benefit of his room at the Great Orient? Or suite; André always saw himself as Upgrade Man. And all the time leaving not one but two rejected beauties on Tung Lung. It was hardly fair, was it? It was fair neither to the beauties nor to Alan. *Great advances have also been made in the field of consumer durables. Hong Kong is now involved in the manufacture of state-of-the-art* – Colin would love that magic phrase – *domestic hi-fi equipment, albeit with a Japanese brand name. Jeremy Choi, managing director of . . .*

Alan was two-thirds of the way through his second draft and into the final thousand when he became aware of the arrival of the five twenty ferry. He rather hoped that Charles would be on board, stealing a Friday afternoon flier in order to get the weekend's drinking off to a good start.

He had forgotten quite how beautiful she was.

Or rather in what way she was beautiful. Partly it was the height, she was nearly five foot six. And her face was long rather than round, not quite so perfect and symmetrical as the faces of other beautiful Chinese girls. Perhaps the point was that she didn't look like a scale model. But it was her clothes that beat him so savagely in the mid-section. Or her lack of them. Well, not precisely that. But the fact that she was out of business clothes made her seem almost undressed; certainly indecent. She had changed from the calf-length black skirt into cut-off jeans; cut off very high indeed, and a great deal of long and lovely leg was thereby available for comment. Her hair had been brushed free of its office style. The white blouse had been exchanged for a white T-shirt, curiously sculpted, and emphasising the slight fulsomeness of the top half of her. She had obviously spent the entire afternoon making herself carelessly desirable. Sophie, of course, emerging from the reception desk of *Business PanAsia*.

Certain of where she was going, a faint smile played about her (freshly reglossed) lips as she turned away and walked along the side of the building, ignoring the open gate, the permanent invitation to Alan's concrete garden. Alan could hear her steps on the stair overhead. No shuffler she.

Should he go to her? Or wait until she returned? He heard her knock faintly. He could almost feel the bewilderment, the realisation, and, materialising in slow motion before her, the betrayal. Second knock, louder, the beginnings of desperation. No sound of retreating footsteps. Was she planning to camp out there until André returned? Or had she collapsed in despair? Or had she silently killed herself?

Better get it over with.

Oh God, not in a sarong. He hurried into his bedroom, found

a pair of black cotton jeans, lightweight and not too disgusting. Yes, and he had bought those T-shirts off a barrow in Causeway Bay, hadn't he, where were they? He selected the black one, very cool, tugged it violently over his head, tucked it into his waist. Thrust his feet into kung-fu slippers. The cool islander.

He walked around the back of the house. Sophie had begun to walk down the stairs: she was descending slowly and bearing a face of desolation: the face of a refugee whose loved ones have all been put to the sword.

'Hello, Sophie.'

'Hello.'

No light of delighted recognition came to her face. 'I'm Alan. André's neighbour.'

'Oh!' And this time a smile, and a very warm one, too. 'Do you know where is André?'

'Yes, well, I'm afraid he's not here, very sorry about it, he's managed to get a message through, asked me to say how sorry he is, sent something for you, if you'd care to come downstairs, I've got it in my flat.'

Alan remembered seeing what Americans call an art movie, one that was called something like *Sorrows of the Kingdom*. Every other shot showed a Chinese face (or was it Japanese, now he came to think of it?) with eyes focused on the far distance, tears flowing regardless down magnificently bone-structured features. It was as if he were seeing the film all over again. Though it seemed to be taking rather longer this time.

Some minutes or hours later, he was making tea for her, while drinking a beer himself. He did occasionally actually drink tea, because jasmine tea was gentler on a morning head than instant coffee. Sophie peered about the flat with a gentler version of the page-boy's disdain. She was sitting ornamentally – she could surely sit in no other fashion – leaning on her right arm, in fact half kneeling and half sitting, her legs tracing wonderful lines across the cushions.

'You have a message from André,' she reminded him. On-jay.

'Well, you know he is travelling abroad for your company, Singapore, selling space.'

'Of course. I help him get the job.'

'Oh.'

'He was supposed to be back today, so he invite me.'

Alan produced the flowers. God, hope she doesn't see the other bunch. Sophie said they were nice. She said the tea was nice. She said Alan was nice.

'You seem very fond of André.'

'I think maybe we get married.'

'Oh.'

'I have known him quite a long time. He is a very kind man.' She smiled elegiacally at a point somewhere over Alan's left shoulder.

He was now sitting himself, at right angles to her, thinking about making a lunge across the cushions in her general direction but knowing he wasn't going to do any such thing and knowing also that even if he was gifted with the necessary reckless courage, it would do no good.

'He is very . . . *romantic*. Chinese men are not romantic. For them, marriage is like business. Like a merger. But André – he *romance* me.' She smiled very sadly and a new tear appeared, and flowed silently down a single magnificently bone-structured cheek.

'Poor Sophie.'

She smiled again, bravely, looking across infinite vistas of ancestral troubles. Another tear followed. Alan, lunging madly, kissed the tear.

That opened the floodgates. She sobbed away for a good while, as Alan held her in his arms, her body, slim and pliant beneath his hands as, lust singing in his veins, he said there there, and said André would be home soon and not to worry, he'd look after her. He kissed face and neck wherever possible, always seeking but never finding lips. Some odd notion of propriety stopped him from aiming kisses further south than her shoulders, bared, though not for him.

'He is a kind man. But very busy. He does not always have the time to be kind like he wants.'

'I always have the time to be kind,' Alan said.

She smiled, even laughed a little. 'You are nice,' she said, comfortably in his arms, now looking up at his face.

'Can I buy you dinner tonight?'

'What time is the next ferry?'

'Seven thirty. I'll buy you dinner in town, if you like, or on the island, at Ng's.'

'Oh, you are kind, Alan, you are very kind.'

'Oh, I am, Sophie, I am.'

She laughed again, almost happily. 'But you see. I must go home now.'

At least I tried; Alan thought. Naturally they debated the question a while, but Sophie really did want to go home, really did not want Alan to buy her dinner, or rather, really did not want to have Alan make an elaborate pass at her. There was no escaping the truth. Absent André had something that present Alan could not compete with. Not, as he believed he had told himself before, fair.

He took the only consolation prize on offer and escorted her down the 176 steps to the ferry pier, she clasping her bouquet. Fortunately, she had not required the bathroom, repairing her make-up on the cushions before him with a hand-mirror, a mermaid run aground on the reef of Jacinta's cushions. Thus she avoided the second bouquet. Alan had managed to think up a lie to cover the situation (Charles had left them there for his non-existent girlfriend) and wondered why he didn't try the truth: André is a lying bastard, you're better off with me. Was it male solidarity? Or the knowledge that it wouldn't work anyway? He wondered about making a dramatic gesture to impress her, leaping across the widening gap as the ferry left, sweeping her off her feet, buying her dinner at the Fragrant Harbour Hotel, sole véronique, back on the ten thirty ferry, yes, André is not the only person on Tung Lung capable of nocturnal niceness.

He enjoyed the thought while it lasted. He promised to come and see her the following Monday, when he delivered his copy. Shift to Quality indeed, he thought, as the gangplank was lowered. Ha.

'Hello, neighbour! Abandoning the island? Night on the town, is it?' It was Charles: arriving passengers had to file past those waiting to embark. 'Why, hello, Sophie. How are you, and what are you up to with this man? Have nothing to do with him. He drinks, you know.'

She smiled sadly. 'Fine,' she said, with great bravery.

'Well well well,' Charles said. 'Have an awfully nice time, won't you?'

'I'll see you at Ah-Chuen's,' Alan said, 'as soon as I have seen Sophie to her carriage.'

'Oh,' said Charles. 'Oh.'

Alan said a nice farewell to Sophie. They embraced; she accepted two cheek-kisses. Then, clasping her dripping flowers, she stepped, the last passenger, onto the boat. The engines grunted softly and the ferry pulled away from the pier. Sophie, standing at the rail now, blew him a kiss, the sorrows of the kingdom etched on her face once more.

Alan walked slowly back along the quay. At Ah-Chuen's, beneath the banyan tree, on the next table to Chuen-suk and his court, Charles sat, two full glasses of beer before him, a nearly empty and a full bottle also on the table. A bird sang four loud plangent notes.

Charles remarked without looking up: 'What occurs?'

Alan sat, drank. 'Sophie had a date with André. André is still in Singapore. I found myself delegated to break the news.'

Charles sat for a while in deep thought, looking out at the harbour, at André's horrible yellow boat. 'Did you fuck her?' he asked.

'No.'

'Hm.'

'Yes.'

'Thought not.'

'Yes.'

Charles turned and looked at him, a bright smile on his face. 'They don't, you know.'

'What?'

'Women.'

'Women what?'

'Fuck one.'

'No. It seems not.' There was silence for a while.

'Alan?'

'Yes?'

'Do you think it is because we're always pissed?'

'I've often wondered about that. But André is always pissed and women never stop fucking him.'

'Good point. Excellent point, in fact. And King's always pissed and Chai never stops fucking him.'

'No.'

'Oh well, another good theory goes out of the window. Not that I was going to stop drinking either way.'

'No.'

There was another longish pause, always something of a feature of conversations with Charles. After a while, Alan got up and acquired from Ah-Chuen another pair of bottles. The bird gave its four notes again. Charles burst into sudden loud laughter. 'One more bottle!' he said.

'Two more.'

'No, the bird. It says, "One more bottle." ' Charles then sang it in the notes of the bird: 'One-more-bot-tle.'

'Very good, Charles.'

'Indian cuckoo.'

'How do you know?'

'I know these things.' He gestured. 'Ask me anything you like about birds.' He allowed a short pause. 'One-more-bot-tle,' he said softly. 'One-more-bot-tle.'

It occurred to Alan that Charles was already pretty pissed.

'Are you already pretty pissed?'

'Yes.'

'I see.'

'Talking of fucking. I was engaged to be married once.'

'Really?'

'When I was a lad of some eighteen summers.'

'Let me guess. A nice English girl from a three-generations-solid expat family, a girl warmly approved of by your parents.'

'Close. Very close. Actually, she was a Chinese prostitute.'

73

'Oh.'

'She was, and no doubt still is, a professional working in Wanchai. I met her in a bar. Like you do, you know. It was called the Seven Seas Bar. It was a nice bar. A very nice bar. A very nice bar indeed if what you like best in life is drinking and tits. Very large drinks and very small tits. You see, none of the women wore any clothes above the waist. I found that an endearing trait.'

There followed another long pause, Charles doubtless recalling endless lost horizons of beers and bosoms. Eventually Alan said: 'And?'

'And what?'

'And then what happened?'

'Well, obviously, I met this girl and went to bed with her and wanted to marry her.'

'What did she think about it?'

'Well, she was all for it, naturally. She thought she was marrying the South China Bank. What more could any self-respecting prostitute want?'

'What indeed? So then what happened?'

'It was the talk of the Peak. The old man's lost his grip, he's let the boy run wild, should have sent him to the university, not that he'd have got in to the university. And I was saying no, it's all quite simple and straightforward. I'm going to get married. And going down to Wanchai and fucking my brains out. I must say, the old man was brilliant.'

'Supportive, you mean?'

'Alan, what on earth, from past conversations, would make you think that my old man would be supportive on this or any other matter? When I say brilliant, I mean just that. He performed a series of brilliant manoeuvres. Though I did have a talk with him once. In his study, it was.'

'Like a headmaster?'

'Like a headmaster. But all terribly human and civilised and men-of-the-world and so forth.'

'How do you mean?'

'I envy you being young, my lad. I was just as wild as you.

Don't think for a second that I will act the heavy father and stop you seeing her. I know what it is to be young and to sow your wild oats. I said, I'm not sowing wild oats, Father, I'm settling down. He smiled, and said, well, we'll give it a few weeks, and then we'll discuss the matter again. He wished me luck. Said I must do what I thought best. Always.'

'So that made you change your mind?'

'Did it buggery! Went straight back down the Seven Seas. I was all set to take out a licence and get married at once.'

'And?'

'Gone.'

'Stood you up? Found someone better? Had second thoughts?'

'Oh Christ, Alan, you do talk wet sometimes. Listen. What do bank managers consider the most important thing in life? I'll give you a clue, it comes in small bits of paper that fold up and fit inside your pocket.'

'All right, got that.'

'Now try another question. What do prostitutes consider the most important thing in life?'

'Oh. Did you ever see her again?'

'Don't talk wet.'

'Sorry.'

'Rather funny, it was, in a way. I was terribly public about it all, while it was going on. All my friends, and all my family and all the friends of my family were positively queuing up to give me good advice. They wanted to be the one that helped me back to the straight and narrow; to do the favour that my father would never forget. You see what I mean? Don't throw your life away, Charles. Charles, she'll ruin your life. I said, I am perfectly capable of ruining my own life without anybody's assistance, thanks very much.'

Another pause. Then Alan asked: 'And then?'

'And then, Alan, old chap, a job was found for me at Hong Kong Estates.'

'A deal?'

'Not presented in those terms. Brilliant, as I say. Suddenly this girl went missing, and suddenly this job materialised, what a fantastic opportunity, I wish I was young myself to take it all on. But as you say, a deal.'

'No thought of repeating the experiment?'

'Whoring, you mean?'

'Getting married, I meant. Or doing something about the girls, anyway.'

'Alan, I've got more important things to do.'

'Such as?'

'Do you know how much beer you have to drink before it starts to come out of your ears?'

'Er, no.'

'Exactly! Nor do I. And until I have found out, I have sworn not to worry about any other aspect of life.'

'Very single-minded of you.'

The bird called again. 'One-more-bot-tle,' sang Charles. 'One-more-bot-tle.'

The bird would not shut up. Alan heard it when he got up for a pee in the night; he heard it when he got up to catch the six fifty ferry. He rose from his bed by an amazing effort of will. By two more of these, he managed not to throw up when the boat entered the traditionally choppy waters of the Tung Lung channel, and to drink a cup of ferry coffee. For a moment, he wondered if the swooping of the taxi – Hong Kong taxi drivers tend to be swoopers – would effect a purgation, but he opened the window, despite the protests of the driver, who was proud of his sick-making air conditioning, and the rush of air kept the various liquids in his system in their place. He arrived in remarkably good shape, considering. Was there nothing he could not do?

Reg was there bustling about with excitement, the little puffs of hair standing from his head more oddly than ever. Odd to think that they would be bouncing about on top of some delicate little Thai girl before the sun went down. Would Reg think whoring a desperate and depressing business in London, or in the Home Counties town he seemed born for? So why was it perfectly acceptable in Asia?

Reg set off for Kai Tak airport with a great fizz of bonhomie and last-minute instructions. Alan made some proper coffee at the office machine, and drank it and felt still stronger. Then he sat at a typewriter and crashed out six hundred words on water politics. It was, he thought, modestly, hilarious. Eventually, the printer arrived, and accepted the fat bundle of deathless prose. Alan had hoped to catch the one twenty ferry back to Tung Lung, but it was not to be. All the same, he was really rather content with himself: Saturday afternoon and already, while waiting for the printer, next week had taken a bit of a battering. Time then for a beer.

He locked up with care and circumspection. God, it wouldn't do to lose the keys. He zipped them into the front pocket of his shoulder-bag and walked over to the Two Brewers. The weather hit him with a very solid blow. This was surely the hottest day of the year so far: bright sun, really not very much humidity at all. Into the eighties, certainly. Better get used to it, then.

The heat gave him a new way of walking. He walked with slow grace: his usual nervous, pecking hurry would make him hot and bothered. He found himself crossing Hennessy Road with a kind of languidness; languidly he entered the pub and ordered a beer and a sandwich, though the beer came before he had finished asking, for he was very much at home.

He caught the three forty home. No matter how languid you were on the 176 steps, you sweated. The humidity found you out. Perhaps the water would be back on. If so, he would take his clothes off and stand beneath the dribbling shower for an eternity or two, and then a drink a beer in his sarong.

But as he turned at the end of the terrace towards the yellow building, he saw that his flat had been invaded; the door was wide open. This was hardly unprecedented. Probably Charles, who must have caught the one twenty. It was only when he reached his gateway that he saw the nature of his invader. A naked girl.

Or all but naked. She was lying face down on the perishing air bed: lean brown body, long black hair, stark black knickers. The tight black pants and the splay of her legs whipped at Bond's senses.

She raised her head an inch; Alan watched the roll of her slim shoulder blades. 'Where,' she said, 'is bladdy-fackin André?'

'Hello, Karen.'

She flowed bonelessly into a sitting potion, knotting the towel on which she'd been lying sarong-wise beneath her armpits. She did so neither ostentatiously nor modestly.

'Is the bladdy-fackin barcer in Singapore?' She spoke a fairly competent version of cockney, an unusual achievement for a Hong Kong Chinese.

'He left you some flowers.'

'I saw the bladdy-fackin things. Tell him to stuff them up his fackin arse.'

'All right. He told me to tell you that he's frightfully sorry, got held up and so forth.'

She folded her arms beneath her towel-wrapped breasts. 'Is he really in Singapore?'

'So far as I know.' Alan sat down on one of his plastic chairs and admired the roundness of her upper arms.

'I bet you he's somewhere else. Hundred bucks.'

'Why do you think so?'

'And I bet a thousand bladdy bucks he's bladdy well fackin somebody.'

'Do you want a beer?'

'I already got one.'

So she had. Alan did not begrudge it. He went to the kitchen to fetch one for himself, abandoning, though not without regret, the plan about taking his clothes off.

He came back to find Karen now sitting on a chair, one foot on the seat, left elbow resting on left knee. White towel, black knickers, gold skin. 'Cheers, Karen.'

'What? Oh yeah, cheers. Do you know why André is a bladdy-fackin liar?'

'Er, no comment.'

'He does it for fun. For no reason. Like bladdy sport.'

'Why stay with him then?'

'He thinks because he asks me to marry him, he can treat me like shit. He thinks you can treat Chinese girls like shit. He never thinks a Chinese girl might have bladdy friends in a bladdy Chinese village. Who might get upset when a Chinese girl gets treated like shit.'

'Doesn't he?'

'You know 14K?'

'Er, no, I don't think so. What is it?'

'It's a bladdy Triad, for Christ's sake. You give André two messages from me. OK? Number one, stick the flowers up his arse. Number two, I've gone to see my friends from 14K. Got it?'

'Got it.'

She looked directly at Alan, who shifted his eyes hurriedly from her crotch.

'I'll miss him,' she said. 'But the barcer's got to go.'

' "Hong Kong has never been able to offer permanence," ' Colin Webb said, the feet on his desk a subtle compliment, giving out the message that Alan was now an accepted person about the office at *Business PanAsia*. ' "It used to play for all its worth the card of cheap labour. But as neighbouring countries took on Hong Kong at its own game, the territory needed to find a new ace of trumps. The name of the suit is precision." Virry nice conclusion, Alan. Virry nice piece all through.'

'Well, thanks, Colin. Glad you're pleased.' Alan, feeling the pressures of a Tung Lung weekend behind his eyes, had nevertheless got his three thousand words completed in time. Now, blinking apologetically in the tough light of a Monday morning, his brain still rattling with dice and with beer, he was nevertheless contriving to look lively, or at least awake.

Colin tugged at the corner of his moustache. Did all Australians have moustaches? 'Virry nice indeed.'

'On time, too.'

Colin snorted faintly. 'I already take that for granted with you.' Alan smirked. 'But listen, Alan, do you know what we never thought of?'

Alan's heart and smirk sank. This sounded to him like a rewrite: plenty more work for absolutely no more money. 'Tell me.'

Colin leant forward, a man confiding a secret. 'Feshun.'

It took Alan a moment to catch up. 'Oh?'

'Designer feshun. Clothes. Manufacture for the big names in Paris and New York, that goes on. But now Hong Kong has designer labels of its own.'

'Sure, Colin. Perhaps I should have thought of that. But your brief seemed very much technology-based.'

Colin waved a hand decisively. 'I'm not making myself clear, sorry. The piece is excellent, no fault to find with it. But I want a side-bar, have a little bit of fun with the same concept. Hong Kong fashion. From crap to couture.'

'From rip-off to the cutting edge.'

'Triffic. Can you do that for me? Virry quick? For the same issue? I've got more space than I thought; we've sold some more ads than we expected, I'm told, good news. Can you do it this week? Copy by Friday? Special rate, five hundred bucks for seven hundred words?'

'I expect so.'

'Any time before close of play Friday. That really is the latest possible time, got to get it to the printer Saturday morning. I only give you a deadline like that because I trust you to deliver.'

'Consider it delivered, Colin.'

The deal was done. They shook hands, and Alan left. Sophie had not been on the reception desk when he'd arrived; presumably she'd been doing clerical duties for Dean. But now he saw, with a mild and more or less controllable lurch of the senses, that she was back in her place. She gave him a sad sweet smile: the Woman of Sorrows greeting the Man Who Understood.

'Hello, Sophie.'

Alan was ready for it, but he was still disappointed. 'How is André?'

'Still not back.' He searched his mind for something warm and comforting to say. Look, Sophie, he's a bladdy-fackin barcer, he's engaged to at least one other woman. I've got a great idea: why don't you step out from behind that desk and come straight out to Tung Lung and fack me instead?

He covered her hand with his own, since it was lying on the desk and she seemed to expect it. 'You should have had dinner with me last Friday.'

'You're very sweet.'

No I'm not. As a matter of fact, I have the sexual energy of a charging rhinoceros. 'Well, you remember that, because there's every chance I'll ask you again.'

Alan heard footsteps behind him and he withdrew his hand. It was Dean. 'Well, hi, Alan,' he said, remembering Alan's name in the unnerving fashion of Americans everywhere.

'Hello.'

'How is your neighbour?'

'André? I thought you'd know more about him than me.'

'How so?'

'I haven't seen him since he went to Singapore for you.'

'Not back?' said Dean, making quite sure.

'No.'

Dean nodded in a thoughtful sort of way and returned to his office.

'André's been doing awfully well,' Sophie said, in a near whisper. 'There was a long telex that came in over the weekend. He's sold an awful lot of space. Dean is very pleased with him.'

'Oh.'

'But he wants to see him, of course.'

'Of course.'

Alan left without any further instalments of the Sorrows of the Kingdom. He caught a minibus down to Wanchai and went to the Two Brewers, which was just opening. He had a beer and a sandwich by way of breakfast, and commandeered the telephone. This was accepted as his right; the Two Brewers had become more or less his second office: the Hong Kong branch of his empire. The first call, to a contact on the Hong Kong Trade Association, was a goldstrike. Yes, there would be a file of written material on the fashion industry available for Alan's collection after lunch. Sure, it was full of quotes he could steal. Any suggestion for a good interview subject? Name? Telephone number? Another call: yes, an interview could be arranged. Any chance for tomorrow? Certainly.

He ordered another beer, and then rang another number.

'*Hong Kong Chic.*'

'Could I speak to Anita Chong, please? This is Alan Fairs.'

A pause and then: 'Hello, Alan.'

'Hello, Anita. Could you use an interview with Sammy Soo?'

'Sure I can. Can you *get* an interview?'

'I can do anything.'

A polite giggle. 'Then get a Sammy Soo frock for me while you're there. Can you do 1500 words?'

'No problem. Next week all right?'

'Perfect, Alan.'

Nothing as satisfying as a win double. Unless it was a treble. Well, get the interview done first. Might not stretch to a third piece. What else? Nothing to do at *HK Biz*, with Reg still away. Some stuff to clear up, but he could do that at home. Which reminded him. Rent was due. Go to the bank and get some cash; King liked folding money. Other than that – oh, yes. Perhaps this was the moment. How long had he been in Hong Kong? Very nearly six months. Very, very nearly six months. He pulled out his passport, which he carried in his shoulder-bag. You were supposed to carry papers in Hong Kong, and he had not, as yet, applied for an identity card. God, he was right, only a couple of days before his six months was finished. He couldn't put it off any longer; he had to go to International House and get organised.

Six months. It seemed like a fortnight. It seemed like a lifetime.

He still managed to make the two fifty ferry. He had seven pink hundred-dollar bills for King, and a stapled addition to his passport explaining to whom it may concern that he had applied for an identity card. The immigration official had explained that in seven years' time, if he was still here – if, indeed! Why, this was home – he would be eligible for Belonger status.

On the ferry, sitting at the very back, with a single beer beside him, Alan read through the portfolio he'd collected from the Hong Kong Trade Association. It was all here. How more than brilliant. The story was a doddle. So crank out a couple of pieces of PE for Reg, and then go upstairs for the rent-paying ceremony. Good. Unless there was another of André's fiancées in the garden, of course.

But there was not, and so Alan pecked out a few words about a company that made office telephone systems. One had, after all, to pay the rent.

And at seven o'clock, he did exactly that. He really did have everything together, did he not? King made him boomingly welcome, gave him beer, accepted his rent. 'No, thank *you*, King. It's a privilege to live here.'

'Alan, it is a privilege to have you and your kind as tenants. The thanks are all mine.' Which was all very fine and splendid. 'But can you tell me, Alan, where is Brother André?'

'Last I heard Singapore, haven't got any more recent news. Are you worried about the rent, King?'

'There are no safe options for rent when André is your tenant,' King said, and hohohoed a bit.

'This isn't the first time he has gone missing?'

'Of course not.'

'You don't mind?'

'Alan, I believe in freedom. That is why I surround myself with free spirits. But André is the freest of you all. All the same, I trust him, you see. André I would trust with my life. I know his heart: he is a trustworthy man, but not one inclined to be tied down. I fear nothing for my rent; André is an honourable man who will pay me as soon as he returns. We are kindred spirits, he and I.'

'You don't believe he will just do a bunk?' Alan was interested in the concept of doing a bunk.

'Not he. He is a bird who flies as he wishes. But this is his roost.'

'I wish I was able to do that sort of thing. I don't seem to fly anywhere.'

'You will, my dear friend. It is in the way of nature. Your nature.'

Alan found this oddly comforting. 'And Charles never flies anywhere either.'

'A bird that has yet to stretch his wings. But he will fly too, perhaps further than any of us. To be young, Alan. Young. See, here, what I have through the post.' He passed Alan a photograph, a snapshot of a girl sitting in a chair with her knees under her chin, holding a cup of coffee. She was wearing a dressing gown, white towelling and modestly crossed beneath her chin. She smiled for the camera: it was a sleepy and contented smile, as if she had just emerged from a prolonged and soul-satisfying tussle beneath the sheets. Alan was afflicted with a brief but terrible nostalgia for time past, for love. 'My daughter Jacinta,' King explained. 'A lovely girl, as you see. And learning to fly.'

'And you?'

King did another of his Boris Karloff laughs. 'I am an old eagle who has flown a million miles.'

'And come home to roost?'

'Laugh if you will, my dear friend, but this old bird has a few miles to fly yet.'

'I don't doubt it, King.'

Charles arrived, fresh from the six thirty, a pink bag, a pink handful of cash, and of course, the dice. King, as was his custom on rent days, took them to Ng's for a meal. Ah-Hei himself served them, a giant on thistledown feet. Alan wondered if it were true, as Charles said, that he was the greatest warrior on the island. Certainly, he moved like a man supremely at home in his own body, in a fashion that reminded Alan of Olympic athletes he had seen on television. While they ate, a sudden dramatic shower of rain fell, and King laughed with delight. 'Summer is coming,' he said. 'The first day of June, and it comes with a bang.'

It was Alan's first glimpse of real Hong Kong rain. It fell not in drops but in a continuous sheet, shattering into knee-high rebounding particles as it hit the ground. They remained where they were after the meal, dicing, drinking, watching the small miracle of the rain. On the way back home, with the rain stopped and the air washed clean and bright, the valley of allotments roared and pulsed with a new sound. 'The bullfrogs have woken up,' Charles said. 'Summer is almost here.'

When Alan arose from his beery slumbers for a midnight pee, the roaring, in the night's stillness, was louder still. The promise of the coming summer was already deafening him.

Reg returned from Bangkok in, so far as Alan could tell, one piece. Alan met him at the office, as arranged, having managed not to lose the keys. This remarkable feat seemed to have elevated Alan from dogsbody to something approaching partner. Reg's first act on return was to consult Alan at length about production schedules and the content of the August issue. No talk of extra money, of course, but it was far more amusing than reading proofs.

The only problem at the interview with the epicene Sammy Soo was to stop Sammy talking. Alan found something genuinely alarming about his careful beauty. It was to do with the almost complete absence of facial hair, and therefore of the hardness of skin that accompanies daily shaving. He remembered a story Bill had told him one evening at the Country Club: 'Twenty years a married man, been all over the world for the British Council, three or four kids. Came out to Hong Kong. Old, old story. After six months, he ran off with the houseboy.'

On Thursday Alan stayed out on Tung Lung and wrote his story on crap to couture for *Business PanAsia*. It was harder going than he expected, but only because the phone kept ringing.

'Hello?'

A woman's voice, Chinese, a near whisper. 'Alan?'

'Yes?' Alan felt a small bead of sweat trickle from his ear, but that was climate, not a nervous telephone manner.

'Alan, this is *Sophie*.'

'Ah, Sophie, you are calling to beg me to buy you dinner tomorrow night when I come into the office. Well, after consideration –'

'Alan, this is serious. It is about On-jay.'

Oh, *fack* On-jay. 'What about him?'

'Have you seen him?'

'No, of course not.'

'Dean is very angry.'

'Oh.'

She lowered her voice again. 'They have cancelled the card.'

'What card?'

She sucked her breath in irritatedly. Alan was an insensitive boor for not knowing which card. 'He is travelling on a company credit card. They have cancelled it.'

'Oh,' Alan said again, but it was quite a different oh from the first one. Alan saw, or thought he saw, it all.

'I don't want him to get into trouble.' Alan remembered that she had 'helped' André to set the trip up. What had the help entailed?

'What do you want me to do, Sophie?'

'Just warn him. Tell him Dean is very angry.'

Alan thought that even André, with his boundless optimism, would be capable of working that out for himself. 'If I see him, I'll tell him. I promise.'

'Thank you, Alan.'

'All right. I'll see you tomorrow, I expect; I'm delivering some copy to Colin in the afternoon.'

'All right.'

'I'll be in just before six, so why don't I buy you a drink afterwards? Say at the Harbourmaster's Bar, at the Fragrant Harbour Hotel?'

'Oh.' There was a pause while she considered Alan as surrogate André. Without doubt, André had taken Sophie to the Harbourmaster's Bar, and impressed her with the lordly waving of a credit card, assuming he had a credit card uncancelled at the time.

'All right.'

Well, sound a bit bloody enthusiastic, then. 'I will count the seconds, Sophie. See you tomorrow.'

'All right.'

My clothes have no zips, no buttons, no fastenings of any kind. They fall away from the throat, they slide off the shoulder. They do not bind the breasts and the hips, they caress. They move with the body. Always you recall that beneath my clothes there is a woman and she is naked. They are clothes that reflect the restless spirit of Hong Kong. He thought briefly about Sophie in clothes that moved with the body, and then concentrated his mind. *Hong Kong no longer relies on volume alone. Hong Kong looks forward –*

The telephone splintered the silence. Sophie again, but not whispering; her perfect secretary's voice. 'Alan Fairs?'

'Er, yes.'

'I have Mr Dean Holdsworth on the line for you.'

'All right.'

A nicely judged pause, one that was almost but not quite impolitely long. 'Hi, Alan.'

'Dean.'

'This is a little unusual, I guess. But I'm a little worried about your neighbour. He hasn't checked in for a day or two. I'm kind of concerned that something has happened to him.'

'I understand.'

'A guy can get into trouble in Asia.'

Especially if he tries to do business with André Standing. 'Very true.'

'So I was just wondering if you had heard from him.'

The flowers? The champagne? Better keep quiet about that. Or would they show up on the company credit card? Surely not itemised as fizz to Tung Lung. Or had Sophie already told Dean about the flowers?

'Alan, are you still there?'

'Sorry, Dean. Just wondering if my other neighbours had said anything. But no, I've heard nothing, and he certainly isn't here.'

'Well, can you just get him to call me when you see him? Tell him I'm kind of worried about him.'

I bet. 'Certainly, Dean.'

'I hear you are doing some good work for us.'

Was that a threat? 'Doing my best, Dean. Colin is very professional.'

'Sure. Well, I'll be in touch. Maybe you'll give me a call if André – ah – drops by for a cup of tea.'

'I'll do that,' Alan said, wondering if he would. Awkward. Very. Bloody, in fact.

'Very good of you. Well, I'll let you get on.'

Alan got on. Damn and blast the man. André clearly had not planned to involve Alan, but all the same, damn and blast the man. Oh well. At least the piece was as easy as that sort of piece can be. Sammy Soo gave him his pay-off line: *Hong Kong is not the city of the future, for it has no future. It is the city of the present, and it always will be. That is why the best fashion in the world can only come from Hong Kong.*

Very, very good. Or very, very adequate, anyway. He rang Reg. Hello old boy. No don't bother coming in today, but can you do a full day tomorrow? I'll have a raft of stuff for you by then. No problem, Reg. I'll have to be away about five, that's all, got an appointment. I can be with you just after half-past nine if I get the eight thirty ferry. You and your ferries. No, that's excellent, Alan, a real load off my mind. See you then.

Alan wondered about spreading Sammy Soo to a third piece, God knows there was enough material. But no ideas sprang to mind. One of those glossy hotel magazines would be the thing, but he didn't know the right people; he needed a contact. Make a few calls, perhaps. But right now it was time for a beer.

Alan and Charles caught the eight thirty together. 'I love this ferry,' Charles said. 'All in all, I think it's my favourite. You see,

I arrive at the office precisely ten minutes late. It tells everyone there that I am a bloody fool. If I caught the ten twenty they'd just think I'd been to the dentist. But this ferry sends the message to the world: Charles Browne is a total waster. That's good, isn't it?'

'I expect so.' Alan had in his pocket a rather exquisite silk tie, decorated with small pictures of polo players. Good of André to lend it to him; he had left it in Alan's flat after a dicing evening some time ago, and Alan had never got round to returning it. 'Do you think we'll see our neighbour today?'

'How long overdue is he?'

'Let me see. It was last Friday that Sophie came out to Tung Lung, and she was expecting to meet André. So that makes it a week today.'

'I propose a wager. Change from dice. Bet you a bucket of shit at Ah-Chuen's that he gets back tomorrow.'

'All right. André becomes the dice. He'll turn up a yah-tze for me on Monday.'

'Done.'

As he and Charles stepped off the ferry, Charles said: 'Hullo-ullo-ullo. What occurs, do you think?'

There was a party of half a dozen gweilos, suited and briefcase-carrying, and with them, two or three Chinese, also suited. This was a business gathering of some kind, so much was obvious from the way they stood around and made jokes.

'Not a clue,' Alan said.

'Trouble,' Charles said. 'Suits on Tung Lung always mean trouble. I must be off or people won't notice that I'm late.'

Alan got the minibus to Wanchai and spent the day writing PE. 'Excellent, old boy. Oh, did you know? Your 'Last Word' on the water politics got picked up by one of the agencies. Reworked it as a hard news story, gone just about everywhere. Even the *Hong Kong Times* ran it the other day.'

Alan laughed. 'I never saw it. How wonderfully funny.'

'Good for the magazine, that sort of thing. It's good working with you, Alan.'

'I'm getting the hang of lying for my living.'

Reg winced. 'Not lying, old boy, you mustn't think of it like that. It's not really lying at all. It's hypocrisy.'

The same warm feeling inside. They worked through to five fifteen, with a brief break for lunch – pint and sandwich at the Two Brewers. Alan then went to the gents, not the most attractive part of Reg's office, and examined himself in the speckled mirror. He did not look dapper in the least. He removed André's tie from his pocket, and tied it. Those polo players looked bloody silly. He looked a complete phoney. But perhaps that was what Sophie looked for in a fellow.

He went down the stairs to the street and caught a minibus from outside the Singapore Hotel. Dodging past the trams, the dozen tightly packed passengers crawled and jerked together towards Causeway Bay. Young secretaries with their knees pressed tight. One man reading the racing form. No eye sought his, no curiosity animated any face. 'Gai how yow lok,' he called, and the minibus stopped on the corner at his request, two or three lithe and slim figures pushing by him even as he descended, disputing for the honour of his vacated seat. A young man in Hank Marvin glasses won, though not without effort.

Alan arrived at *Business PanAsia*, greeted Sophie in a business-like way, but with, he hoped, a confident rather than phoney smile, and walked through to Colin's office.

'Triffic, Alan,' Colin said when he had completed his reading.

'Good.' They exchanged amiabilities.

'No worries, Alan. I'll be in touch next week about the next ish.'

'Good, Colin.'

Sophie was waiting for him. She was clad in business chic, in clothes that did not caress or fall away, but the slim golden V between the points of the collar of her white blouse was as ever worth inspecting. 'I was hoping you'd be wearing a cheongsam for your visit to the Fragrant Harbour Hotel.'

'Oh, Alan.'

Alan handled all the business of Mr Singh and the lift and Helen's greeting and the cheongsams (he thought of Charles and the Seven Seas Bar) and the sirring and the smiling reasonably well, he thought. 'What do you say, Sophie? Why not a Singapore Sling. Two Singapore Slings, please.'

The word Singapore did not provoke as he had feared the cataracts of the Nile. This was real progress. He had taken the risk of introducing the name because the drink itself had the virtue of not tasting like a drink at all. And he chatted, airily, urbanely, about business. A real Hong Konger, was he not? He talked about Sammy Soo, about office telephone systems, about Colin's professionalism. All this shop went down very well.

'I like Dean,' Sophie said. 'He is kind. Colin is nice, too, but he makes jokes and sometimes I don't understand if he is joking or not. But Dean is a very honest man.'

Alan could feel it coming. But he was buggered if he was going to say the name first.

'André is very honest too,' she said. 'But in a different sort of way.'

Very true, yes. A dishonest sort of way, on the whole. Alan ordered more drinks, overriding Sophie's little ritual yelp. Soon she was sipping away merrily. Good. Not that he had any hopes of a seriously happy outcome, but you had to do your best. It did not seem, however, to be making her giggly and seducible. He had thought, on the whole, that it wouldn't.

'Do you think anything has happened to André?'

'Well, something has.' That did not really sound excessively sympathetic, did it? 'But not necessarily something bad.'

'If anything happened to him I should want to die.'

Oh God. 'That's a bit extreme, old girl.'

She looked at him through her lashes. 'Do you think he has found another girl?'

You mean apart from Karen? 'How can I know, Sophie?'

'I think if he found another girl, I would kill myself.'

A tear, nine parts of Singapore Sling to one of saline, formed in each eye. Oh bladdy-fackin hell. 'Ah, but you wouldn't be able to.'

'You think I would not have the courage?'

'All the courage in the world, Sophie. But you wouldn't get

the chance to try, because I would sweep you off your feet, cover your upturned face with kisses and marry you on the spot, and you'd be so busy you wouldn't have *time* to kill yourself.'

She gave a sad tiddly giggle. 'I want to marry André.'

Oh, *fack* André. 'Why don't you have dinner with me? I warn you, I'll treat you so nicely you'll be aching to marry me long before the pudding comes.'

Alan was very sweet. But she really did have to go home. They discussed the idea for a while, but she really, really did have to go home, and Alan really, really was very sweet. So he paid for the drinks, not with a lordly credit card but with cash, rather a lot of it. He steered her to a taxi, the door opened for her by the Sikh. Should he leap in after all, and get cosy with her in the back? No. Give the driver ten bucks to take her home. Cheer up, Sophie, he's not worth killing yourself for. Cheek-kiss cheek-kiss. You kill yourself for me instead. Giggle. No seriously, Sophie, if you feel bad just ring me up, and I'll leap on the nearest ferry and come and rescue you. Sad smile. One more cheek-kiss. So very sweet.

No he wasn't, he was a charging rhinoceros, and *damn it*, he had missed the eight fifteen and the next ferry wasn't till ten thirty. After running through a few thoughts on ferry timetables and the people who devised them, an idea struck him. He went back into the hotel, found a telephone and rang the *Hong Kong Times.*

'Yes of course we will, what do you think we are, responsible individuals or something? We'll be there in about fifteen minutes, since you ask.'

Alan swooped up to the Country Club in a taxi, and there were Bill and Wally waiting for him, a third can of beer already on the table along with the lavatory paper and three bags of unshelled peanuts.

'No trams or buses for the young freelance,' Bill observed.

'We staff men can't afford taxis, can we, Bill?'

'True,' Bill said. 'But I catch them anyway. Two things you can be sure of in Hong Kong. Death and taxis.'

'You can have both together most days,' said Wally. 'Pick the passengers out of the wreckage and take 'em straight to the QE Hospital to finish them off. Why do we live here?'

'I've just been drinking with a girl who kept talking about killing herself.'

'What, if you don't marry her? Or if you do?'

'Did you ever think about topping yourself?' Bill asked seriously.

Alan got up and bought three cans of San Mig. This was to buy time, because he still had a fair amount in his can. 'I suppose everyone who ever had a teenage love affair *thinks* about it,' he said on his return to the table.

'I wouldn't mind a teenage love affair,' Wally said. 'Have you ever seen a troop of Chinese girl guides? I mean, really studied them?'

'It's the method that's the problem, of course,' Bill said. 'Ropes, pills, razors. All that sort of thing is enough to put you off.'

'Forward the blue tit patrol!'

'Drowning is supposed to be particularly pleasant,' Alan said.

'But how do they know?' Bill asked. 'On whom do they rely for their information? It's not to be trusted.'

'Take up smoking,' Wally said, breathing smoke. 'It's the best way. A mite slow, that's my only complaint.'

Eventually, it was time for Bill and Wally to do the second half of their shifts, and for Alan to catch the ten thirty ferry. Pleasant farewells were spoken. Alan bought beer from the Country Club, four cans just to be on the safe side, and took a taxi, one that retraced the steps of his Great Walk. Would stories of his good cheer and good income get around? Would Simpson hear of them? The taxi reached the ferry pier at ten twenty-five, and ten minutes later, the boat itself arrived. Alan walked on board, nodded to a stylishly suited youth with gold spectacles, one of the Ng clan, the number one son, Mark. He took his place at the back. Heaving a long sigh, the boat moved reluctantly away from the pier, to make its long journey across the South China Sea once again. As it pulled away, Alan removed the top from his beer, tossed it over his shoulder, raised his can to his lips. It tasted quite as it should.

'Do you have another of those, by any chance?'

'My God.'

'My dear, how good to see you.'

André looked wonderful; glowing with health. He had picked up a bit of a tan, and his teeth shone with especial brightness. He, the hunted fugitive, exuded self-confidence, self-delight. He was in one of his darker suits, a quiet tie, one of the old school or club ones. At second glance, his hair looked a trifle wilder than it usually did: not as if it needed cutting, but as if he had been running his hands through it rather a lot. The eyes looked a trifle wild, too, or maybe just tired.

'How are you?'

André opened his beer and drank with great delight. 'Excellent. Rather superb, in fact. Nice trip, very, very rewarding.' He raised his can to Alan. 'Still, good to be home. A thousand thanks.'

'One or two people have been wondering where you were.'

'I rather supposed they would. Still, got to keep people on their toes, haven't you? God, I was ready for this beer.'

'I suppose you have. Which reminds me, thanks for the champagne.'

'It got there all right, did it? And the flowers?'

'They got there too.'

'Went down all right? I mean, with the ladies concerned?'

'Not quite as well as the champagne. Sophie says she'll kill herself if you don't marry her, but she took the flowers. Karen didn't take hers, and asked me to tell you to stick them up your arse and she's going to set the Triads on to you.'

André leant luxuriously against the back of his bench and laughed in a pleased sort of way. 'How splendid to be back on one's own ferry. I say, isn't that my tie you're wearing?'

'It is, as a matter of fact.'

'Frightful cheek,' André said, without rancour.

'You're not worried about these death threats?'

'You mean Sophie? Or me? Tell the truth, not terribly. Sophie's always been a bit of a weeper, that's just her way. And Karen threatens me with 14K every time she catches me fucking somebody. All it actually means is that she has a good old whinge with Ah-Chuen.'

'Goodness, is Ah-Chuen —'

'Still, best not discuss it at the top of our voices, even if it is in English.'

'And Dean is anxious to talk to you, of course.'

'Is he going to kill himself? Or set the Triads on to me?'

'Maybe both.'

'He'll be all right. I've got a ton of ads for him. I'll reassure him on Monday morning or something.'

'Well, I think he'll be at the office Saturday morning —'

'Let him sweat a bit. You wouldn't have another of these delicious cans of beer, would you?'

'Sure, André. Here.'

'Thanks, old thing. Which reminds me. Congratulate me. Drink my health. I am engaged to be married.'

'I know. So these women of yours keep telling me.'

André made a huge gesture with his beer can, sweeping Karen and Sophie and all the women of Hong Kong into oblivion. 'Real thing this time. Met a wonderful girl in Malaysia — Bumiputra. Between you and me rather a nice change after all those skinny Chinese girls. Very beautiful, very loving, very rich. Wonderful contacts, first-class business brain. She's a princess, actually.'

'André, I don't really believe that. I expect you are having me on. They don't really have princesses in Malaysia any more, do they?'

This, after all, was too André-esque to be credible. 'Well, sucks to you because they do. Frightfully complicated system of aristocracy, as it happens.'

'And you are going to marry into it? What does her family think?'

'All in favour of it, naturally. Couldn't have been nicer. There was talk about whether or not I should have to become a Muslim, but they're pretty relaxed about it. Pretty advanced lot. But I'm prepared to do it, naturally. A really wonderful girl, you see.'

'And will she come and visit you on Tung Lung?'

'Very soon, I hope. You'll love her.'

'I'll do my best, anyway. But, André, what were you doing in Malaysia? You should have been in Singapore.'

'Oh well. A bit of everything, really.'

Alan looked at André in admiration. Chaos lay all behind him and, if Alan had understood Sophie and Karen and Dean aright, chaos lay all before him. But André was untroubled. Alan recalled watching a Buster Keaton film, Keaton walking through a nightmarish landscape of collapse: buildings falling all around him and each one missing him by a hair while he walked on, his face perfectly blank, not so much untroubled as completely unaware of the disasters all around him.

'But how have you been, my dear? How is business?'

Alan talked of *HK Biz* and *Business PanAsia* and *Chic*, and André listened with his customary attention, his customary sympathy.

'Oh, that reminds me,' he said. 'I met a nice girl at the Great Orient in Singapore. She was there for a meeting. She edits *Orientique*, the hotel chain's glossy mag. Name of Kate something or other, English girl, debbie but nice. Got her card somewhere; I'll look it out for you tomorrow. Talked you up no end, I did, she said she'd like to meet you and discuss business. Also met a smart chick who edits the Hong Kong mag *Asian Hotelier*. Belinda Chowdury, really sexy little Indian girl. I'll give you her number too, when I find it.'

'Thanks, André,' Alan said, genuinely touched.

'And that reminds me, do you want a hi-fi? Absolute rock-bottom dirt cheap?'

'New line of business for you.'

'Met a chap on the plane coming back, actually. I can get you a very nice system for a grand. Costs twice that in the shops.'

'Wouldn't be a shady deal, would it?'

'Don't you worry your head about things like that. Are you on?'

'I suppose so.'

'But tell me, how is everybody?'

Alan told him, and the normal routines of gossip took them onward across the inky sea. The ferry arrived at last at the Tung Lung ferry pier, and they walked downstairs at their ease, allowing the hurrying Chinese first use of the gangplank. And then André was talking in Cantonese, indicating a pile that stood in the goods bay beneath the stairs.

Two of Ah-Chuen's understrappers had boarded the ferry, and they seized the luggage at André's instruction: two small suitcases and one very large cardboard box. André and Alan ambled after the luggage along the pier.

'No typhoons yet?'

'Not even the number three up.'

André sighed. 'Too early, really. Still, the season of typhoons is almost with us. You haven't had a good typhoon yet, have you?'

'No.'

'You'll enjoy it, my dear. Very stimulating experience, a typhoon. Meanwhile, how about a sail, tomorrow? I think it might be a good idea to sail round the island. But a beer at my place right now, don't you think?'

'I want to get some milk from the village first, I'm out of it. I'll join you in a moment.'

'Good man.'

Alan never got his milk. He got as far as Ng's restaurant, where he saw Karen. It would, he thought, be the act of a friend to tell her that André was back. She was sitting at a table talking to Ah-Hei, who was surveying her with a brooding expression as they drank tea. Old man Ng was also sitting at the table. Alan realised, rather too late to stop, that he had interrupted an important discussion.

'Hello, Karen.'

It was as if these innocent words called into being a tidal wave of hate: but not from Karen. From Ng and Ah-Hei. Alan moved in an instant from drunken joviality to bowel-churning terror. Their anger hit him like a wall.

Ah-Hei got to his feet without Alan quite seeing how he managed it. It was as if Ah-Hei had just materialised in front of him. He seemed to have doubled in size: taken upon himself an aspect of ferocity. Alan could hear Ng shouting at Karen in Cantonese, and Karen shouted passionately back, while Ah-Hei stood in front of him, still in silence. Then Ah-Hei did a terrible thing.

He prodded. He prodded Alan in the middle of the sternum with his finger. It was a little like being rammed with a poker. Alan felt not so much his space as his person invaded, his psyche overwhelmed by this giant's outpouring of strength into this one small prod. He reeled back three paces; Ah-Hei, stalking him, moved forward another triplet of steps. Alan was aware that Ng was on his feet, and was shouting at him, that Karen was on hers and shouting at Ng. And Alan's head sang in bewilderment as Ah-Hei launched another devastating cattle-goad prod at him. In a couple of seconds, he found he had backed up against Ng's high counter, where Ng's vast wooden abacus no doubt sat awaiting the play of the master's calculator fingers. Ah-Hei was standing with his chest not quite touching Alan's own. Alan had read that Bond's mind was miraculously cleansed of all distraction by the threat of violence, that danger and tension relaxed him. Alan did not find this the case at all. His head was a Hallelujah chorus of disbelief, his eyes slithered wildly, looking for the return of normality.

And then Ng was waving a newspaper in his face. Why, it was the *Hong Kong Times*. Since when had Ng learnt to read English? Ng was expounding some matter in Cantonese, impatient of his own halting command of Alan's language. He then reached to the counter and, wonder of wonders, took a copy of *HK Biz*. What was this all about?

And Ng was showing him the page with the 'Last Word' on it, his hilarious piece on the water-politicking pixies of Tung Lung. Ng stabbed the page with his forefinger a dozen times, and said more complicated things in Cantonese.

And then Alan's head did clear. Oh dear, he thought very

precisely. I am about to get the most terrible beating. I hope it won't hurt too much. I do hope they don't want to do anything, as it were, long term.

He turned to Karen for at least an explanation, but the treacherous bitch had gone. There was nothing for it. No point in launching a frenzied counterassault. That would, perhaps literally, be fatal. Ah-Hei asked a sharp question of Ng. What shall I do with this bastard? Which bones shall I break?

And Ng was talking to Ah-Hei more quietly now, more decisively. And then, a sound like a gunshot.

Even Ah-Hei, whose eyes had not left Alan's for a single fragment of time, was forced to turn at this sound. Not a shot, Alan realised, but flesh on flesh. A handclap. And there was Ah-Chuen standing at the entrance to the restaurant, but not like a customer. And Karen standing beside him.

Ah-Chuen barked out something. Ah-Hei replied in a couple of monosyllables. Ng spoke with renewed anger.

And then Ah-Hei turned. Away from Alan, towards where Ah-Chuen stood: big, portly, eyes like two small stones. Ah-Hei stood in front of Ah-Chuen, not quite close enough to touch, half a head smaller, but a man in perfect training. For a long moment, they locked eyes on each other. And then Ah-Hei moved.

It was beautiful, in a way; Alan registered that even in his fear. Ah-Hei, a cat in human form, spun on his left foot and sent out a whirling blow with his right foot: a reverse roundhouse kick, the most showy of kung-fu moves, a staple of all the martial dramas that Alan had ever seen. It passed in front of Ah-Chuen's face, missing him by the breadth of a hand, as was clearly intended. Ah-Hei was politely reminding Ah-Chuen that he, Ah-Hei, was a master.

Ah-Chuen's response was not beautiful. He raised both his hands and gave Ah-Hei a shove in the chest. Not quite an assault, that, not a real blow. Ah-Hei, slightly off balance from the completion of his kick, found himself powered half a dozen steps across the restaurant, cannoning onto a table. He spun, feline, and dropped into a fighting crouch. Alan awaited with resignation the most terrible outcome.

Ah-Chuen folded his arms. He looked down at Ah-Hei with an almost beatific expression, and then spoke a single word. What did it mean?

'Get out. Now.' Karen's voice, and Alan obeyed it. He walked without bending his knees, because his joints seemed to have locked. He walked towards Karen, towards the ground behind Ah-Chuen: Ah-Chuen standing like the statue of a conqueror. Ah-Chuen nodded once to Ah-Hei and Ng, and then turned. The three of them walked away.

At the bottom of the 176 steps, Alan found himself once more capable of speech. 'Ah-Chuen,' he said, 'thank you.' He reached and briefly placed a hand on Ah-Chuen's shoulder.

And then unexpectedly, Ah-Chuen giggled – fluting and delighted. Playfully he pushed Alan in the chest with his finger-tips. 'Fu' o',' he said. And Alan sat on the steps and laughed.

After a while he heard Karen's voice again. 'I take you home,' she said.

'I'm all right.'

'Sure.'

They started the ascent. 'Karen?'

'Yeah?'

'What's it all about?'

'Oh, you bladdy gweilo, you. You make trouble, that's what it's all about. You know a big party from the PWD came to Tung Lung today?'

'PWD?'

'You know nothing about Hong Kong. Public Works Department. They read all this crap you write about water and wells and the Ngs and the Chuens. And so they come out to talk about putting Tung Lung on to the main water supply.'

'But isn't that a good thing?'

'Bladdy fool. Ng and Chuen control the water on Tung Lung. Good money. Now if the mains come, everybody gets water. So no money.'

'Oh Christ. But I thought it was that grey-haired guy, Chuen-suk, that owned the other well. So what's it got to do with Ah-Chuen?'

'Bladdy fool. Ah-Chuen is the number one son of Chuen-suk. Both called Chuen, right?'

'But I thought it was a different name, Chuen-suk.'

This time she sighed, her anger with him apparently gone, dashed against the wall of gweilo stupidity. 'You call the son Ah-Chuen because that is friendly. You call the father Chuen-suk out of respect. He is an important man, and older than you. Most people call him Chuen-suk out of respect. It means Uncle. You really don't know anything, do you?'

'Then why did Ah-Chuen rescue me?'

'He likes you, you silly barcer.'

They had reached the gate in Alan's concrete garden. 'It's all right,' she said. 'I know André is home. I'll go and see him now.'

But she walked beside him to his front door, perhaps postponing the moment, perhaps needing to regroup after the turbulence the night had already brought. Alan opened the door, pressed the light. 'Karen – thanks for rescuing me. I'm so –'

His voice broke and for an appalled second he thought he might blub. Out of sheer panic he started kissing her. This seemed increasingly to be a good idea.

A few moments later, he saw that he was lying back on the cushions, and she above him, tonguing him unexpectedly with delicacy and taste. He looked up at her wildly, his appalled blood singing. She smiled at him, and was beautiful.

'I like you,' she said. 'You bladdy gweilo.'

Alan gently took the hem of her singlet in his two hands and, with whimsically pedantic care, began to roll it upwards half-inch by half-inch. She smiled benignly at him while he did so. Quite unresisting.

And then a strange thing happened, something that Alan never really did come to terms with. Still with the gentle smile on her face, she untrousered him with considerate movements and then with brief kind fingers brought about a small miracle. Alan watched the brief ballet of her upper moiety as if to commit it for ever to memory.

And then she was lying with her head cradled on his shoulder, his arm about her. If it was tenderness she craved, she had gone there by the most direct route. 'I like you, you bladdy gweilo.'

'I adore you. I always have.'

'You liked that?'

'Of course, Karen, but – well, why?'

She sighed gustily. 'I like you. But I can see the future, sometimes. I don't mean like a fortune-teller. Just think ahead, see round the next corner. Just obvious things. Like if I make love to you properly, I fall in love with you, and maybe you fall in love with me.'

'Is that bad?'

'Yeah. Because I still love that barcer André. So all you and me can do is make a terrible mess. Bladdy gweilos.'

'Why don't you go and find a nice Chinese boy? Or are you a bloody gweilo too?'

'Gweipo – I'm female, remember.'

'I remember,' Alan said, remembering.

'You know nothing. But come to think of it, maybe you do know something. I'm too much a gweipo. I don't mean blood. Pure Soho Chinese, me. Came to Hong Kong when I was sixteen. I know about gweilos. I understand the barcers.'

'And the bastards don't understand you?'

'Barcers don't even try. Bladdy Hong Kong. Hey, I got to go. Go upstairs to that barcer André.'

'Do you have to?'

She was sitting up, smiling down at him with love. 'Yes.'

PART III
SUMMER

Always the bloom of sweat on your skin: even in the morning, in bed, beneath the electric fan that whirled inside its little cage on the wall. Like being lightly and permanently covered in wallpaper paste. It was, Alan thought, really rather pleasant. You never, for an instant, forgot where you were.

It was Sunday. He knew that without opening his eyes. The sounds from the garden told him so. The first time he had heard these sounds, he had wondered if several people were performing complex sexual acts on the concrete. Sharp little cries: staccato grunts: fast thick pants.

He was accustomed to it now, for no Sunday began without it. But it always woke him. And so Alan got up, not without reluctance or a mild hangover, and wrapped his sarong about his waist. He put the kettle on, and then opened his front door. 'Morning, neighbour.'

'Morning, Charles.'

Charles did not for a moment cease his rhythmic lashing of the air. Right hand, right hand, a sudden unexpected left; fists curiously clenched. Each piston-shot was accompanied by a snorting exhalation through the nose.

Charles turned slowly, on his heel, through 90 degrees, his hands now held in front of his face, palms outwards, relaxed, like great soft paws. He swayed gently, made a feint with his left and then struck. Left, left *foot*, amazingly high, if not quite so beautifully as Ah-Hei, then snapping back at once to his ready position. Charles was wearing only a pair of shorts, and these exiguous, yellow and satin. Sweat rolled from his surprisingly hairless body: he was like a water creature, a seal perhaps. Alan went back to his kitchen to pour boiling water onto brown powder and to add UHT milk. Charles, he knew, would not drink; not coffee and not yet.

Alan went to sit on one of his plastic chairs, admiring Charles's ritual frenzies. They took place in his garden because Charles's flat was too small to permit such excesses. Besides, Charles liked to be outside and, Alan thought, liked to be watched, too. So Alan sipped coffee and watched.

'Lazy – unnh! – bastard.'

'Sane bastard.'

Charles brought his assault to a close. What marked the end of a bout? Did the air submit? Or had it been struck a lethal blow? Charles, breathing heavily but still through his nose, sank easily to the ground and sat, resting his back against the wall of the house. A pair of running shoes lay before him: sockless, Charles laced them to his feet.

'Today's the day.'

'Never.'

'Foolish words.' Charles flowed to his feet, and walked through the gate. He turned to face along the path. He laced his fingers together, extended his arms before him, palms facing outwards, and slowly raised his arms high above his head, at the same time bowing his chin to his chest. It was always this way: no doubt an important part of the callisthenics, but it looked like a brief obeisance to the might of the sea. Very slowly, he rose onto the balls of his feet. Then, softly, he lowered his heels, freed his hands, raised his head. He then lifted his left arm, touched his watch, and struck the air a single savage blow.

'Aaaa!' he called, from the bottom of his lungs, and at once he was gone, running pell-mell towards the 176 steps.

Alan opened his mouth to call out something derisive, but closed it, realising that Charles was already beyond the reach of his voice. And so he made himself two slices of toast and Marm-ited and ate them. Another Tung Lung Sunday was off and running. The sky was a deadly blue, the humidity so high that the smallest movement left its trace in liquid, and the temperature was soaring inexorably towards the hundred mark. Good. That was what weather should be. Perhaps the heat would inspire

Charles to the breaking of barriers; but all the same, he expected that it would be more than an hour before he was back, looking as if he had swum over the mountains rather than run, huge with self-delight and demanding beer.

André appeared on his balcony over Alan's head. He was wearing a shirt covered with parrots and a pair of ragged cut-off jeans. He looked immensely distinguished in these garments.

'Morning, André. Not joining Charles on his run then?'

'My dear, I can think of a dozen better ways of killing myself without even leaving the flat.'

A few minutes later, André came down to join Alan on his plastic chairs, bearing a pot filled with real and freshly made coffee. Alan looked at him with mild interest. 'Are you going domestic on us?'

'Not at all. It's Charles's.'

They drank the coffee together, content in silence. Alan thought of Charles: running across the island where Alan had walked that Christmas Day; where, indeed, he had walked once or twice since with his island companions to eat a meal at the distant Christmas restaurant, as a change from Ng's. No one trod the path much in the way of business, but in the spring and the autumn, Chinese schoolchildren would march across in large packs, carrying elaborate rucksacks and wearing stiff new hiking boots. Alan liked the walk, though the steep ascents made him pant.

'It's going to be a touch draughty today,' André announced after a while.

'Happy for you,' Alan said.

'Oh, Alan,' André said. 'It's ridiculous, this affectation of yours.'

'No.'

'It's perfect. Look at the conditions, it could hardly be easier.' He waved his mug seaward: deadly blue and flecked here and there with white-capped wavelets.

'No.'

'And I'll take it really quietly this time. I know I can make you love it.'

'No.'

André laughed quietly, sipped coffee. 'My dear, you are a man of steel today.'

'Every day. At least on the subject of boats.'

'I pushed you too hard that time, didn't I? I really didn't want to frighten you; I thought you would like it, you see.'

'A misjudgement.'

Alan's strength of will was something of a ritual joke on Tung Lung: evening after evening he would refuse and then accept a final beer, while Charles shouted 'Man of straw' as he opened his can. But after the first outing, he had not been back on André's boat.

André had taken him sailing on the first weekend of his Tung Lung life. It was supposed to be something of an initiation. Alan cared nothing for boats but, flattered to be asked and desirous of being liked, he had accepted the invitation. It had not been a success.

The boat turned out to be the baffling arrangement of yellow plastic canoes he had seen on his first visit to Tung Lung that Christmas Day. 'It's a yacht for hooligans,' André had explained, unaccustomed pride in his voice. 'Or if you like, a yacht for Spitfire pilots, or Hell's Angels. It is the fastest thing without an engine in Hong Kong, and I can sail the crap out of anybody.'

It was called a Hobie Cat, André explained, because it was invented by a man called Hobie and it was a catamaran. It was built on minimalist lines: the two yellow hulls connected by a yellow trampoline. From the centre of this rose a ludicrously high aluminium mast. Once the rainbow sail had been raised the boat comprised nothing but wind. The single refinement for passenger comfort was four sockets, one at each corner of the trampoline, designed to hold cans of beer.

Not that travellers in André's craft had much opportunity for relaxing over a beer. The simplest manoeuvres required the concentration and commitment of a Hell's Angel surfing through Hennessy Road traffic. Alan became aware of this before they had even begun, when, after a relatively event-free crossing of

Tung Lung harbour on an inflatable toy boat, André had strapped him into something like a baby-harness, and then attached him by a long wire to the dizzy top of the mast.

All went well for the first minute and more. Then, as the gawky craft approached the mouth of the harbour, André instructed him to push himself away from the boat. Almost at once they were travelling with quite preposterous speed, far faster than Alan had believed the wind would permit. Their passage was also far bouncier than seemed right. Alan's only point of contact with the boat was the balls of his feet, and the long wire. He and André lay suspended side by side, their bodies parallel with the water, the sea inches from their shoulders. The sea leapt and spat at them as they creamed a path across its surface. It was terrifying, freezing, soaking and sick-making all at the same time.

On they went, for what seemed endless hours, bumping and soaking, across the endless viciousness of the sea. Alan lost track of time and direction: all that mattered was keeping his feet pressed hard to the edge of the trampoline, while André chattered away and occasionally whooped. At one stage, Alan was made to clamber across the trampoline and fling himself out again on the opposite side, while André fired a running commentary of nautical terms at him.

'Back towards the bay,' André said. 'Let's show them what the old girl can do, shall we?'

Again, he caught the stabbing breeze to perfection, and they were away at doubled speed. 'Look at the wake!' André said. 'Reckon we could tow a water-skier?'

No doubt they could have towed several: a long, die-straight line of cream marked their progress. 'We can do better than this,' André said. 'Come on, baby! Another knot!'

And Alan was flying through the air; in slow motion he saw the plimsolled foot of André rise upwards to smash him in the face, then felt the collision with the stiff wires that supported the mast. And then the bite of the sea: colder and crueller even than he had imagined.

He rose to the surface spluttering, thankful, appalled. The

first thing he saw was André's laughing face, his dripping curls. 'Unreal,' he was saying, every time he could draw breath. 'Unreal, baby, unreal.'

'Stop saying baby,' Alan said.

'Yeah, but that was cool, wasn't it?'

Alan, wet, freezing, appalled, asked: 'Did you do that on purpose?'

'Not exactly on purpose. Just wanted to see how far we could take it. You know how one does.'

'Why aren't we wearing life jackets?'

'Life jackets are for wimps, Alan. Haven't got any. Come on. Let's right the old girl.'

This took a bit of doing. One hull was below water, the gaudy sail undulating hapless on the surface, a single hull standing clear. The two of them had to line up on the emergent hull and pull.

'When I say go, dive onto the trampoline.'

'Dive,' Alan said unhappily. 'Right.'

'At once.'

The sail rose from the sea at last, André called dive, but Alan made a poor second when the moment came. His weight, remaining too long on the wire, caused the righted boat to keep on coming. Gracefully, it completed its turn, performing a second capsize on the opposite side. Again, they emerged from the sea; again, André was laughing. They seemed to be drifting faster and faster towards Cheung Chau. They performed the manoeuvre again; this time Alan was quicker. And, with André laughing again or still, they turned back towards Tung Lung harbour with what looked like the speed of terminal insanity. Bizarrely, they slowed at once to a crawl as they passed at last into the arms of the harbour. This was, no doubt, the most skilled and flashy watermanship.

André lowered the sails and tied up to his buoy, his face radiant. 'Enjoy?'

'No.'

'Oh, my dear. I'm so sorry.'

'Sorry, André, I don't think it's my thing.'

'Oh dear, oh dear. I pushed you too hard, didn't I? So sorry. Next time I'll take it easy, all right?'

'I don't think a next time is really on.'

'Oh, my dear.'

But Alan had stuck to this with rare firmness of purpose.

'Alan, come. This afternoon. With a beer or two inside you. A really gentle sail. Are you sure I can't tempt you?'

'Not with boats.'

'Ah well. Charles, as ever, will be my companion for a somewhat more robust excursion. After lunch, I think. Lunch at Ah-Chuen's?'

'I expect so.'

'And dinner at Ng's?'

'I expect so.' Dinner at Ng's had no terrors for him. After that terrible nocturnal discussion with Ah-Hei and Ng, Alan had thought he would never be able to set foot on Tung Lung again, never mind in Ng's restaurant. But King had given him safe passage, and as he had re-entered the restaurant the first time, Ng had given him an infinitesimal unsmiling nod. The only real difference was that Ah-Hei never served them any more. He occasionally regarded Alan with lizard eyes. Always motioning one of his minions to take the order.

'Will Karen be joining us?'

'I expect so.'

'My young friends. Good morning to you.' King was standing on his balcony, high above them, apparently to give his blessing to the city and the world.

'Morning, King. Coffee?' André waved the cafetiere amiably in his direction.

'A fine thought. I shall descend.' A few minutes later, he joined them, taking one of the plastic chairs, greeting them both once again with his ponderous bonhomie. 'And Charles – he is on the mountains?'

'I expect so.'

'And we shall lunch at friend Ah-Chuen's?'

'I expect so.'

'And dine at Ng's?'

'I expect so.'

'Fine thought. A Tung Lung Sunday. What more could any man want?'

'Well,' Alan said. 'Perhaps a beautiful girl in the middle of the night. But nothing else.'

'On Tung Lung, all things are possible, my friend. It is our good fortune to be honoured guests on this island. For the real people, life is harder. The fishing has been bad all week. They say it will get worse.'

'Shame.'

'And our neighbour, Mr Ng, has had a profound disappointment. The planning department has refused him permission to build a street of houses where the vegetable gardens now stand.'

'Quite right too,' Alan said with spirit.

'My friend, I understand what you say. That is the romantic in you. But Tung Lung is still a part of Hong Kong and that means all things must change. He who does not change is lost.'

Alan laughed. 'I'd never have thought it. And you such a traditionalist.'

'I am a traditionalist, Alan. And the tradition of Hong Kong is change.'

It really was very hot. Alan manoeuvred his chair a little deeper into the shade cast by André's balcony above him. A huge butterfly, white with orange tips to its wings, passed flapping with absurd deliberation. It looked like a work of origami.

After a while, they heard the slap of Charles's feet. Blowing typhoons, he ran through the gate and halted. Sweat was running in odourless millraces about his body. 'Curses!' he said, dabbing a finger at his watch. He dropped into a crouch, resting the knuckles of his left hand on the floor.

'Time?'

'One hour four. Curses!'

'You'll have to try harder,' Alan said comfortingly.

'It's the damn downslopes that do it,' Charles said, breathing with deliberation, inflating his chest like a bellows with each inhalation. 'Going up, I'm cruising. But going down, you have to let go. Really let go, stride out, risk turning an ankle. If I can speed up on the downslopes, I'll have it.' His breath was already returning to a normal rhythm.

'You let go on those downslopes,' André said, 'you won't turn an ankle. You'll break your bloody neck.'

'Put that on my tombstone,' Charles said. 'He went downhill too fast. Wonderful. Let the day begin.' And he took himself off to his flat for a shower.

'Seriously crazy,' André said benignly.

King slapped the table with a curious decisiveness. 'Seriously sane!' he said. 'Each of us is an outlying island of sanity to the madness of Hong Kong.'

'I wonder,' said André, 'if it's time for a beer.'

'Well, Charles will be down soon enough.'

And he was, but it was Charles transformed. He was dressed, not in his traditional Tung Lung uniform of shorts and flipflops and nothing else, but with finicky care: black shoes with a high polish on them, white socks, white trousers, clean and pressed, a virginal white shirt buttoned at the cuffs and neck, knife-edges along the sleeves, and a plain black tie that was surely silk. His hair, instead of being worn in a boyish flop, had been Brylcreemed and combed back abruptly from his forehead. And in his hands he carried a tray.

On the tray were four pint glasses. Each was filled to the brim with opaque red liquid. Ice floes clanked against the glass; celery sprouted from the ruddy depths. A smirk of self-delight shone from Charles's face.

'Good morning, neighbours.'

'Charles, what the bloody hell are you playing at?'

'You sound like my father. Cease doing so. Taste. Drink.'

Alan took a glass, and a precautionary sniff that revealed nothing but a briny sensation and a tickling of the nostrils from the celery. He sipped, and was aware of an electrical sensation about his lips. More courageously, he drank. At once, a spectrum of tastes assailed him. The first level hot, the second very hot, the third a furnace. And then the long finish: the sour bite of vodka.

'Golly,' he said.

'These,' Charles explained, 'are the Bloody Marys that history has been waiting for.'

The recipe was cajoled from him. A quarter-bottle of vodka per glass to start things off. Half a can of V8 juice. Celery salt. Soy sauce. Worcester sauce. 'The merest hint of Tabasco', perhaps a dessertspoonful. Fresh lemon juice. A few capers. Lurking sharklike in the depths a couple of jalapeño peppers. And floating on the surface, poured in over the back of a spoon, chilli oil.

There was a long pause. 'Perfect,' Alan said at length. For it was, in its appalling way, delicious.

'My father always told me that it was very unwise to drink beer on an empty stomach. So I made this, so we won't have to.'

'The perfect drink to have before a sail,' André said brightly.

'It's rather *like* having a sail in your bloody boat,' Alan said. 'The difference is that you overdo the Tabasco.'

King and Alan had stationed themselves at a convenient distance from the vat of boiling oil. They were drinking beer at Ah-Chuen's, having watched Charles and André set sail on the ghastly boat, a can at each corner of the trampoline. Charles had changed, with affected reluctance, out of his bridal finery.

On fine weekends, Ah-So would position his vat, or foodstall, or dai pai dong, outside Ah-Chuen's, and would fry fishballs, sausages (which he would snip into pieces with a huge pair of scissors), vegetables daubed with fishpaste, and other delicacies. Ah-Chuen's customers, passers-by, arriving and departing ferry customers, bought and ate throughout the day. 'Each augments the other's trade,' King said. 'It is typical of Hong Kong, of business goodwill. Which reminds me, my friend. I have something to ask of you. I would like you to place some information in your magazine, ah, *Hong Kong Business*.'

'If I can, King.'

King looked at him very solemnly. 'It would be as well to do so, Alan.'

'You mean it's the quid pro quo? For Ng?'

'I say nothing, Alan. I merely advise you very strongly to find a home for this information. I will supply you with it, if you like, on Monday morning.'

Alan felt his heart sink. King had told him that, after the night of the nocturnal prodding, Ng had wanted him to leave Tung Lung, never to be seen again, but King had interceded on his behalf. 'Ng says you can stay, Alan. It's a favour, Alan, and a favour to me. And in Hong Kong, a favour always gets called in. Remember that.'

It seemed no great problem at the time – anything to stay on Tung Lung. But Alan felt a little touch of fear now: fear of Ng's malign golden smile; fear of Ah-Hei's whirling paws; fear, above all, of being lost again, lost as he was on the night of the great walk, when Simpson had told him never to darken the doors of the *Hong Kong Times* again. 'I'm going to have some more fishballs,' he said.

He rose and asked Ah-So for another bowl, a matter that did not overstretch his Cantonese. There was hardly a dish he could not ask for now. He came back, peering out at the sea beyond the harbour, but saw no sign of the rainbow sail.

'Be easy, Alan. André and Charles will be back shortly.'

'Oh, I know. But it scares me to death, that bloody boat. André is crazy once he gets the wind in that sail.'

'There you go again,' King said. 'Back to that. André is *sane*, when he is close to the wind. Which is always. Besides, you need have no fear for André. He is a fine sailor. He and Charles took part in many races with the Hong Kong Yacht Club last summer, and won a good few. He would have won his class, had he completed the season.'

'Oh,' said Alan, interested. 'Why didn't he? Business commitments?'

'André is perhaps too free a spirit for the Hong Kong Yacht Club.'

'You mean he got thrown out?'

'The details elude me.'

'Talking of free spirits,' Alan said, 'I gather Karen is joining us tonight.'

'Free!' King said. He was in one of his not uncommon oracular moods. 'She is a prisoner of two cultures. André is the key to her prison.'

'André isn't a key really, is he, more like the credit card you use to slip the latch? But no, sorry, King, I know what you mean. I think.'

'A fine woman.'

'Yes,' Alan said, seeing without difficulty the ballet of her upper moiety. 'Oh thank God, there they are.'

The brave rainbow sail was making its way towards the harbour. Alan watched, with pleasure now, to see what flashy watermanship things André would do on his approach. This time, there was a dramatic unfurling of the sail in the midst of a controlled drift to the mooring buoy. He watched Charles and André tie up, paddle ashore in the little inflatable. Soon, they were walking towards Ah-Chuen's with that enviable slouching gait that follows certain kinds of physical repletion.

They ordered beer, fishballs from Ah-So, noodles from Ah-Chuen. Alan ate some of the fishballs, ordered some more. Ah-So, standing behind the vat of oil, was sweating more monstrously even than Charles after his double crossing of the island. An uncomfortable business, but what is comfort, compared with the joys of business? The Tung Lung Sunday unwound its ritual summer pattern. André and Charles slipped into one of their ritual arguments.

'But I could do it.'

'It's not designed for single-handed sailing, Charles.'

'But all the same, I could do it.'

'It is designed right to the edge, so you're always going to get capsizes. And one person can't right it.'

'I damn well could, you know.'

'Well, I can't do it alone. I've tried.'

'Well, we'll both go out. Capsize. Then you watch, and I'll right it.'

'What's the point? There's no way you're going to take the boat out on your own. I won't do it alone, after all. I do have some sense, you know.'

'But, André, I could *do* it. Don't you see?'

The bickering, amiable enough, continued through lunch. Then King, perhaps making a judgement of Solomon, asked if he might go for a sail, by no means an invariable part of Sunday's patterns. André agreed willingly, and they continued. One more beer and we'll do it.

Ah-Chuen came to sit with them, and conversation continued half in Cantonese, half in English. André was speaking with exaggerated humorousness, loud and theatrical. Ah-Chuen replied in English: 'If it no bloody good, I box you good.' Much hilarity and backslapping.

Ah-Chuen brought a round of beers, explained that they were on the house, and left them, to attend to a new batch of customers arriving on the ferry.

'I do like that man,' Alan said.

'Very wild as a young man,' King said. 'Great bruiser and brawler. He was a champion beer-drinker, won a competition for the fastest drinker, something sponsored by San Mig, got quite a lot of money.'

'You're in trouble, then, André,' Alan said. 'Once Karen gets him on her side.'

André smiled lazily, catlike. 'I think you'll find that Ah-Chuen's first loyalty is to me. Besides, when it comes to ducking, I'm pretty good. No one has ever landed a blow on me. King, are you ready for your sail? We can take the beers with us.'

They set off to the harbour steps.

'I hope André doesn't drown King.'

'Serious loss, that. I'd be an orphan.'

Alan was at a loss to know if this was a joke, and if so, how funny it was. 'Has your father ever been out to Tung Lung?'

'Once. When I was getting set up here. Knows King from the old days, you see. That's how the deal was swung. Kind of in loco parental thing, I suppose.'

'You don't see much of him. Your father, I mean.'

'No, I don't, do I? The deal was that I had lunch with him every Sunday. But very soon, I realised that it would rather bugger up my Tung Lung Sunday. And also that my father didn't really want to have lunch with me every Sunday either. So we both of us let it slip, without regrets. So I never go at all. Well, hardly ever. Just occasionally when there is a summons.'

'Does he mind?'

'Well, he pretends to, obviously. But I really don't care. Because, you see, I like it here. It is the first time in my life I have ever lived in just one place, you see, and I find that really rather restful.'

'What do you mean? I thought you have always lived in Hong Kong?'

'No. My father has. I was always going to school in England and then coming back to Hong Kong. Living in two places. Only difference was that at my father's place the rules were stricter. Even when my mother was alive.'

'When did you first go to England?'

'When I was five. Prep school, nothing but the best for little me. In fact, one of my earliest memories is arriving at Kai Tak airport and feeling extremely proud.'

'Because you had flown all the way from England by yourself?'

'Because I recognised my parents.'

'Golly.'

Charles took a long pull at his beer and gazed at the horizon. Alan said nothing, thinking that Charles's mind must be filled with troubled reflections, but when he spoke, he said: 'I love that little boat, you know.'

Alan looked out to sea. Distantly, he could see the silhouetted rainbow forming a surprisingly acute angle with the horizon.

'I want to steal it,' Charles said softly. 'I really do. I was lucky, actually. When I see the mess most people make of bringing up their kids. King's kids. I mean, they lived with King for fourteen years or so, before he and his wife split up and she took them back to UK. And believe it or not, they are much more fucked up than me. Jacinta was a right little bitch, always giving her dad a hard time. And Byron was a proper little tick.'

'Byron and Jacinta, for God's sake. Are they the names a caring father would choose?'

Charles gave a sudden bellow of laughter. 'Exactly the names a caring father would choose. Spent months thinking about them.'

'The daughter looked rather tasty, from a picture King showed me.'

'I think you might find her a touch indigestible.'

Alan yawned extravagantly. A fine sleepiness had come upon him. 'Talking of women, I hope there won't be a scene tonight.'

'Should there be?'

'Karen's joining us at Ng's.'

'Are you in love with her?' Charles asked with distressing suddenness. 'You used to look longingly at her tits. Now you look longingly at her face.'

'Very humorous. Would you like to sail her single-handed?'

Eventually, King and André returned. They had not, it seemed, capsized. The light was failing fast, as it did at this time of year: a brief dusk, during which the mosquitoes snapped at your ankles. The air did not cool at all with this sudden darkness, and there seemed no reason to move ever: the four of them, seated round a table, a detritus of ringpulls and spat-out bits of fish all around them.

Eventually André said, 'Look, chaps, I said I'd meet Karen off the ferry, getting soft in my old age. I'd better go up and change first.'

They decided to join him, and to mount the 176 steps as a party. They settled up with Ah-Chuen, always an especially complicated business on a Sunday, with beer and snacks taken at random throughout the day.

'Do you think we should have another Bloody Mary?'

'Good idea, but I only bought the one bottle of vodka. Still, perhaps I should put my tie back on.'

'All right,' Alan said. 'I'll put a tie on as well. Keep you company.'

Alan went to the length of ironing one of his few clean shirts. Must take another load to the laundrette next time he went in to town. From his small tie collection, he selected one with paisley scrawls. He regretted that he had returned the polo players to André. He sat on a plastic chair in the wet dark warmth of the night, waiting for arrivals. Charles was first, clad once again as the perfect waiter, hair Brylcreemed to iridescent perfection. King was next, in striped shirt, plain maroon tie. André, however, kept them waiting.

'Prinking himself in front of the mirror.'

'Stealing my shirts.'

But he was not. When at last he appeared, he was in full evening dress: a white dinner jacket, thin strip of bow tie, modestly opulent shirt with a few tucks in it, black trousers with ribbons of silk along the outer seams, simple black cummerbund. His hair looked newly sculpted.

'What, no tails?' Alan asked. 'I positively refuse to be seen at Ng's with a man who doesn't wear tails.'

'Have you noticed,' Charles asked, 'how André always goes that little bit too far?'

André made a minuscule adjustment to his bow tie. 'It's called style,' he said, 'if you but knew it. Shall we descend for aperitifs? It is about the cocktail hour.'

As they passed along the main street, Alan cast sidelong glances at their fellow villagers, looking for astonishment, resentment, open laughter, disbelief, shared delight. None of these came. Ah-Hei greeted King with perfect impassiveness; Mr Ng's cold nod from his usual eminence beside the clacking abacus betrayed only fiscal interest.

They ordered aperitifs, four bottles of beer, *now*, and don't bother with any tea. 'They all seem to think this is perfectly normal,' Alan complained as the beers came, Ah-Ko, Ah-Hei's number two, understanding the need for hurry.

'You misunderstand the Chinese mind,' King said. 'They see before them a party of gweilos. They already know we are crazy. You could run up and down in a gorilla suit; or you could behave with sober decency all your days on the island. Neither would make a jot of difference to the way the villagers see you.'

'Even for you?'

'Even for me, to an extent. Even I am an outsider; at best an honoured guest. You see, you think the Chinese are crazy. But the Chinese *know* you are crazy.'

'That reminds me,' André said, 'I'd better go to the pier.'

It was a while before André reappeared. When he did so, he and Karen were entwined, his arm about her shoulder, her arm about his waist inside the beautiful white jacket. She was wearing a very short denim skirt and a black garment with a lot of straps that made it clear to those that did not already know that her body was lean and sinuous and the palest of pale brown. Snake, Alan thought. Traditional Chinese term for such a woman. Snake. She had brushed her long hair several thousand times and it shone with a blackness that dazzled. She had made herself up with the care of a Chinese calligrapher.

'What's all this bladdy crap?' she said, in friendly greeting to the well-dressed table.

'We thought we'd make an occasion of it,' André said. 'It's not every day that something as important as this occurs. Gentlemen, please rise. Charge your glasses. May I propose a toast? To the future Mrs Standing.'

They stood, drank; Alan could have sworn that Karen blushed. Looking down at her, Alan was able to observe the tiniest strip of the upper curvature of a tiny pale brown breast. Alan was enraptured; also with André's daring move, his hijacking of their joke and using it for his own purposes.

They sat. Karen was furnished with beer. Food was ordered, not without a lot of arm-waving and argument, mostly between André and King, both on the top of their form and bellowing instruction and counterinstruction in Cantonese. Course followed course in the usual aleatory fashion.

'All you crazy guys,' Karen said contentedly. 'In your crazy clothes.'

'Don't you know?' Alan said. 'White men go to pieces in the tropics if they don't change for dinner every night.'

'Surely going to pieces is the whole point of being in the

tropics,' Charles said. 'We've all gone to pieces or we wouldn't be here.'

Charles's remark set the table in a roar.

You acquire a method for dealing with these things. When you begin that long, slow, graceful parabola backwards into the vastness of space, there is yet no need to despair. To strip and find his bed had been the work of a moment: but at once he was joined by a familiar unloved companion. Bedspin. When the bed soars and arches beneath you, you know you have progressed into the deeper regions of drunkenness.

But Alan was still just about bearably drunk. *Capably* drunk. He opened his eyes, and focused meticulously on the light-switch. This was the core of his method. The point was to hold it there. It showed a tendency to slide away, up and to the left – always to the left, why was that? – but Alan subdued it with his will. Man of steel. Alan knew that if the light-switch broke away, he was lost. It swayed, made skittish little darts for freedom, retreated unwillingly back into the centre of Alan's vision. Stayed. See what I mean? Sleep struck him like a sandbag.

It would take a nuclear explosion to wake him. Alas, a nuclear explosion was what took place. An enormous crash was followed by the most tremendous roaring. For a moment, Alan panicked, sweat breaking out in dramatic cataracts, but soon he knew exactly where he was. Was someone knocking down his flat? After a moment, things became clearer: someone was knocking down the flat above.

'You fucking little bitch, do that again and I'll –'

The rest was lost in a passionate reply, the words indistinguishable, though no doubt bladdy-fackin barcer came into it. How strange it was that André, so charming, so unflappable, was able to give himself without restraint to these tiresome disputes. Another crash: something had been thrown, perhaps a table upset.

'Right, you little bitch . . .'

More inscrutable bladdy-fackin stuff.

'I'll teach you to believe me. I'll teach you.'

More screaming. The sound of feet treading hard. This was surely a physical struggle. Alan counselled himself: get ready. The orgy of reconciliation is at hand. Screams of ecstasy any minute.

Alan had retreated to a half-doze when the sound of a slamming door roused him again. Then a passionate hammering on its surface. Her voice rose, clearer now that she was in the stairwell: 'You can't leave me like this, you barcer! You can't!'

André's voice, calm, muffled, words indistinct. They raised Karen to new peaks of frenzy: 'Where can I go? Where can I go?'

André's voice was again unclear. Alan savoured a pause by falling into a doze. Then loud histrionic sobbing drew him close to the surface. This was followed by a shotgun blast of sound from André's stereo, absolute rock-bottom dirt cheap. There was a little more hammering on the door, but the pristine ferocity of the first assault had abated.

None of this was exceptional. It might even be considered an aspect of Tung Lung routine. Drunk or sober, he would let it wash over him. Lulled by the thunder of the bassline overhead, he gave himself up to beery slumbers.

Some time later – he was never sure afterwards whether the interval was to be measured in minutes or hours – he was awake again, with a terrible feeling of being adrift in the universe. Terror seized him: an invisible hand, gnarled and skeletal, took a light grip on his intestine.

The noise came again. It was a tumultuous knocking at the door. His door, he worked out before terribly long; it was *his* door that was being so savagely knocked. He was in the midst of some terrible emergency. Deal with it then.

He got to his feet with remarkably little trouble, hearing another terrific volley of knocking. He covered his nakedness with a sarong. And then went to the door. 'Hello?' he said through its thickness.

'For Christ's sake open the bladdy door.'

Karen then. 'Isn't it open?' Why was he asking this?

'Course it's not bladdy open or I'd be inside, wouldn't I?' She sounded pure cockney *in extremis*. But how odd, the things you do when you are – no, not drunk, when you have had a few, that's all. Pressed the button in the middle of the door handle, in that mood of meticulousness that sometimes comes upon you in these late-night circumstances. Pondering on the phenomenon of memory, he opened the door. And came within an inch of passing out from pure shock.

Karen was there outside, alone, and naked. Quite naked. Completely naked, *perfectly* naked. She had no clothes on. She had no clothes on at all. Not one. He stared, not in lechery but bewilderment.

'Aren't you going to ask me in?'

A light sweat broke out on his brow. It spread, like a little fire, over his face, bursting from beneath his arms, forming on his shoulders, coursing down his back.

'Sorry, Karen. Come in.'

A second and much heavier sweat followed this, cooling miraculously the instant it formed.

'You don't look very pleased to see me,' she said.

Alan wanted to lie down full length on the floor. But he did not do so. However, in the hope that such a move would look natural, almost inconspicuous, he lowered himself to one knee before her. It was impossible to know what to do with his arms, and with the hands at the end of them. 'Hello.'

She looked at him, disappointment in her eyes. 'What kind of bladdy welcome is this?'

Alan made the effort of his life. 'You know, all of a sudden I feel most unaccountably unwell.' He looked up at her: she stood over him, framed by the open door, the blackness of the tropical night behind her. Tiny dark-nippled breasts, slim pale gold body, small lank patch of black fuzz. She was, he was aware, beautiful.

His body was seized by a violent and quite unstoppable need. He leapt, with surprising athleticism, to his feet, turned, ran, sarong cascading round his ankles. He made it to the bathroom, more or less. And voided in long agonies of vomiting. Dripping with sweat, blinded by the violence of the seizures that shook him, indifferent to all save the need to empty himself. At one stage he was aware of a cool hand, not his own, on his brow.

At last he was spent, quadrupedal on the tiled floor. Weak. Horribly weak. He wiped his horrible face with his towel, wiped as an afterthought, some of the mess.

'Poor Alan,' Karen said. She put her hand back on his brow. Alan remained a long moment on all fours, feeling some ease in her hand.

'Sorry,' he said after a while.

'You need to drink tea,' she said decisively. 'Go and sit down. I will make some.'

'All right.'

She turned and walked away from him. For a moment, Alan considered her golden buttocks. Then he went to the basin, washed, spat, spat again, noseblew disgustingly. This was degradation. Shame filled him. Perfunctorily, he cleaned the floor with his ruined towel, threw it into a corner. Picked up his sarong, but from the weight of it he knew that it was too disgusting to wear.

He paused for a moment, considering the possibilities of vomiting anew. The storm was subsiding now, but the brief illusion of sobriety brought on by purgation was rapidly vanishing again. No, he really was going to throw up again. Anything but that. Lie down then, lie down fast.

He turned to his bedroom; at once decided that that was too provocative an action. Cushions, lie on the cushions. He walked across the sitting room in a few hurried strides, lowered himself with care. Halfway down, he was aware of his own nakedness. This was no good. This was terrible. But if he got up and looked for some garment, he really would throw up again. He lay down on the cushions, unscathed; unclad.

The scent of jasmine reached him as Karen scalded the leaves. He heard the soft slap of naked feet as she came towards him across the tiles. He opened his eyes. She was carrying a teapot in one hand, two mugs in the other, and, she was, as he noticed before he noticed the teapot and accessories, still naked. 'This will make you feel better,' she said, meaning, he supposed, the tea. She sat beside him on the cushions, but on the other stroke of the L. She set the mugs and teapot on the low table.

'Thank you,' Alan said. 'Look, Karen. I'm awfully sorry.'

'You drink too bladdy much.'

'I suppose I did.'

'I didn't say did, I said do,' she said, inaccurately, though perhaps, when you came to think of it, accurately. Contemplation of these verbal niceties brought about a mild attack of bedspin, or cushionspin.

'Look, Karen, shouldn't you put some clothes on?'

'I haven't got any bladdy clothes. Bladdy André locked me out without any.'

'Yes, I suppose so, but why don't you borrow a shirt or something? Or anything?'

'You haven't got any clothes on.'

'Look, I know, I'm sorry, I'll put something on in a second, I just feel awful —'

She made a gesture, one that meant anything you wanted it to, and poured the tea. The scent of jasmine doubled. It was good. Alan sat, greatly daring, but nothing happened amiss. He took the mug, sniffed, sipped scalding liquid minutely. 'You're right,' he said.

He sipped again. To his amazement, he was not lying. Death no longer seemed imminent, nor even desirable. Upstairs, the music had abated. The night was silent, bar the grating of cicadas. He heard a soft chirp from the wall, and a gecko made a foray along his wall.

He became aware that Karen was observing him very seriously, as if she were wearing clothes and he not. 'Why do you drink so bladdy much?'

'Why do you keep on seeing André?'

That made her look a fraction less clad. He sipped again the cooling liquid. They gazed at each other, over the horizons of their mugs, at 90 degrees to each other, gazes meeting or not quite meeting at right angles. Alan stole a little glance at her little breasts while she considered his remark.

'You're bladdy smart,' she said after a while. 'If you mean André makes me feel good, and then he makes me feel real bladdy bad and I maybe want to throw up.'

'Perhaps.'

'Or maybe you mean I ought to give him up.'

'Perhaps that, too.' Well, perhaps he did mean some of those things.

'But I don't give him up, do I? I stop for a bit and then I start again. So maybe it's permanent. Maybe I have to marry André and you have to become a bladdy alcoholic.'

'Oh God. Is life so terrible for us both?'

'I don't know. Maybe. I still want to marry the barcer. And you will have a drink tomorrow.'

'I suppose I will,' Alan said, sadly. Though it wasn't such a bad idea as all that, when you came to think of it. 'Do you think you will?'

'Marry him? I don't know. You don't know him. You only drink with him. But André can be – you can't know – so fackin *nice*. I mean, he treats me like a bladdy princess. We go to the best places, he acts like I'm the fackin Queen. Then he goes to some place and comes back full of bladdy lies. You know he always lies, André?'

'Well, no.'

'Bladdy gweilos. Always on the same side, against the bladdy Chinese.'

'No, Karen. I only mean that I don't know about what you say from personal experience.'

'Yeah. Maybe you don't. After all, you don't fack him and you don't do business with him.'

'Maybe.' Alan sipped. The scalded flowers calmed his body, cooled his brain. He looked again at Karen, across the right angle. She was looking straight ahead, and his glance was not intercepted. He inspected the tops of her knees, over the table, her arms, the long line of the side of her, elbows hiding, though neither intentionally nor entirely, her breasts. A longing seized him. He wished to lie with her: his head in her lap, her cool hand on his brow. For about a year and a half.

'Because he was fackin somebody in Singapore that time.'

Alan's head jerked away from her. 'Why do you think so?'

'Stop being a bladdy gweilo. Because he's André, because he always facks somebody when he goes away. And because he always bladdy tells people.'

'Karen –'

'All right. Don't bother lying. All gweilos together. Don't tell the truth to Chinese girls. Bladdy bad form.'

Alan sighed. Replied honestly: 'I'm sorry, Karen.'

'Why do gweilos drink so much?'

'Got to keep up your liquid level in the tropical climate,' Alan said automatically.

'All you do is drink. You all drink so bladdy *much*. I think maybe you all kill yourselves.'

'Really, Karen, I mean –'

'If I don't wake you up tonight, maybe you throw up in your sleep and choke to bladdy death.' She turned to him with sudden vigour at the thought, and caught Alan looking at her.

'Thanks for saving my life, Karen.'

'Bladdy gweilo,' she said. Almost tenderly.

Alan had drunk his tea. He lay back a little on the cushions, closed his eyes. That was rather good. Somewhere, far and distant, he could hear the voice of conscience calling him to order, instructing him to seize Karen in his arms, and make wild loving love to her. The thought made the room spin just a little, and so he silenced the voice.

'Let's go to bed,' Karen said.

Alan spoke without opening his eyes. 'You go, Karen, I'll stay here.'

'I mean sleeping.'

'So do I. I'll stay here.'

'You going to throw up again?'

'Don't think so.'

'Ah, Christ, Alan, let's just go to bed and bladdy sleep. In the morning, we feel better.'

'Lovely,' Alan said. 'That will be so lovely.' He drew his knees up towards his chest, discovering as he did so that he was lying down. A decade or so later, he felt a soft fluttering, and something descended gently onto him. He thought a few words of gratitude but he did not speak them, or even move.

Alan found that he was singing to himself, very softly, as he made his coffee. Really hardly any hangover at all. I must throw up more often. Waking up had been slightly disconcerting. He had to work out why he was sleeping on the cushions, and then how he had acquired a sheet to cover him, and finally, why he was alone in the flat. The solution to these mysteries shamed him a little, but perhaps it was all for the best. He had been bitten a few times on the face by mosquitoes, sleeping unprotected as he was, but nothing too desperate.

He fetched from beneath his bed the tough and well-travelled holdall that he used for his laundry runs to Wanchai. Good bag. Alan liked to think it made him look tough and much travelled. From this, rummaging through his dirty laundry, he found a towel that was at least usable. He washed without problem, for the Ng well seemed to be having a good run of late, used the towel, returned it to the bag with his other towels, unregarded, unsmelt, and likewise his sarong. He would take everything in on his way to Reg's that very day. He dressed in cotton trousers, rumpled, and a shirt that really ought not to have been asked to do another day. He could have sworn he had one cleaner than that about the place.

He drank his coffee. Had he handled things extremely well last night? Or on the contrary, extremely badly? Had he succeeded in being a gentleman? Had he failed to be a man?

Catch the twelve o'clock ferry. And no urgent work, so why not make a few calls? – ones he had been putting off for too long. Then take the laundry to the laundry, before it walked there. Lunch in the Two Brewers, yes. Good.

Steps walking around the house. Who? Steps coming through his gate. Karen, come to make up for the lack of love the night before? But the caller was fully clad, and André. 'Hello, my dear.'

He opened the door, and left it open, letting the morning in. 'Seen the weather?' André asked. 'One of those.' Alan could not see the sea; could hardly see the Ngs' house. 'Real wonton souper of a day. Don't move a step without your brolly.'

The day was of a perfect stillness, the heat not diminished a jot. Mist rolled into the flat in thick waves. 'Anyway, your shirt, I believe.' He wafted a fairly unexciting pale yellow shirt, which hung on a hanger.

'Oh.'

'Karen borrowed it to come home in.'

'Yes.'

'So I made her iron it.'

'That was kind of you. Or her.'

'I say, are you all right, old thing?'

'Sorry, André. Not at my best this morning. Do you want some coffee?'

'Adore some.'

André strode across Alan's flat as if it were the lobby of the Great Orient Hotel, hanging the shirt with some care from the top of Alan's bedroom door. He was wearing the bottom half of a suit and what was even for him a notably smart blue, and a white striped shirt. He wore cufflinks and a tie that hinted at membership of some privileged organisation. He sat down on the cushions, where, though presumably he did not know it, Karen had sat naked the night before, and accepted graciously a cup of coffee at Alan's hand.

'Interesting night, my dear?'

'I'm glad you brought it up. What happened, André?'

'Precisely what I was going to ask you.'

'Well, let's do it chronologically,' Alan said, taking his own place of last night on the cushions, at right angles to André. 'You start with your bit and then I'll cut in with mine.'

'Seems rather a waste of time, that,' André said carelessly, 'since there is only one point to the story, no matter how we decide to tell it. I mean, did you fuck her or didn't you?' He asked the question soothingly, almost pleadingly.

'I didn't as a matter of fact.'

André looked at Alan, disconcerted; almost disappointed. 'That's what Karen said.' He seemed to be finding this a very hard concept to grapple with. 'Why on earth not, old thing? If you don't strenuously object to my asking?'

'Should I have done?'

'Well, I would have, had the positions been reversed. And, she was yelling through the door that she was going to sleep with you.'

The thought raised a sudden warmth of desire in Alan's mind. Oh well. 'Not how it worked out.'

'Never thought of her as a tease.'

'Not that. But then there is a difference between going to bed with someone who really wants to go to bed with you, and someone who wants to go to bed with you solely to make trouble for a third party.' Elucidating this point brought a slight memory of last night's dizziness.

'Rather a fastidious point.'

'Perhaps you're right.'

André leant back against the wall, and delicately placed his feet, crossed at the ankles, onto the low table. They were clad in loafers of sublime softness. 'Alan, has it crossed your mind that you are a very odd person? A naked girl walks into your flat in the middle of the night, and you don't sleep with her. Come to think of it, the only reason she didn't try Charles is because she knew he wouldn't sleep with her either. A strange pair, you two.'

'You sound as if you wish that I *had* gone to bed with your fiancée.'

André pressed his palms together before his face, all the fingers touching. 'Interesting. You know, on the whole, I rather think I do. It would certainly hand me the moral high ground. If she had slept with you, I could have claimed it all back. Shame.' He was silent for a moment, and then he started to laugh, silently, in perfect ecstasies of private delight.

'What is it, André?'

André looked at Alan, and said: 'Perhaps I shall choose to believe that she slept with you anyway. Why not take a high moral tone with her? You can't talk to me like that, you bitch, not after what you got up to that night with Alan.' And he returned to his laughter of silent delight, quite transported with the beauty of it all. Alan had no idea at all whether or not he was serious. 'That reminds me, Alan. Did you ever call that English woman, Kate something, at *Orientique*?'

'Funnily enough, I was planning to give her a call this morning.'

'Putting this shirt on this morning, I found another card I'd been meaning to pass on. Laundered but legible. Belinda Chowdury, *Asian Hotelier*.'

André reached inside the pocket of his shirt, and tweezered a card between two fingers. Alan took it: 'Thanks again, André. I'll call her this morning too.'

André brought his feet to the ground with a soft, decisive thud, and flowed forward to a standing position. 'Well, I must go and make a living. You on the ten twenty?'

'Twelve o'clock, me.'

'Well, see you later. Be good. Though come to think of it, you already have been, haven't you?'

The traffic had gone sticky-solid, like nougat. After a despairing five minutes looking for a minibus or a taxi to take him to Central, during which the entire traffic system remained unmoving, Alan switched to his Hong Kong street-lore Plan B. He fought – the word was not a metaphor – onto a tram, employing a kind of overhead fencing technique, his umbrella a light sporting sabre. The rain was not rain, rather a solid continuous sheet. There was no break between drops either vertically or horizontally.

Stuck. The traffic was stuck, the pedestrians were stuck. In the rain, everyone in Hong Kong uses an umbrella, it being far too hot for raincoats. And so they get jammed overhead and have to be wrenched free. Smart brisk girls of five foot in height carry their brollies at gweilo-blinding height. But between Wanchai and Central the trams run in a fenced-off, trams-only lane, and provide the answer to what was, almost literally, a sea of sorrows. Alan boarded the tram as a pirate boards a ship. It was done with the fervour that only a man with a ferry to catch can muster.

Odd day. He had seen King, and obtained from him the information he was supposed to publish as the calling in of the favour: the favour of his continued health, his continued residence on Tung Lung. It was innocuous stuff, quite the opposite of what he had feared. It told merely of the founding of a new Hong Kong company, backed by unnamed overseas Chinese, to be called Island Holdings; a pep talk from someone King told him was a 'spokesman', Jeremy Kwan, about how much money they planned to invest in the New Territories if things went their way; some thoughts on the 're-Sinification of Hong Kong'. And that was about it. He had tapped this guff out, relieved, and put it straight into the magazine without troubling Reg about it.

He knew better than to stay on the tram once it had swung into Des Voeux Road. There it left its private lane and rejoined the nougat. Five minutes to ferry time: well, looking good. But no beer, damn it all to hell.

Taking a fast track through gutters, swerving round groups of shuffling dawdlers, dodging in front of becalmed taxis, Alan scurried along Connaught Road towards the pier. The top of the House of a Thousand Arseholes was lost in clouds, like a Himalayan peak. Was there really no time for a quick side trip to the supermarket by the Jordan Road ferry terminal? No, foolish person, there was not.

It was your ankles that got wet, what with the puddles and, above all, the splashback from the rain, which fell too heavily to rest quietly. He pulled a dollar from his pocket and, turning to the pier, fed it into the turnstile. A cascade of whistles blew as he walked, with unconvincing nonchalance, to the gangplank.

'The three's up, neighbour.' Charles was sitting along the back. The rain did not hit him directly, because the open area was now shrouded with canvas, making a sort of murky green booth. The atmosphere was filled with a million atomised droplets.

Alan sat alongside him, and received his can, punched into his hand with emphasis. The ferry departed, the ringpulls were pulled. The three, Alan knew, was a typhoon warning. There were three degrees of severity for the typhoon signal, which had all the logic of the scoring system of tennis. The three was followed by the eight, at which point all ferry traffic ceased, and most of the rest of Hong Kong business as well. And after the eight, the ten. That was a real blow, generally 'a direct hit' in Hong Kong talk.

'Did you hear some kind of kerfuffle from André's house last night?' Charles asked him.

Alan told his story. At first with embarrassment, latterly with *élan*. For Charles was utterly delighted by its every detail.

'Projectile vomiting!' Charles bellowed out the term, enraptured with delight. 'Nothing women appreciate more than a good bout of projectile vomiting. Did I tell you I saw Bonelli's eagle last Sunday when I was out on my run?'

'Is that good?'

'If you mean is it rare, then not very. What I mean is, it's bloody wonderful.'

'You're sure it was a – what?'

'Bonelli's, yes, don't insult me, pale leading edges, dark brown and white underwing, longish tail, black band on it, thin white terminal band.'

'Charles, what the bloody hell are you talking about? What do you know about birds?'

'Practically everything,' Charles said vaingloriously.

'All right, what's the bird that makes all the racket outside the windows in the morning? The one with the hangover-piercing screech?'

'Chinese bulbul. Nice little things, head like a badger.'

Alan looked at Charles. The damp had made his thistledown

hair stand away from his head like a little fuzzy halo. 'I only recognise the house sparrows myself,' Alan said.

'No you don't,' said Charles rudely. 'You only recognise the tree sparrows. There aren't any house sparrows in Hong Kong. So tree sparrows behave like house sparrows.'

'Golly.' This was for Charles, rather than for the ecology of the sparrow. 'How come you know all this stuff? And why have you never told me?'

'Didn't think you'd be interested. And I'm right, aren't I?'

'I'm interested in how you know.'

There was too much canvas hung around the boat for Charles to toss his can over the back, so he placed it on the floor below him, helped himself to an additional can, ringpulled the ringpull and drank. He settled himself comfortably back into his seat. He seemed to be moving into his Scheherazade mode.

'When I was a little lad, my father didn't own Hong Kong. He only owned half of it. He owned the half that's called the New Territories and Outlying Islands. So he had a place out there, north of Tsuen Wan, a proper house with a big walled garden. My mother was alive then, and she filled the place full of animals. Dogs and cats and parrots and terrapins, bloody great ponds full of fish, huge aviaries, and all the garden was filled with free-flying birds. She put out tons of food every day for the wild birds. I used to come home for the holidays and just sort of roamed about the place. It really was quite big, you see – enormous for Hong Kong. My mother never went out, never at all, sort of a semi-invalid even then. Sometimes she talked to me, told me what the birds were. And it was all I was really interested in, all I really liked. For years, really.'

'You don't seem to do much about it these days.'

'Funny, isn't it? I wanted to be a vet, you see. But then I fucked up my A levels, got chucked out of school for going on the piss. So I was brought back here. University not being an option any more, you see. My father wanted me to do a dirty job, a manual job, so I could see what life was like without any qualifications. Let that be a lesson to you, that sort of thing. Well, you know the Botanical Gardens?'

'Sure, little half-arsed sort of zoo halfway up towards the Mid-Levels.'

'That's the place. Well, I got myself taken on there. Paid about ten cents a week, cleaning up birdshit. My father saw it as a kind of cooling-off period. A spell in chokey.'

'So it was pretty unpleasant?'

'I didn't like it there, Alan.' Charles slowly spread his arms wide, like an umpire signalling a wide. 'I loved it. I adored it. I thought I had died and gone to heaven.'

'So what did you do?'

'I've told you, cleaned up birdshit. That was the beginning and end of my responsibilities. But you know the azure-winged magpies? They escaped, years back, and there's a small colony of them in the gardens. I used to carry crumbs and stuff in my pockets, and feed them, and they followed me all over the place like dogs. And the other birds – I used to go into the aviaries, and I just really – well, it sounds stupid. It is stupid. I just felt they liked me. Liked having me about the place. Especially the big birds. The Changas are good with small birds, songbirds, long tradition of looking after little birds in cages. But they weren't happy with the big ones, so I sort of specialised in them. The owls especially – the Chinese don't really like owls, super-stition thing. I could go into the owl cages, and the owls would come out to see me. Gave them a good old headscratch. One of the barn owls used to perch on my shoulder when I was trying to clean the floor.'

'So why did it end, Charles?'

'It ended because my father wanted it to end. If you own Hong Kong, you can't really have your son working as a coolie, can you? But anyway, he thought I had learnt my lesson, so he took me away from the gardens.'

'But you were happy.'

'What's that got to do with anything?'

It was impossible to tell if Charles was enjoying these con-fessions, or whether they were wrung from him on a rack of pain. 'So he made you leave the job with the birds and start your apprenticeship with Hong Kong Estates?'

'Precisely. And then I went to the bad, or if you prefer, from bad to worse.'

Alan knew something of the next part of the story: the friendship with a group of marine policemen, the patrols, the parties, the insanely dangerous drunken stunts, the vandalism, the scandal, hushed up, of the smashed-up bar in Wanchai. That was one of Charles's Scheherazade set pieces, and Alan had heard it in two or three different versions. Alan always enjoyed Charles's confessions. He seemed to delight in presenting himself as a comic character whom no one could take with any seriousness. But then, with startling inappropriateness, would come more vistas of desolation and despair. Alan's response to this latest tale was perhaps appropriate. He took a can from Charles's pink plastic bag, ringpulled the ringpull and drank.

'Shall we dine together tonight?' he asked.

'I was going to suggest a bucket of shit at Ah-Chuen's.'

'Got the dice?'

'Naturally.'

'That's all right then.'

It was always one of the hardest decisions of the day: whether to fag up 176 steps, deposit one's bag and change into Tung Lung chic, or to commence the evening with a quick one at Ah-Chuen's, which was, of course, seldom either quick or one. But with rain like this, the steps would be Niagaras. It might or it might not ease up, but certainly one should give that possibility every chance.

Naturally, they had to enter the inner fastness of Ah-Chuen's café; there was no dalliance under the banyan tree that evening. Customers were pushed together by the storm, in elbow-cracking distance of each other's folding round tables.

The air was steamy, and loud with music from Ah-Chuen's new stereo which was, not by coincidence, identical to Alan's own. The voices of two separate groups of card-players rose above it: perhaps fishermen who had been sheltering here all day. Alan rang King, but got no reply; Charles ordered beer and food, Alan requesting Singapore noodles.

Over post-prandial beers the dice began to rattle. At once they were absorbed by the eternal computations and decisions and disappointments that make up the game of yah-tze as the dice rolled and teased across the hard wooden surface of the table. The noise was part of it; and good. Not so noisy as mah-jong, where the shuffling of tiles sounded like a demolition crew at work, but the harsh, purposeful rattle was balm to the soul. Night had fallen with no noticeable decrease in warmth or wet.

'Rather impressive,' Alan said, 'this weather. This number three.'

Charles made a largeish gesture, indicating infinite contempt for any weather as feeble, as altogether impotent, as to be designated by a mere three. 'Did you read your *Hong Kong Times* this morning?'

'More or less.'

'Thing called Typhoon George been mashing up the Philippines. They reckon this current disturbance could hot up into the next typhoon.'

'And that's good?'

'Sit right on top of us for three or four days. Sit in the bunker with a good supply of beer till the damn thing blows away. Tonight, a small tropical disturbance, tomorrow the real thing. And Hong Kong stops dead.'

'I can't believe it can be that bad.'

'It isn't. It's worse. Your throw.'

Alan produced a workmanlike three threes and noted them down carefully.

At nine the eight fifteen ferry pulled up at the pier. They inspected the arriving passengers: 'March past of the bloody mushrooms,' Charles said. Neither King nor André was part of the umbrellaed throng. 'Don't believe King is on Hong Kong,' Charles said. 'He'll be up to no good with Chai.'

Alan wondered what André was doing. Proposing marriage to Sophie? Making love to her in the honeymoon suite of the

Fragrant Harbour Hotel, loaned for the purpose by a cringing management? Still, he reflected, he had done good business himself that day. Both Kate somebody – actually Burdett – from *Orientique* at Great Orient Hotels, and Belinda Chowdury of *Asian Hotelier* had been guardedly enthusiastic about taking his work. He was to meet both the following week. André had passed on the genuine goods. Once again he thought, as he had thought intermittently throughout the day, of Karen's body, the little knife-blades of her hips, her cool hand on his brow. The memory would have been more agreeable had he been able to edit out his shame. He saw, unbidden, the least revealing view of her, sitting, her gaze at right angles to his own, the long bare side of her all that was visible to him, a slim crescent of breast behind her unintentionally concealing arm.

There was a thump on the table and Alan jumped. Three large bottles of beer appeared, all in one meaty paw. Ah-Chuen had come to join them: he carried in his other hand a single glass.

'Fuck off,' Charles said, without looking at him.

Ah-Chuen giggled. 'Fu' o',' he replied.

I really must learn Cantonese, Alan decided again. Perhaps Ah-Chuen thought he really must learn English, though he spoke English better than Alan spoke Cantonese. By a hair.

He thumped Charles on the shoulder, as he took a seat. 'You get fat.'

Charles was outraged. He pressed his shoulders back, rippled his pectoral muscles, slapped his stomach with an open palm. 'Not an ounce of adipose tissue,' he said. He poked Ah-Chuen in the gut with a finger. 'It's you that's fat, you Changa bastard.'

An expression of horror lit Ah-Chuen's face. 'Not fat!' he said. 'Little beer maybe.' And he laughed, or rather giggled, high and piercing, always an unexpected sound from so substantial a citizen. He clapped Charles on the shoulder again. 'Beer is good.'

'Ah-Chuen, you never spoke a word as true.'

'San Mig is best beer.'

'Like a book thou talkest, Ah-Chuen.'

'Beer of Hong Kong.'

'It is the best because it is the cheapest,' Alan said.

'Chippus?'

'Money,' Alan said, selecting a word he was sure no Hong Konger could fail to know. 'Coca-Cola –' he raised a hand to head height, palm down, pursing his lips in disapproval, '– San Mig.' And he lowered the hand to table-top level, grinning and nodding. 'Cheap,' he said. 'So I don't drink Coca-Cola. I drink San Mig.'

Ah-Chuen understood, and laughed in delight.

'A purely financial consideration,' Charles said. 'The reason I'm a piss-cart, m'Lud, is that I couldn't afford Coca-Cola.'

It was true. San Miguel really was the cheapest canned drink available in Hong Kong. Coca-Cola, lemonade, sugar-cane juice and chrysanthemum tea: all these cost more. Ah-Chuen got to his feet to serve a group of customers at the far end of the steamy room. He then returned to the table, and added to everybody's glass. 'San Mig,' he said. 'Chippus.'

Alan bought a round. They drank for a while. 'Where is On-jay?' Ah-Chuen asked.

'Still in town.'

A reverential look appeared on Ah-Chuen's face. 'Business?' he said. 'Good.'

'I expect so.'

'On-jay is very clever man,' Ah-Chuen told them. He tapped his skull meaningfully. 'Like Chinese man.'

Charles laughed very loudly. 'André is a Changa!' he said. 'Now I understand. Now it all becomes clear. The bastard is a fucking Changa!'

The phone rang, and Ah-Chuen got up to answer it. For a while he listened, and then bellowed a bit in Cantonese. Then he said: 'Hokay, On-jay. Hokay.' He crashed the handset back into its cradle and returned to the table. 'On-jay,' he said. 'Good business!'

'What business?' Alan asked.

'Crooked business, I bet,' said Charles.

'Aaa?'

Charles looked very severe. 'No good. Police.'

Ah-Chuen giggled, and mimed some rather sketchy kung-fu in Charles's direction. 'Good business. No police, or I give you Chinese kung-fu.'

Charles waggled a finger beneath his nose. 'Try that with me, you Changa bastard, and I'll throw you in the fucking harbour.' Ah-Chuen had no difficulty in understanding this jocoserious challenge.

'Hokay.'

'Listen,' Charles said. 'Chinese man, business, OK.' Then he changed his smiling face to one of sniffy disapproval. 'Chinese man, drinking –' he took a hefty swig of air to make his meaning quite plain – 'no good.' He made a gesture of utter dismissal.

'Aaa?' said Ah-Chuen, in a tone of cosmic outrage. 'I am champion! I am beer king! I win!'

Charles shook his head sadly. 'Years ago. Many years. You old man now. Old man. Fat man. No good any more.'

'Not old! I beat you!'

'Never. Never in a thousand years.'

'I beat you now. I beat you *easy*.'

'Never. Bet?'

'Bet?'

'Money, you fat bastard. Ten dollars.'

'Hundred!'

'Done.'

Ah-Chuen explained the course and distance over which he had won so gloriously in his youth. This was a single tooth-glass filled with beer. Each contestant placed his glass on a table, and was forbidden to touch it. On the word go, they drank. The winner was the first to bang his empty glass down onto the table.

The commotion of this exchange had attracted the attention of Ah-Chuen's other customers. They pushed back their chairs, exchanged knowledgeable comments. An informal amphitheatre was created. Outside the rain hissed.

'You're sure you haven't overtrained?' Alan asked.

'I'll have him. The Changa bastard is too fat.'

Ah-Chuen poured two glasses, holding each in turn at eyelevel as he did so, glass inclined, gradually returning it level, lowering it to the table-top as he filled it to the brim. At last the two glasses stood side by side, ready, waiting. Alan had never seen beer look threatening before. Ah-Chuen looked at both glasses with concentration. His face was hard, tight. Was there a warrior gleam in his eye, a Boxer rebel, a Triad enforcer? Charles was mucking about: Ah-Chuen was in deadly earnest. What did the Chinese really think about losing face? 'Shall I be the starter?' Alan asked.

'Hokay.'

'Stand up, Charles.' Charles stood, shook hands solemnly with Ah-Chuen. 'Gentlemen, your glasses are before you. I shall say one two three go. Got that?' Two nods. 'Gentlemen, prepare to drink. One two three *go*.'

Charles seized his drink, raised it, dispatched it in three massive swallows. Ah-Chuen did not raise his glass at all. Instead, he lowered himself. He bent his knees, bringing his head almost down to table-top level, and simply poured the beer into his mouth, keeping his throat open by an extraordinary act of will. It was the swallow of a boa constrictor. He banged his glass down a good half-second ahead.

'Well played,' Charles said, gasping a little, taking his hand. 'Bloody well played.'

'You good. Very fast.'

'You were faster. However –' Charles made a sweeping gesture – 'I'm not really a sprinter.' He pointed at the two empty glasses. 'Too small. We drink in the English way, I win.'

'Aaa?'

'One glass no good. Three glasses, I win easy.'

'No. I win. One glass, hundred glasses.'

They agreed on three. The notion of double or quits was introduced: Ah-Chuen took it up with a gambler's instinctive understanding. The rest of the clientele or audience buzzed and disputed.

A feeling of recklessness arose in Alan. 'Anyone want to bet?' he asked. 'I'll take any bets against the gweilo champion.'

Ah-Chuen explained this readiness. After a low growl of mistrust, Alan soon had liabilities of $190. A double worry assailed him. Wouldn't it be rather awkward to collect money from these people? Wouldn't it be rather awkward to pay up himself?

Ah-Chuen reached down four glasses from a shelf by the fridge, and with the old ones, made two lines of three. Then, glass by inclined glass, he filled each with pedantic care.

Alan made a little performance of crouching to check the levels. Ah-Chuen, uncharacteristically, for Chinese do not in the main go in for such displays of affection, clapped him on the shoulder as he did so.

'Shall I start you again?'

Charles stood, and rotated his shoulders. He then clenched his fists, down at his sides, and inflated his biceps. He looked huge. Ah-Chuen patted his stomach, and laughed. Then again his face darkened, and he turned to his row of glasses with an air of menace. With a sound like a rifle-crack, he slapped one palm against the other. He bent his knees, very slightly, softly touched the first glass with his fingertips, and then lowered his hand to his side.

'Gentlemen, once again the game is drinking. I shall say one two three go. You have three glasses before you. Please drink them. One two three *go.*'

As before, Ah-Chuen's superior technique gave him the lead: the knee-bend, the python-swallow. Again, his glass hit the table with half a second's lead. He repeated his single swallow for the second glass, but emerged pink-faced, gasping. Charles, with his triple swallow, was gaining. Ah-Chuen picked up his third glass, his eyes bulging with effort, the joy of battle, even as Charles banged down his second. Ah-Chuen opened his throat, poured. But stopped, gasping in mid-pour. Charles swallowed massively, once, twice. Ah-Chuen opened his throat again, poured, Charles swallowed frantically, heroically. Crash! The glasses hit the table almost as one, but there could be no doubt about it. Ah-Chuen had won by a whisker.

But no triumph lit his face. Instant desperation. And suddenly he was spraying liquid from his mouth, as if the beer were a liquid yoyo. For a second Alan saw him as an ornamental fountain, an angry sea-god that permanently vomits a stream of cool, refreshing potable liquid. It was too instantaneous even to be disgusting: pure beer, three glasses, nothing added, nothing taken away. Helpless in the violence of reverse peristalsis, Ah-Chuen vomited the entire course and distance onto the floor of his café.

And then Charles took three long and stately paces to the door and stepped into the rain. There he gargoylely vomited. Alan went to his aid, hovering in the doorway, trying to avoid the still streaming rain. Charles turned to Alan, himself streaming at eyes, nose and mouth. 'The bubbles. Christ, the bubbles. Sweet Jesus, what an indescribably sordid scene.'

Ah-Chuen walked, weak and tottering, to the door, where Charles stood, still bent. He placed a hand on his shoulder. He too was laughing. Perfunctorily, they embraced, and then shook hands formally.

'I win.'

'You win.'

'You like brandy?'

'Not normally,' Charles said. 'But on thinking things through, I find that brandy is exactly what I need.'

Once again Ah-Chuen patted his broad belly. 'Is good for stomach.'

They returned to the table. One of Ah-Chuen's many minions had cleaned up already. Ah-Chuen rapped out an order, and the same or another minion fetched three clean tooth-glasses, a brandy bottle, a towel. This last was given to Charles, who removed his shirt, rubbed himself down, arranged the towel about his shoulders like a stole. Ah-Chuen barked again, this time impatiently, and the three tooth-glasses were filled with ice. Ah-Chuen then filled each to the brim with five-star. The ice cracked in merry greeting to the spirit.

There was little to say. The contestants, wet with sweat, beer and rain, were too spent to speak much. The three of them sat, sipped, in mostly silent companionability. Shame, pleasure, pride.

The march past of the mushrooms began again: the ten thirty had arrived. It was nearly half-past eleven. Alan watched them dimly through the open awning. Last of all was André. He walked into the café, lowering his umbrella, scanning the scene before him with an air of infinite tolerance. 'Greetings, people. Ah-Chuen –' and he spoke briefly in Cantonese.

Behind him appeared Ah-Chuen's mopper-upper pushing a trolley: umbrella-less, soaked. There were a dozen boxes on the trolley, each sealed with tape.

'On-jay! Good. Ve'y good!' The two of them shook hands, both smiling very broadly. Then Ah-Chuen personally supervised the unloading of the trolley. André went to sit with Alan and Charles.

'What occurs, children?' he asked.

'I was going to ask you the same question,' Alan said.

'A little business. What else?'

'What's in those boxes?'

'You're very inquisitive.'

'Sorry.'

André smiled, relaxed, winning. 'My dear, I didn't mean to offend. A little brandy, nothing sinister. Ah-Chuen sells it to the nobs on the island. I can get it for a good price.'

'But it needs a lot of ice-cubes?'

André smiled very gently. 'Perhaps so.' He stood again, and fetched three bottles of beer from Ah-Chuen's fridge. 'Who's got the dice? I feel ever so slightly lucky.' A rattle as Charles wordlessly scattered five dice across the table. 'The typhoon will hit tomorrow. Big bastard. Direct hit. Take my word for it. Get ready, chaps. Typhoon Hope is coming.'

PART IV

AUTUMN

No need even to think about awaking the bad purple herring-bone from its aestivation, but it was slightly less like living up to your ears in soup. For some reason, this was displeasing. Alan had complained about the weather of the summer whenever it had seemed appropriate, but never with a full heart. In summer every sudden movement, every moment of hurry, every access of panic called into being a gallon of sweat; and as summer progressed, Alan found that the weather imposed a wonderful pre-emptive calmness on him. He lived, it seemed, in a world of calm, slow grace: something unknown in colder climes. From this came a strange summer-long content: something, he was sure, unobtainable in the arctic wastes of the air-conditioned apartments of the expats of the Mid-Levels on Hong Kong Island.

But now, the scarcely perceptible fading of the summer heat brought autumnal restlessness. For the first time since he had taken up residence on Tung Lung, he thought seriously of travel, of going to those places that loomed so large in André's personal mythology. Perhaps he would drop hints here and there among his stable of editors. I may be making a trip – André never said 'going' – to Singapore, anything you might need from there? And Singapore had no autumn.

Alan caught the four thirty back to Tung Lung, and as was usual on this ferry, he was alone. The ferry timetable patterned his days as the seasons patterned the farmer's year. Sipping his San Mig, but a single can (though there was a second in his bag should he have need of it) he journeyed in unaccustomed soli-tude, wondering if any of his magazines would pay for his actual fare. That was the tricky bit, of course.

The climbing of the 176 steps produced less sweat than it had done a few weeks back. Still, never forget the importance of maintaining your liquid level in a tropical climate. He would have beer in his concrete garden after he had showered, or splashed in a red bucket if the well had run dry, of course. Yes, and some loudish music on his excellent rock-bottom dirt-cheap stereo. He was in control, was he not?

He saw from the end of the terrace that his door was open, but the sight gave him no qualm. It might, after all, be a beautiful girl lying naked on his cushions. A weak memory of black pants and golden skin warmed him.

But no. Two strangers sat on his chairs before his house, both fully clad, and both male. On the table before them were two cans of beer, presumably from his fridge. They were in animated conversation. One appeared to be about his own age, but wearing, of all things, a white suit with a startling turquoise shirt, unbuttoned deep. He wore pilot's gold-framed sunglasses and his hair was vividly blond. The second was a boy, perhaps fifteen, but with an elaborate haircut that was obviously supposed to give him an air of toughness and experience.

Both leapt to their feet as Alan turned in to his own gate, and both began to address him in terms of evident enthusiasm. Alan blinked. 'Can we start again?'

The white-suited one took charge. 'G'day,' he said. 'James James,' and stuck out a hand, surprisingly hairy wrists protruding from his ice-cream seller's suit.

'Oh really? I'm Alan Alan.'

'Yeah yeah yeah, most people say something like that.' But James James seemed only delighted by this as he shook hands with great purpose. 'But it's my name, you can call me James, or Mr James. Cool or what?' He laughed, and Alan laughed too.

The tan was too careful, the teeth were too white: Australian, flashy, stranger on his island, in his house, drinking his beer: how many wrongs could one man do in five seconds? He seemed utterly confident that Alan would like him; so much so that it seemed a shame not to start at once.

'I've just flown in,' said the boy, not yielding an inch. 'God

Almighty, what a terrible flight. Hit an air pocket coming in over the chequered rock. Nearly crashed. Nearly died. Kai Tak airport always does me in. Did you know the pilots have to do a whole year of instruction before they're allowed to land at Kai Tak?'

'Fascinating,' Alan said. 'I'll get myself a beer, if I may.'

'Get me one while you're up,' the boy told him.

'James?'

'Jim'll do, yeah, thanks, triffic.'

Alan removed three cans from the fridge. That left two, plus the one in his bag. He would have to get some more. How long was this pair going to stay? For ever? Was that actually true about Kai Tak?

Alan took his place back at his table, copiously thanked by James, or Jim, and at least acknowledged by the boy, who sat back in his chair and put his feet on the table. 'So where's Dad?' he asked.

'Dad?'

'Oh my God, don't you know who I am? Did you think I was a spy or something? I got arrested for spying once, out on the border near Lok Ma Chau. In jail for a week. Talked my way out. But Christ, didn't you recognise me from my photos? I'm Byron. Byron Kingston. Get it?'

'Oh. You're King's son.'

'Congratulations! Give the man a cigar! Yup, John Kingston is my old man. Great man, my dad.'

'Indubitably.' Alan began to wonder if this small boy was drunk.

'So I thought I'd drop by and see him.'

'Why not? Does he know you are coming?'

'Bloody well should do, shouldn't he? I rang him up and told him. But it doesn't matter if he doesn't show up for a while; you've got plenty of beer, haven't you?' And he laughed uproariously.

'I thought you were at school in England,' Alan said.

'Walked out last week. Nothing they could teach me. Decided to come out to Hong Kong to start up in business. Why waste time? I intend to retire at twenty-five, you see.'

Jim stretched out his legs; white moccasins and yes, turquoise socks. 'Great plan. Yeah, me too. Mica fackunmillion.' All one word, a single grandiose concept, not a mere measure of currency. 'Only thing is I'm twenty-seven. Hold on, guys! I'm at my most dangerous when I'm behind schedule. And look out! Because I'm *always* behind schedule.'

Alan, bemused by all this, had neglected to open his beer. He did so, not exactly to give himself time to think, but to give himself time, anyway. He drank a very large mouthful very slowly. A small bird with a flash of white perched for a second on the wire fence; Alan wondered if it was one of Charles's Chinese bulbuls.

'Are you here to do business with King?' Alan asked after a while. 'I thought he only ever did business with Chinese.'

'Kinda,' Jim said. 'I may be taking a flat out here.'

'I didn't know it was ready,' Alan said. 'Who told you about it? André?'

'Tall guy with curly hair? Bloke with a kangaroo loose in the top paddock?'

Alan was taken aback by this description. 'That's André.'

'Said it was all fixed. Arranged to meet me here and introduce me to this Kingston bloke. Byron here introduced himself to me on the ferry and took me up here. Your flat was open, and Byron here said it was kinda the custom to walk in and help yourself. Seems a bit of a liberty now I think about it. Hope it's OK.'

'I'm a believer in liberty. I expect André and King will be here soon enough. But you probably didn't realise that you enter a different time zone when you come to Tung Lung. It's a difference of quality, really.' Alan was rather showing off. He had written a piece on Tung Lung life for a magazine (the credit card magazine *Hallmark*) and that had been the substance of his opening paragraph. He had been paid $750 for 1500 words; what do you expect, Marcel Proust?

'I like the looka the place,' Jim said. 'It looks pretty wild.' He waved his can vaguely at the pointy hills.

'Very dangerous when the mist comes down,' Byron said. 'I went climbing one day, got caught in the mist. Walked around in circles for two days. Nearly died of exposure. Finally, I climbed to the top of the highest peak. God, they were worried about me. They couldn't put a helicopter up to search for me, because of the mist, right? But just for a second, the mist lifted when I was on top of the peak, and I got a glimpse of Tung Lung harbour. Just for a second, right? I made a mark on the ground, an arrow. And then I walked. Followed the arrow. Straight as a die. Didn't turn left or right, didn't walk on the path or follow a stream. I knew if I went off the straight I would be lost. And that would be certain death. Finally, I reached the houses. And at last, in the end, I found the harbour. Walked up the steps to home. They'd given me up for dead.'

There was a pause, in honour of Byron's near-death. And then Jim said: 'Wow.' Alan began to like him.

'Tell you what,' Alan said. 'Have a quick look around my flat. Chances are you'll be offered the ground-floor flat next door. It's just the same as mine only backwards.'

'Nice one. Great. Thanks. Are you sure it's not mine that's the right way round and yours that's backwards?'

Jim got up and went into the flat. Nothing too shaming lying about was there? Not even too many empty cans: he had carried a load out to the bins at the bottom of the steps that morning.

'Tell you what,' Byron said. 'Punch me in the stomach. Go on. Hard as you like.'

'Not just now, thanks.'

'Go on. Hard as you like.'

'I'll get a friend to do it later.'

'A friend of mine thought he could do it. Take a blow in the stomach, I mean. But he couldn't. I punched him and he passed out. Swallowed his tongue. Nearly died.'

'How terrible.'

'I saved his life. Stuck my hand down his throat. Grabbed his tongue, incredibly long, you've no idea how long a tongue is. Yanked it out, and got his breathing started again. He would have died if I hadn't been so quick.'

'Well done. How long are you staying with us?'

'What do you mean, how long? This is my home, man.'

'Oh.'

'Got no place back in Europe, have I? UK's gone. Shot. Finished.'

'What about the rest of your family?'

'Ain't got no family but Dad. My sister's vanished, just hopped it, gone to India or somewhere, probably dead by now. And Mum doesn't care. She never liked me. Lives with her fancy man. I had to slap him around a bit. He can treat Mum like shit, because that's what she likes. But I draw the line when it comes to treating me like shit, know what I mean? So I slapped him a bit. But I couldn't stay after that, could I? So here I am.'

'Just like that?'

'Dad left me an emergency bank account. If ever Mum should get completely out of order, we could just grab a ticket and fly back home.'

'Very considerate. We?'

'My sister had an account too, but she cleared it out when she pissed off.'

'How do you mean?'

'Gone to the bad. Ran off with a man. Drug addict. Gone to die of dope and hep in India. Shouldn't take long.'

'Love it. Love it to bits.' This was Jim, returning to the concrete garden. 'Look, I see these are the last of your beers. I'll go and fetch some more when we've drunk 'em. But like hey, what a nice pad. And I mean the ferries are OK? A guy can commute?'

'Hundreds do. It works well enough. What line are you in?'

Jim sat down and put his ankle on his knee, in the James Bond Position. His left hand clasped lightly the right turquoise sock; a gold bracelet hung from his hairy wrist. Even so, Alan still liked him. 'Background in advertising, worked for several of the big agencies in Sydney. Came here to set up on my own. One blue-chip client and I'm a rocket, yeah? Mica fackunmillion. Saw the typewriter – you the writer bloke André told me about?'

'That's me. Journalism, you know. Bit of this, bit of that.'

'Do advertising and public relations?'

'No.'

'Well, do you write bullshit?'

Alan was affronted. 'I make my living by writing. What the hell else do you think I write? I am the world's undisputed master at paid editorial.'

'Well, hell. Maybe we can do some business.'

'Always open to offers. Outside drinking hours, anyway.'

'Tell you what,' said Byron. 'Punch me in the stomach. Go on. Hard as you like.'

'It vexes me,' André said. 'It really does.'

'Unlike you to be vexed,' said Alan.

They were sitting outside at Ah-Chuen's, enjoying the beauties of a Tung Lung Saturday; less perfect than those of a Tung Lung Sunday but fairly considerable all the same. Ah-So tended his vat of boiling oil, and the scent of fishballs filled the air. Alan was wearing around his shoulders the grey and hooded garment he had bought from a Causeway Bay barrow to counteract the chills of the *Hong Kong Times*'s air conditioning. André was wearing a Harlequins rugby jersey, extremely ancient, its colours faded, testament of a thousand salty drenchings. In fact, André had just returned, relatively dry, from what was clearly a powerful and exhilarating passage around the North Point of the island in the Hateful Boat.

'You can't see any flaw in him,' André said. His tone was as languid as ever, but there was a note of peevishness there as well. Quite unwonted. 'You can walk all the way round him. Front, back, sideways. And he is still perfect.'

'Trick lighting,' Alan said. 'Makes him look three-dimensional.'

'That's what I thought at first,' André said. 'But I've looked very close, in direct sunlight. And he still looks real. That's what bothers me. He's so perfectly plausible.'

'But so are you, André.'

'But I'm *genuine*.' This, by the standards of André's drawling conversation, sounded almost like a cry of anguish. 'I've always got a lot of schemes going, of course I have. I'm always up to something; but I've never made any bones about that, have I? I never cheat anybody. Not my style. And the thing is with Jim, you can't even tell that he's up to something.'

'He must be.'

'But what? Tell me that. What? I mean, he's off on Hong Kong now, on a Saturday afternoon, and I have no idea what he is doing. And it troubles me.'

'Mica fackunmillion.'

'He's always talking to me about my work and my business. I keep thinking he is about to buy me out.'

'Does the same to me, with journalism, and I agree, there's something rather spooky about it. I keep thinking he's going to take me over, too. But really, André, how could Jim buy you out? He couldn't stand the pace. No one could.'

'Now there you speak the truth.' André was a little mollified by this.

'Any trips planned?'

'As ever. Might make a little run over to Taipei next week – remember Angel?' Alan didn't but merely nodded. 'She'll be there, plus a friend of mine in electronics has some kind of notion. And I have some possibilities of doing some work in Chinese medicine, oddly enough. Angel's father is involved in the business, actually.'

Alan laughed out loud. 'You're going to remove snake's gall bladders and grind up deer antlers in a pestle and mortar?'

André smiled, pleased at this. 'Very astute remark, my dear. Who would ever imagine a gweilo involved in Chinese medicine?'

Alan thought about this for a while. And then said: 'Are we talking Customs here, by any chance?'

'Alan, do I look the sort of person that would carry bear bile and tiger bone through Customs in a suitcase?'

'No, you don't.'

'Well, there you are, then. Ah, here they come.'

The rainbow sail appeared around the northward arm of the harbour, running hard before a cheerful wind, a long white wake scribbled across the surface of the sea. Alan could see the nearer of the two hulls bobbing rhythmically into the waves like the head of a galloping horse. 'I see Byron is still on board,' he said.

'Ah well. Charles had his chance, but he blew it.'

'One of these days, I shall have to tell Byron that nearly dying just isn't good enough. How did any son of King's get to be like that? Which reminds me, I meant to ask. You've met his sister, haven't you?'

'Jacinta? Yes, of course. Worse. Ten times worse.'

'Not possible.'

'I assure you.'

'I suppose that means she wouldn't sleep with you.'

'The question never arose, my dear. A most insulting suggestion, as you would know had you set eyes on her yourself. Too much lip and too much arse.'

'She sounds overwhelming.'

'If she tried it on with me, she wouldn't just nearly die, I can tell you. I like Asian girls, as you know. I haven't slept with a European women for years. Unless you count – but no, really, the principle is the thing, and besides, I was awfully drunk. Where was I? Yes, the point is that Jacinta is just about the perfect opposite of everything I find dear in Asian ladies.'

'You'd think someone like King would be able to keep his family in better order.'

'The wife's ghastly, of course. That's the problem. Melbourne bourgeoise, the very worst kind of Australian. And, of course, King was never really cut out to be a family man, was he? That's why he is so happy in the current setup, for all that he moans about missing his wife and kids. He's much easier with just us, with the occasional visit from Chai, of course.'

'I get the idea that the real love of his life is the entire Chinese race.'

'Quite good, that, my dear. Fact is, that wife of his just annexed him and King went along out of sheer goodness of heart. Have you noticed how Charles always lowers the sail before coming into harbour? Never gets up to any fancy stunts?'

'I've noticed that you always do the exact opposite. Coming in with one hull up in the air and the bloody sail parallel with the water. I don't know why you bother; I'm sure Chinese people don't impress with such monkey tricks.'

'Don't see why not. It always impresses me.'

'You're so easily taken in, André. At least, by yourself.'

André enjoyed this. 'You'd think Charles would be the reckless one, wouldn't you? But he's terribly meticulous. Conservative, even.'

Charles, walking towards them from the small beach where he had left the inflatable, was shirtless, as was his wont in all but the cruellest weather. Byron was shirtless in imitation.

'Alan,' André said suddenly, 'do me a favour. Come for a sail.'

'André, I'd do anything for you. Except that.'

'If you don't, I'll have to take Byron out again.'

'What's wrong with that? He might do more than nearly die.'

'My dear, if I were sure of that, I would take him out instantly. But the prospect of another near miss is too much for me. Charles my dear,' he continued smoothly, as Byron and Charles approached them, 'do you think we should take a turn across the bay once you've had a beer?'

'I'll come,' Byron said.

'Byron, I'd adore for you to come. But I promised to teach Charles a particular method of hull-flying, and that simply can't be done with an extra passenger.'

'Oh my God. All right then, I'll forgive you. But you'd better take me out tomorrow.'

'Not possible, alas. I have a long-standing date with Charles to perform a complete circumnavigation of the island. Have I not, Charles?'

Charles, a trifle dim about picking up André's mute appeal, said: 'Eh?' And then real sadness suddenly clouded his features. 'Oh André, what a bloody wonderful thought.'

'I mean, there's some real weather out there.'

'It's certainly whipping it up in the Tung Lung Channel. Christ, remember the last time we did a circumnavigation?'

'My God, I should think I do. Day after Typhoon Hope.'

'Was that hairy or what?'

'Right to the limits.'

'Didn't capsize though.'

'Daren't.'

'All we could do to keep the old girl upright.'

'If you weren't such a big bastard, we'd have been gone. It was a wonderful feeling, having you out there on the trapeze.'

'Remember how I had my arms out over my head, to get every last ounce I could away from the boat?'

'Couldn't even see the wake behind us, the sea was so unstable.'

'30 knots gusting to 50, wasn't it?'

'At least.'

'Crazy.'

'The best.'

The two looked at each other fondly. 'Tomorrow then? Hope for some nasty little autumn squalls?'

Charles's face, briefly alight with joys of remembered peril, saddened once again. 'Oh André. You'll never forgive me. But I can't. It's impossible.'

'How so?'

'My father. What else could it possibly be but my bloody father?'

'Since when did you start caring about him?'

'It's not that. I have been summoned. Summoned to the Peak. We have to have what he calls a Little Talk.'

'Oh God,' Alan said.

'Precisely,' Charles said. 'It bodes no good.' Charles's voice took on deep, magisterial tones. 'Charles Browne – your name is Charles, isn't it? Yes, Dad. How many times must I tell you? Don't call me Dad. Sorry, sir. Charles Browne, your manner of life is unsatisfactory. You are going to the bad out there on Tung Lung. You must give up beer, abandon your friends, start working properly at that wonderful job I fixed for you. Why don't you take up with that nice prostitute again? In retrospect, she was such a good influence, at least compared to your friends on Tung Lung. Better her than a beery end on an outlying island. But, Dad – I mean, sir – I want to come to a bad end. It's what

159

you've been preparing me for all my life. We are not talking Casual Whim here. We are talking Career.'

Alan, laughing, was aware that Charles was in some distress. 'Do you really think he will take you away from Tung Lung?'

'He can try. He can do anything, my old man. He owns Hong Kong, you know.'

'I believe you've mentioned that before. But he doesn't own Tung Lung as well, does he?'

'Nothing is beyond my old man. Tung Lung is as far away as I can get, but one little tug on the string, and I come jerking all the way back up to the Peak. But what else can I do? Besides, I have a cunning plan. I will agree to everything, promise anything, then come sneaking back to Tung Lung and get on with the job of going to the bad.'

'Are you absolutely sure that means you can't get back for a sail?' André asked, beseechingly.

'No good. There's also a lunch party. One for my special benefit, if I read the signs correctly. A lunch full of Useful People. Contacts for my future career. Reclaim the lost soul. God rot the lot of them. Do you think the boss of San Mig will be there? Or the Chief Brewer?'

'That's a thought.'

'Chief taster. Charles Browne, these are the conditions of the job. Arrive at nine thirty every morning and drink yourself paralytic until six. I won't tolerate any slacking. I want you arseholed from breakfast-time on. If I once catch you sober in office hours, you're fired. Is that quite clear? Of course, Mr Brewer. I'll do my best, sir, I really will. But God, could you imagine it, meeting someone at my old man's place, someone you really wanted to meet, someone who really could fulfil every dream you have ever had?'

'Ah well,' Alan said, to comfort, 'you'll be back in time for an evening meal at Ng's, so we can restore a bit of reality.'

'No, it gets worse. I've got to stay the night, go to work from his place on Monday. Bastard.'

'Couldn't you just not go?' André asked. 'Haven't you thought of that? Wouldn't that be the simplest solution?'

'Of course I've thought about it. But it just wouldn't work, would it? So I'll give him an easy victory, and hope he won't bother me for a bit. That's all I want, you see. Not to be bothered.'

'I went out in a typhoon once,' Byron said. 'Went for a walk, just to see what it was like. Everyone told me not to be crazy, but I didn't care. Saw this old Chinese bloke, he had his head cut off by a flying slate. Just in front of me. Came spinning across the street, hit him in the throat, took his head clean off. Body fell on the pavement, but the head blew away. Last I saw of it, head bowling down the street, caught by the wind, going faster and faster.'

The Sunday ferry timetable was subtly different to the weekday service, carefully designed to catch you out if you were not on your toes. Not that it mattered, because no one ever went to Hong Kong on a Sunday. It was a day of various ritual observances.

The mid-morning ferry left at ten thirty rather than ten twenty. Charles joined Alan for a cup of coffee before catching it. The suit was grey, and looked smarter than usual. Alan suspected he had had it cleaned and pressed for the occasion. The shirt was white, perhaps the shirt he had worn on the day of the Bloody Marys. The tie was not black, though perhaps it should have been to match Charles's face.

'I've just thought of something,' he said, as he entered.

'Oh-ah.'

'My father might have invited a Nice Girl for me to meet.'

'Oh God.'

'I have no objection to girls. But Nice Girls are a different matter.'

'I can see that.'

'Oh Charles, what do *you* do? I drink myself paralytic every night. How *fascinating*.'

Charles set off for the ferry a good ten minutes early; this was as uncharacteristic as his gloom. Alan took the remainder of his coffee out to his concrete garden, and arranged himself comfortably on two chairs. He heard more steps from outside: not easy, contented steps coming to demand coffee, but firm paces signalling business. Who else was catching the ferry?

King emerged from the side of the house, suited and stern. Byron was beside him, also grim, not suited, but wearing jacket and tie. 'Morning, chaps,' Alan said, for they had their eyes hard in front of them. His cheer met with scant response. 'Where are you off to, in all your finery?' he asked.

'We have business in town, Byron and I,' King said. Byron said nothing at all, as they passed on towards the 176 steps, which should have told Alan something.

But then, at ten thirty precisely, André himself emerged, suited and flying, garment bag over his shoulder, attaché case in his hand, shirt unbuttoned to the navel.

'André?'

'Running for a plane, my dear, slight change of plan.' As if on sudden impulse he threw to Alan a small object that he had held in his palm. It landed on the concrete at Alan's feet. It was a key. 'Water the plants for me,' he said. 'Byeee!' And was gone.

Alan finished his coffee, now lukewarm, feeling not a little bemused.

The shouting had roused Jim. He stepped from his door into the shared concrete garden, not suited, though rather too exquisitely dressed for a Tung Lung Sunday: perfect white jeans and a scarlet shirt. 'Hey,' he said. 'What's happening, my man?'

'Everybody on the island has gone raving mad,' Alan explained. 'Everybody has put on a suit and gone rushing like lemmings to the sea.'

'Then you'll just have to talk to me,' Jim said.

So they went and took breakfast at Ah-Chuen's, sitting before the harbour in some content, and then cautiously began the day's drinking. At noon, the next ferry arrived. Sundays always brought swarms of visitors. Jim and Alan watched them, school children in mufti, each lethally armed with a three-foot pitchfork, viciously barbed at the tines. Each was carefully and inadequately protected with a piece of cardboard.

'What the hell?' Jim asked.

'They come out here in gangs of at least twenty, to escape the noise and bustle of Hong Kong. It's a rural idyll. They buy charcoal bricks and meat in the village. They listen to music on those suitcase-sized ghetto blasters. They singe meat, giggle, get botulism, set the island on fire and then go home.'

'Alan! Is that bladdy-fackin barcer at home?'

'Hello, Karen. My, you look stunning.' She did, too, striding purposefully off the ferry in cut-off jeans that revealed her body at its most snakelike.

'Never you mind that, you fackin barcer,' she said, smiling affectionately. 'Where is bladdy-fackin André?'

Here we went again, Alan thought. 'Karen, I don't know how to say this . . .'

Eventually, she accepted a beer. How, Alan wondered, had André managed to avoid her at the ferry pier in Hong Kong? He must have performed some kind of jungle belly-crawl. Or perhaps he just relied on his luck: a pretty reliable commodity, it must be said. Meanwhile Karen explained that this had been André's last chance, and if the barcer thought he was going to marry her now, he had another fackin think coming.

Jim had been introduced in one of Karen's pauses for breath, but otherwise had merely looked at her, a useful enough way of passing the time. There was a small gap between the top of her shorts and the bottom of her singlet, over which she wore a short satin garment a little like a battledress. Alan thought he could detect in Jim a certain concentration on the thin strip of pale brown thus revealed.

But eventually, even Karen paused, and Jim leapt in. 'What kind of work do you do, darlin'?'

Darlin'? Alan thought she would bridle at this uncompromising approach. But on the contrary. She smiled at him, in a modest fashion. She seemed to become in an instant a wholly different person. She told him, quite humbly, that she was working as a secretary, and named the company.

'Ever thought of going into selling? Things like advertising space?'

'Why should I?'

'Because you'd be bloody good at it, that's why.'

She tilted her smallish chin at him. 'Why do you think that?'

'I just happen to be pretty bloody talented at spotting that sort of thing, darlin'.'

'Oh.' Karen, for once outmanoeuvred in the delivery of shock tactics, retreated into silence.

'Look, sweetheart, I'm going to do a very forward thing. I'm going to ask you to have lunch with me tomorrow. On a purely business basis, all right?'

She gave him a look of deep cynicism. 'Purely? Oh, sure.'

Jim gave a huge, exaggerated shrug. 'Look, darlin', I hope I ain't *insulting* you by talking strictly business. But if you want to talk business with me and nothing else, that's how I'd like it. Cool?'

Karen looked at Jim, considering her options. And quite uncharacteristically, she opted for defence rather than attack. 'What do you know about me?' she asked. It was almost as if she really wanted to know.

'Nothin',' Jim answered with great delight. 'But I can see you're Chinese, and so you understand about Chinese people. And I can see you understand about gweilos. You know how our stupid minds work, don't you, sweetheart?'

Karen smiled modestly, almost winsomely. 'So?'

'Most people in Hong Kong can only do one of those things, though a lot pretend they can do both. And you're a lippy chick, and I like that. One o'clock Monday? I'll pick you up at your office.'

'No. Best meet outside.'

'You're in Causeway Bay, right? Meet in the lobby at the Fragrant Harbour, go to their dim sum place, or do you prefer French?'

'I don't mind,' Karen said.

'Well, I prefer to eat Chinese, but we can change our minds. See you tomorrow.'

'OK,' Karen said. And after a pause she clearly decided to quit while she was ahead. She took her leave.

Jim and Alan watched her retreat the entire length of the harbourside and it was, Alan thought, worth every step. 'More beer?' he stated rather than asked. 'And by the way, Jim, she's a maniac.'

'Yeah, I can see that. But what if she was my maniac?'

'You mean –'

'I mean business, sweetheart. Smart chicks like that ain't so common. Ah-Chuen!' he added in a sudden bellow, as if he had lived on Tung Lung for a lifetime. 'Ah-Chuen, leung goon San Lig, m'goy!'

Ah-Chuen appeared at his elbow with the beers. 'Fu' o',' he said. Was this total acceptance?

They pulled the tops from the beer and contemplated the cans for a while. Then Jim continued what was perhaps a train of thought by raising the subject of *HK Biz*. 'I mean, I've been reading the copies you gave me.'

'Good God. No call for that.'

'It's a neat little mag. Great potential.'

'Been doing very nicely for years.'

'Sure, and you don't want to change any of that. Gotta keep that intimate touch going, that's what works for you. But there are obvious areas for expansion. Computing is going to be a skyrocket: you want to get in on that before it starts.'

'I can't really see computers taking off for our sort of people.'

'Well, you're wrong. It's all going to change.'

'I'm sure there's a lot in what you say. But Reg likes the quiet life, you see.'

'Then maybe he needs a partner.'

'What a sweet idea.' Sitting sipping beside his own harbourside on a sunny Sunday, Alan felt there was no amount of nonsense he could not listen to in good humour. Who was it who said you could negotiate the price of almost everything, but there was only one price for being a millionaire?

Eventually, after dining that evening at Ng's, they returned home, climbing the 176 steps in some hilarity. It was then, over last beers in their concrete garden, that Jim chose to sing his version of 'I Loves you Porgy'. He sang it falsetto, and rather beautifully, holding the tune perfectly and knowing all the words. It was an eerie business. Alan looked down over the roofs of the village, while the words rolled out over them: 'I loves you Por-geeee . . . bud I ain't *wur*-theee . . .'

The week had gone well for Alan, though neither André nor Charles had been sighted since the Sunday of the Suits. On Friday, Alan rang Reg to discuss the next week's schedule. Reg had planned what he kept calling a Spotlight on Printing, and wanted Alan to interview three or four executives from printing firms.

'Is this a normal method of paying your printing bills, Reg?'

'How could you suggest such a thing?'

'Hard to say. Perhaps it's because I've known you for getting on for a year.'

'That reminds me, Alan. You remember that short piece you did on the "Hong Kong Round-up" page? About a company called Island Holdings?'

'Yes?' said Alan warily. He had not forgotten the calling-in of the favour, the payment for his permission to stay on Mr Ng's island.

'As you doubtless know, they started making a few waves after that. Spoke to a friend of mine, researcher for a stockbroking firm, had a drink with him last night. And he told me that Island Holdings don't exist. Never have done. Complete phoney.'

Alan felt as if he had hit a massive air pocket, like Byron coming in to land at Kai Tak. 'Jesus, I'm sorry, Reg. I –'

'Don't worry. We were hardly alone. Everyone else was conned by them, we just had the honour of being first. But I thought it would amuse you to know. Look, do you think you could get those interviews set up? It would be great if you could do them next week while I'm away. No hurry, but as soon as possible, if you know what I mean. Make it the priority. I'll do all the office stuff today, don't bother coming into town for that. And you're still all right to come in tomorrow morning, and to do your stuff with getting the edition to the printer while I get the plane?'

'It'll drop off, Reg.'

So before starting on the list of printers, Alan began on a few connections of his own. 'Hello, Kate, how's things at Great Orient? No, still lovely out here on Tung Lung, eternal summer, you know. Look, remember the piece on Kowloon Walled City we talked about for *Orientique*? I can deliver it some time this week, if you like.'

Kate rode horses at the Jockey Club's place at Bee's River every morning before work, and her voice seemed to boom down the telephone from several fields away. 'Ya, okay, sure, why not, it'll make good pictures.'

'Good words, too, Kate.'

'Temperamental bloody artist. But it's a good coincidence that you called me, actually, because our PR person was talking to me about you this morning. Well, she was talking about Tung Lung, actually. Her name's Laurel Chen, mind if I put you through to her?'

'Sure.'

'Come and have lunch when you deliver the Walled City piece.'

There was sharp click on the line, and then a voice started boasting about the Great Orient Hotels' cooking. Alan actually began to reply before he realised it was a tape. He really was not quite on top of his game that day. Then a bell sounded crisply, and a voice, equally crisp, spoke to him. 'Good morning, Mr Fairs, this is Laurel Chen.'

'Hello,' Alan said jovially. Did she want him to write the new brochure or something? 'What can I do for you?'

'Mr Fairs, I believe you know André Standing.'

'Sure,' Alan said agreeably, and then instantly panicked. The plane hit another air pocket, a big one. 'That is to say, he is a neighbour of mine, I see him now and again, though I believe he's out of town —'

'So I believe also. He is staying at the Great Orient Hotel in Taipei.'

'That sounds like his style.'

'He says he is working on behalf of a magazine. He gave your name as a reference.'

The plane lurched again. Alan nearly died. 'What's going on?'

'Precisely what I asked myself, Mr Fairs. Have you asked him to write a piece for one of your magazines?'

'What? I haven't got any magazines.'

'I rather got the impression that you were in magazine publishing.'

'I suppose you could put it that way. I write things for them. Magazines, that is.'

'Oh,' she said. 'You're a *journalist*.'

The tone was wounding to Alan's self-esteem. 'Look, Miss Chen, what magazine am I supposed to be publishing? Why not tell me? Then I can check things out from their end, since there's obviously a major misunderstanding somewhere. I could make a few enquiries and then get back to you.'

She seemed ever so slightly mollified by Alan's change of tack. 'That's very kind. But be discreet, all right?'

'Certainly.'

'The magazine in question in *Asian Hotelier*. But please do not mention my name, or the name of the hotel. Or say that there is any official enquiry. It is just for my – personal curiosity.'

'Mine too. I'll call you back.'

'Thank you, Alan.'

'My pleasure, Laurel.'

Alan rang off. Y*b**nna mat! He stood up and walked around his room a few times in rather small circles. Best call Belinda at *Asian Hotelier*.

'Alan, darling, what have you been doing with Great Orient Hotels? I was just going to ring you. I have been having the most appalling morning, too dreary.'

'Remember the chap you met in Singapore, at the Great Orient there? Man by the name of André?'

She giggled, 'Of course I remember. Too delicious.'

'Belinda, you didn't, did you?'

'Un peu trop louche for little moi.'

'I'll fight a duel with the man if he claims to love you more than I do.'

'Oh, you darling. But, Alan, do you know what is going on?'

'What's happening your end?'

'Well, I got this absolutely brutal telex from Great Orient in Taipei. Positively demanding to know about the magazine, and your part in it, of all things. I'm trying to work out what to say.'

'Laurel Chen over here is also in a great flap, so they've obviously been in touch with her as well. And she tells me that André is at the thick of it.'

'What is going on, Alan?'

'You know what André's like.'

'I think that is a rather indelicate assumption. But, Alan, what should we do? Do you think André is in trouble?'

'I'm damn sure he is. André is always in some kind of trouble. The thing is that you must concentrate on looking after yourself. And me, of course. Don't worry, André is far better equipped than we are to do the same thing for himself.'

'You don't like him very much, do you?'

'He's one of my best friends in the world, Belinda. But let's try to look like innocent bystanders, yes?'

'OK, Alan. Look, thanks, for being in touch. Can you make lunch next week? I'd love to see you, and we can talk about stories.'

'That would be lovely.'

'And you can tell me how naughty André really is.'

'I was hoping you would tell me.'

Giggling, she rang off. The phone rang again immediately, making Alan jump. It was Kate again. 'Look, Alan, awfully sorry and all that, but your name is a bit of a sensitive issue round these parts. I really don't think I'd better run your Walled City piece after all. Which is a blow for me too, but there it is.'

'Oh God. Look, Kate, I've put a lot of work into this. It's

going to be a nice piece, too, I promise you. Why don't I do it under a pseudonym?'

'I'll think about it. What pseudonym?'

'Er, Sam Coleridge?'

'Ha bloody ha. I'll get back to you in the week.'

Alan walked around the flat for quite a long time, saying fuck quite a lot. After a while, he stopped and made himself coffee. He went and drank it on one of the outside chairs. He watched Chai walk, tall and straight and proud, into Ng's palazzo. They exchanged greetings.

'Josun!'

'Josun.'

Pretty good, eh? And he considered matters more deeply. Why was he not angry with André? If anybody else in the world had done this, he would be murderously angry. Was this just a lovable peccadillo? Bastard. I mean, really, bastard. All the same, it was rather jolly of him to hold an entire international hotel chain up to ransom. Any more betrayed girls to come weeping or cursing to his door? Look girls, here is lovely Alan Fairs, and he is not, repeat not, a bastard. Oh darling, poor you, how unerotic. Bastards, too delicious.

The phone rang. It was Reg. 'Look, Alan, who is this guy who keeps ringing me up?'

'Which guy? André Standing?'

'No, not *that* bastard. Some idiot called James James, says he's a friend of yours, wants to have lunch with me, supposed to be meeting him today. Who is he?'

'An Aussie loudmouth who fancies himself a crash-hot businessman. I'd trust him as far as, er . . .'

'André Standing?'

'Well, maybe a bit further than that.'

'Has he got money?'

'If you can make gold from bullshit, he's loaded.'

'Well, you can, I'd have thought you'd have learnt that by now. How are those printing interviews going?'

'Slave-driver. All set up.'

'Alan, you are lying through your teeth.'

'Ah yes, well, maybe, but it's all under control.'

'Call me back after lunch. That reminds me, come and have lunch with me next week after I've got back.'

'Love to.'

So many lunches. Too delicious. He thought for a while about making love to Belinda Chowdury, and it was pleasant thinking. But he wasn't really rich enough, was he? He rang the first name on Reg's list of printers and fixed an interview. Chap kept wanting to discuss computer technology there and then. Well, tell me all about it next week. Look forward to it, Mr Fairs. Too dreary.

The telephone splintered the silence once again. 'Hello, my dear.'

'André, you bastard, what the bloody hell's going on?'

'My dear, I know, but I can't talk now. Do you think you could meet me off a plane this evening? I get into Kai Tak about eight.'

'What on earth for?'

'It would just be quite tremendously useful, you know. Thanks a lot, Alan, I really appreciate that. Oh, and that reminds me. You know my kitchen? In the coffee jar there is a left luggage ticket. Could you fish it out, and then go to the left luggage office at the Departures hall at Kai Tak? And then meet me down at Arrivals with the bag. Be awfully helpful.'

'All right.'

'And then perhaps a spot of dinner? My treat, of course.'

'What a kind thought. Where are you now?'

'I'll see you at eight then. In the coffee jar, yes? Thanks so much, my dear. It means a lot, you know?'

How strange to be on the five twenty ferry. It was as if the world was turned upside down. In fact, Alan couldn't remember ever having caught that ferry before. Why would anyone wish to leave the island for the night?

He took his place at the back and waited for the boat to pull away. Ritual associations were more important than mere warmth, and besides, feeling the bite of the early evening air, he had for the first time taken his unfortunate tweed jacket from the wardrobe. It would have been a good idea after all to have had it cleaned during the summer. He wore it over his shoulders, without thrusting his arms into the sleeves, seeming in this way less irrevocably committed to the turning of the seasons. He had two cans of beer in a pink plastic bag at his feet and *Octopussy* in his jacket pocket. He was self-contained.

But in the end, self-containment was unnecessary. To his surprise, a tall suited figure climbed the stairs. It was King, striding rather majestically into sight; King, he might have added, of all people. King was not a great catcher of ferries: his business affairs seemed inextricably bound up with Tung Lung. And not a great wearer of suits, either. This, the second time in a week, was unprecedented.

'Good evening, my young friend.'

'Hello, King. Has the world gone mad? Every time I look up I see all my friends streaking away from Tung Lung in their best suits.'

The ferry hooted and pulled off from the jetty, and Alan lifted his bag. Ungrudgingly if perhaps a trifle wistfully, he handed the second can to King.

'A thousand thanks, young Alan.'

'Just as well you haven't got that hard-drinking boy of yours here. Somebody would have had to go without.'

'That hard-drinking boy of mine has gone back to UK, Alan.'

'Oh. I thought he was all set to stay here for ever.'

'I would have been happy with that outcome, Alan, believe me. But I had his mother on the phone every night. It transpires that the boy was due to appear in juvenile court last week. But he came here instead.'

Bald statements of misfortune are hard things to deal with. 'Oh. What has he done? I mean, allegedly done, as we were taught to say when I was on local papers.'

'No allegedly about it, Alan. He was involved in credit card fraud.'

'Quite enterprising of him.'

'Not very. The cards belonged to a schoolteacher. From his own school, I mean. He says he found them in a corridor. He ran up several hundred pounds on three or four credit cards.'

'Just the sort of initiative you expect from a young lad with a Hong Kong background.'

'An amusing remark, Alan. But the problem is his mother. The boy is not truly aware that what he has done is wrong. He is honest, you see. Now, I see that you may have trouble with that idea. I brought him up that way. He is *too* honest. Too honest for his own good, alas, because his mother has kept him cocooned from the real world. That is how he got into this mess.'

'So how did he get over here? On the cards?'

'I left both my children a little money when I was last in UK, so that they could make a trip to see me at Christmas. He got his hands on it when his court case came up. It shows a wonderful faith, Alan. He really believed that I could make everything turn out all right.'

'We all want to believe in somebody like that.'

'I would have done it were it possible. I would have done anything. But he is in too deep. I was forced to buy him a ticket home. I put him on the plane myself. That was the worst part of it all. I felt bad, Alan. Very bad. I think it is something he will find hard to forgive.'

'Oh, King. How dreadful for you.'

'But the business with Jacinta grieves me still more.'

'Oh God. What's happened to her?'

'That is precisely the problem, Alan. I don't know. Her mother has let her run wild. And you see how they reward her. She too has left her mother, taking the money I left for her Christmas visit to Tung Lung. She explained that she was travelling east. And nothing has been heard of her for a month. I fear, Alan, I fear the worst.'

'How ghastly for you, King.'

'And she so beautiful a girl. No, a woman, now. A beautiful

woman, but lost in the maw of Asia. Alan, I would die for my children. But I can't see any way that would help.'

Alan let a pause develop after this. He had been taking rather rapid sips from his beer, and was seriously regretting the lack of the second, or rather third can. Eventually, he said: 'What brings you into town, King?'

'Business, my friend. What else? It grieves me to leave my island, and even to spend a night away from its shores, but what must be must be. I am bidden to a banquet with some Chinese friends of mine. Much business will be talked, at the proper time of course, and much brandy will be drunk, also at the proper time. Brandy is a drink I have never liked. But as you must know, Alan, no banquet is a banquet without a bottle of five-star on the table, and no man is a man unless he drinks most of it.'

'That reminds me, King. I heard a buzz about Island Holdings the other day. What was the truth of that story you and Ng planted on me?'

At this, King cheered up immensely. He slapped Alan cordially on the thigh. 'Ah yes, my friend. Island Holdings. The major international company funded by overseas Chinese.'

'That's the one.'

'Would it shock you to know that it never existed, save on paper?'

'No, King, it wouldn't.'

'It was a front to conceal the involvement of my friend and partner Mr Ng.'

'Oh.'

'The planning department did not look kindly on his ambitions of building a hundred houses on the market gardens. But the government is prepared to bend the rules for the sake of investment from overseas Chinese. Major part of policy, you see. And now, I am happy to say, Island Holdings has won planning permission for the great Tung Lung housing development. And appreciate the irony, Alan: one of the reasons it is going through is because the island will have mains water next spring. Ng can go ahead with his plans, and I can go ahead with my part, which is the supply of building materials.'

Alan allowed his mouth to hang open for a while, to collect the moist warm evening air.

'Is Ng not a genius, my young friend?'

'I suppose so.' Alan did not say that it grieved his heart to think that his Chinese scroll was to vanish. That he had helped to destroy it.

'When this evening is over, Alan, I expect to be a very rich man indeed. This banquet is something I have been working towards for perhaps ten years. All my plans have come to fruition. And I and my Chinese friends, colleagues and partners, will drink a great deal too much brandy and swear undying fealty to each other, and to the mighty dollar. I will go to bed at three a.m. and my bed will spin as if I were a boy unused to drink. I will go to bed drunk and I will wake up as I once was: sober and a millionaire.'

'Wonderful news, King. I hope all goes well.'

'My thanks, Alan. And what brings you to Hong Kong on a cold evening?'

'I'm meeting André at Kai Tak.'

'Is André not capable of finding a taxi himself?'

'Well, he wanted me to fetch something for him from the left luggage place.'

'Oh.' King spoke this syllable with great solemnity.

'Yes,' Alan said. 'I've been thinking that as well. Ever since I put the phone down. What do you think I should do, King? I mean, he asked me, as a friend –'

'I can tell you one thing with complete confidence, my friend: André would be very sorry afterwards.'

'Oh God. I can just see him being sorry. What should I do?'

'Listen, Alan. There are some ways in which André, like Byron, is an innocent. He is a very trusting person. Everything he says, he believes utterly.'

Alan was still dithering as the ferry pulled into Hong Kong. Together, he and King walked into the ferry building, Alan's eyes automatically flickering across the barrier to see if any friends were lurking, awaiting the next departure. The next boat to leave would, after all, be the six thirty. He looked for Charles, and saw Jim, in his white suit, this time with a red shirt and red tie.

'Hi, guys!'

Alan approached the mesh of the barrier to speak.

'Look, Al, great things to tell you,' Jim said. 'Had a triffic meeting with your mate Reg today. We must talk.'

'Look forward to it, Jim.'

Alan and King walked on. 'Be very careful, Alan.'

'I try.'

After more than usually affectionate farewells, Alan left him to walk to Star Ferry, paying his fifty cents, wild extravagance, for a first-class passage. There were at least half a dozen boats fussing about across the harbour as the Star Ferry reached its evening peak of business. Alan took his place on the waiting boat, regarding suited gweilos reading their *Hong Kong Times* and their *Asian Wall Street Journal*; suited Chinese reading newspapers that ranged from the many-charactered quality press to the mildly pornographic newspapers at the other end of the market. He observed expressionless eyes contemplating smudged, minute and grainy tits. Others pondered the enigmas of racing form, for there was a meeting at Happy Valley the following day. The new season had started again after its summer lay-off. Alan had never bet on the Hong Kong horses: the clattering dice of yah-tze offered him not adventure and hazard but comfort and security. He thought again of his own manner of life, in touch with the wild magic of Hong Kong, yet apart from it. He had got it right. Perhaps he, alone on the ferry, was happy and free. He thought, with a thought that surprised him: was the allegedly beautiful Jacinta happy and free in the maw of Asia? Or a lost and bewildered stray?

Alan, ignoring the charms of the volume in his pocket, looked back to the wall of buildings at the greater harbourside behind him: the lights still shining in the House of a Thousand Arseholes. Here and there were gaps in the ramparts, like missing teeth, giant construction sites, their jackhammers silent as dusk came.

The ferry docked on Kowloonside, and Alan strolled towards the taxi rank. This was always the best way for the un-luggage-encumbered to get to Kai Tak, or any cross-harbour destination, when traffic was heavy. Pleased with his Hong Kong street-lore, he reached the head of the queue.

'Kai Tak, m'goy.'

'Aaa.'

What to do about André's luggage? Toss a coin? Roll the dice? Well, he was in very good time. So have a beer first, at the very least; read *Octopussy*. His Cantonese failed him at the airport, but by shouting 'li-do' a few times, he was able to persuade the driver to take him to Arrivals rather than Departures. Perhaps he would be making a departure himself one of these days. Little trip to Singapore. See if Belinda had a freebie to offer him.

The Arrivals building gave him an unexpectedly violent pang of remembered terror. He had not been here since his own arrival in Hong Kong. He remembered the failure of the promised airport meet, the telephone call to the *Hong Kong Times*. Well, he had travelled far since that day: of that there was no doubt. He went to the small café, and sat before a beer for a while, as he fingered the left luggage ticket inside his pocket. Slowly, the hall before him filled with greeters. Sorry, André. Didn't have time. Only just got here. Got stuck in traffic. Dreadful congestion at the cross-harbour tunnel. Not your fault, my dear. I'll get it myself, only last week's dirty laundry. You should have caught the Star Ferry, you know.

No, he really ought to get the bag. No he oughtn't. André was a friend. André was a barcer. Come to think of it, was he either?

Alan was drinking his beer in extremely small sips. He thought of Bond, carrying the diamonds into America, hidden inside his golf balls, and how even he had made such a mess of the cheery question of the Customs man. He would finish his beer and then do it. It was five to eight, though. And what if André found him drinking beer? He watched as people began to emerge from the automatic doors, to be greeted with whoops and smiles, but never with hugs. The Chinese didn't hug. They shouted instead. Children and old people and pregnant women and impossibly young fathers, all grinning. Apparently longing to hug but not doing so.

Alan's beer was finished. A quarter past eight. Customs never stop me, my dear. Until they do, of course. Ah yes, the old counterclockwise deodorant trick, eh? But let him go, see if his accomplice is waiting for him outside. Then we'll pounce. Get the whole gang.

Alan left his glass and walked into the crowd, for they were now coming thick and fast through the automatic doors. A gweilo businessman, carrying only a shoulder-bag and an attaché case, a stratospheric jay-walker. A Chinese lady with unconvincingly curled hair, pushing a cart laden to the ceiling with cardboard boxes: a rice cooker, a child's tricycle. Where would the poor little bugger ride that? Better move him out to Tung Lung.

And suddenly there was André, strolling through the automatic doors which, it seemed, pulled back with especial deference for him. He was pushing a trolley: attaché case in the basket at the back, garment bag clearly visible on top, containing, no doubt, silk shirts, silk ties, spare suit. And beneath the garment bag, Alan could see two very large, brand-new holdalls. André looked even more composed than usual; perhaps that was a giveaway.

Alan felt terribly shabby, tieless in his tweed jacket, even if he had thrust his arms through his sleeves to counteract the added chill of the airport's air conditioning. André's eyes skimmed the crowd; finding Alan, he raised his eyebrows slightly and walked over to meet him. No hugs. 'Evening, old thing.'

'Er, hello, André.'

'You've got it all right?'

'Look, I don't know how to tell you this, André. I'm sorry. I haven't got it. I lost my nerve.'

André stood before him lost in thought for a while, his face unreadable. After a while, he said, still looking into the crowd: 'Don't quite know what you mean, my dear. Just last week's laundry. Still, no bones broken.'

'I'm sorry, André, but I just –'

André silenced him with a gesture. 'Have you got the ticket? I mean, you do have the ticket?'

'Sure.' Alan wanted to retract this the instant he had said it. But he would be firm, would he not? Sorry, André, I can't do it. If you want it, you'll have to get it yourself. But he said nothing.

'I suggest we walk to the taxi queue,' André said, terribly quietly. They did so: the line was perhaps fifty people deep. 'Excellent,' André said. 'About ten minutes, then. Look, just get a cab, would you? I'll get the bag from left luggage. You might as well take my luggage, all right? Tell the driver to take you to the Departures building. But make sure you tell him we're going to Hong Kongside afterwards, or he'll refuse to take you, won't do a three-dollar run, will he?'

'Well, if he speaks English –'

'You'll make yourself understood. See you up at Departures in ten minutes. Then we'll go for that meal I promised you.'

'But, André, that's not necessary. I mean, I hardly –'

'Give me the ticket. Thanks. See you in a jiffy.'

'All right, André.' Oh Jesus. What is in these bags? He looked down at them, fat and bulging holdalls. Oh God, Oh Christ. Oh fucking fuckfucks.

He stood in the queue, feeling horribly conspicuous, as if he was dressed as Batman in the erroneous impression that the party was fancy dress. The line crawled and shuffled. He willed every taxi to pick up three or four passengers, but each time, it seemed just a single person climbed in. He kept giving his baggage cart little pushes forward, once ramming the calves of the person in front, a Chinese man in a caramel-coloured suit, and apologising profusely. Then suddenly he was three from the front, repeating his calves-ram and apologising still more fervently, hoping the man would not seize his bags in a rage, tearing them open and scattering God knows what the length and breadth of the airport. And then the caramel suit was climbing into a taxi, and the taxi behind was pulling up for Alan himself. The boot clicked open automatically as he stopped, a little refinement some of the taxis possessed. Alan filled it with André's luggage and climbed into the back.

'Aaa?'

Oh God, a monoglot. 'Go Departure!' Alan said, pointing skyward. 'Then Hong Kongside. Heung gong-ah. Fragrant Harbour! Fragrant Harbour Hotel!'

'Aaa?'

'Dip-ah-cha! Then heung gong-ah! First dip-ah-cha! Then Fragrant Harbour Hotel.'

The driver pointed skyward. 'Dip-ah-cha! Hokay! Flay-gan huppa ho-tay!'

'Hoho. Hoho.' Meaning jolly good, there being no word for yes in Cantonese.

And the cab swept around the airport roads, swung about, climbed the slope upward, there to the welcoming group of Customs men, policemen, soldiers brandishing sub-machine guns, searchlights, grenades, flashing lights, loudspeakers. Hokay, Mr Fairs, come out with your hands high.

But there was André, standing tall and easy, a large suitcase on the pavement beside him. Unhurriedly he stooped, spoke to the driver in Cantonese, and then placed a suitcase into the front seat before joining Alan in the back. He spoke another sentence of Cantonese, before adding: 'Fai-dee, m'goy.' Alan knew that one: hurry, please.

And the driver fai-deed, and soon the taxi was streaking clear of the airport, and André was smiling at Alan with just the least hint of a patronising smirk.

Alan spoke first. 'How the hell did you get me involved in all this, André?'

'All what?'

'You know what I'm talking about. What's in that bloody case?'

'I told you. Last week's laundry.'

'And in the ones in the boot?'

'Oh, that's this week's laundry.'

Alan felt the tensions of the evening rise to a head. 'Fuck off, André.'

André was instantly contrite, instantly understanding. 'Alan, I'm sorry, I really am quite tremendously grateful to you, and please take the dinner tonight as a small token of gratitude. But best we drop the subject now, don't you think? For all our sakes. All right, my dear?'

Alan found himself reluctantly mollified. 'All right,' he said, just a trifle sulkily. 'All right. I suppose you're right.'

'I am always right, Alan. That is the secret of my success.'

'Thanks for explaining that, André. I feel much better about it all now.' But he didn't. 'All the same, André – well, you do live, don't you?'

'But barely, my dear.' The taxi carried them through Kowloon, the same non-pretty way that had appalled him so much on the day of his arrival. Soon be his anniversary, would it not? They plunged beneath the waves, through the now uncongested cross-harbour tunnel – it always seemed longer than Alan remembered – and turned over a curling flyover that brought them to the door of the Fragrant Harbour.

'Good evening, Mr Singh.'

'Good evening, sir.'

Alan, crawling across the seat after André, saw the doorman accept a folded note, presumably ten dollars. 'Could you be awfully kind, Mr Singh, and get these three bags to the concierge? And have the ticket brought to me in the restaurant? The Continental, not the Pagoda.'

'Of course, sir. Thank you, sir.'

'Oh, and just leave the garment bag at the desk, would you? I'll collect it myself later on.'

'Certainly, sir. Thank you, sir.'

'Not at all, Mr Singh. Come, Alan. Do you share my feelings that this is an appropriate moment for champagne?'

'I feel more in need of a powerful sedative, but I expect you're right.'

André led the way across the lobby with immense strides, so that Alan had to hurry to keep up with him. 'I think so. Good evening, Mr Wong, a table for two, please. Thank you so much, and could you send the sommelier over right away? Alan, I do indeed have something to celebrate. Perhaps the most brilliant day of my life. Good evening, yes please, a bottle Veuve Clicquot, please. Yes that one, of course, right away.'

The champagne arrived, was poured. A page-boy came to them bearing a small salver on which lay three numbered tickets. Alan took them with gracious thanks, sprinkled a few coins onto the salver, for which he was thanked with enthusiasm, and placed the tickets with some care into his wallet. He turned to Alan and smiled with perfect brilliance. 'Well, Alan. Thank you for your very present help today. To the future, yes?'

'To the future.'

Alan drank: pale, sharp, infinitely lifting of the spirits.

The champagne giggles consumed them as they swooped towards the ferry. At ten forty, André paid off the cab, and Alan followed him, only slightly less easy in his heart, towards the ten thirty ferry which, as they could see, had yet to depart. The gate clanged shut behind them; they crossed the gangway even as it began to rise beneath their feet. Announcing departure with its crack-of-doom hoot, it pulled away from the jetty as they ascended the stairs. 'Perhaps,' André said, 'it's as well you didn't let me stop for the beers. In a way.'

'I lack your faith.'

'How shallow you are. Why, there's Charles.'

Charles sat on the back bench, jacketless despite the chill, tieless and shirt undone two or three buttons deep. Both arms were spread out along the back of the bench, his feet on the seat before him. His smile was both colossal and unfocused.

'Have nothing to do with him,' André said sharply. 'The man's drunk.'

Charles slowly placed his hands behind his head. 'I suppose you bastards want beer.'

'Only to save you from yourself. I wanted to stop for some on the way, but André was panicking about the ferry.'

'Charles, you clever old stick,' André said, ignoring this facetiousness. Placing his arms and legs in more conventional positions, Charles rummaged on the floor and produced a six-pack.

'Muchee coldee,' he said proudly.

Seated, the ringpulls consigned to the deep, they drank deliciously.

'So how was the meeting with your old man, Charles?'

Charles held up his right hand like a policeman. 'Wait. Wait. All in good time. I want to hear everybody else's news first. It is practically a week since I last set foot on my island, and I need to catch up with the news. Once I have done that, I will be in a position to impart some news of my own. Now listen, you two, I want you to try really hard to make your stories interesting. Because I have some quite colossal stuff to tell you. The most colossal news you will ever hear in your lives.'

'What's that?'

'No. Your news first. Sum up. Alan, you first. Tell me everything. I bought the beers. I have a right to insist.'

'A very fair point. Well, it's all been pretty much the same as usual, except that I have had a little trouble – hey, André! I meant to take this up with you. You make me forget everything. What's this about you using my name at the Great Orient in Taipei?'

André smiled kindly. 'Oh dear, I was afraid that might get back to you. Fact is I needed somewhere to stay in a hurry. Cleaned out, you see. Great Orient seemed the right sort of pub, but I needed a line to get in there.'

'Why not try somewhere cheap for once? It might not necessarily have been fatal.'

'You know nothing about the world, Alan. It is ten times easier to work something on a five-star hotel than it is on a dosshouse. A dosshouse expects you to try something. I'm sorry if you had trouble, Alan, but I really was in dire need. You don't really mind, do you?'

'Well, it's probably cost me a commission worth fifteen hundred bucks, plus I might not be able to work for two magazines again.'

'I'm so sorry, my dear. Look, I'll make up the fee as soon as this deal has gone through – least I can do. And as for the rest – well I have a couple of ideas that might interest you. That might be worth something to you.'

'All right, André. We'll talk about it later.'

'What's André been up to?' Charles asked.

'I haven't the faintest idea, Charles.'

'He's a bastard, that André. Have nothing to do with him. He drinks too much. Where were you?'

'André, as you know, has been to Taipei. You saw King and Byron on the ferry when you went into town, did you know what was going on?'

'Tell me.'

So Alan explained about the fraud charges. 'And King is pulling off some major deal, he says. He's going to be a millionaire again tomorrow. Oh, and Jim's going to be a millionaire any second too, apparently. He's up to something; I expect to see him in the bankruptcy court any day now.'

'Very good summary. Thank you. André, anything to add?'

'As a matter of fact I have.' André took a sip from his beer. 'Wanted to wait till we were all together before I made the announcement. Remember that girl I used to know in Taipei? Angel? Well, she and I really hit it off awfully well, and we're going to get married. She is beautiful. And tiny. Really the tiniest girl I have ever slept with. And quite quite lovely. Soon she will be coming out to Hong Kong. It is just a question of getting a passport. When she does, I will certainly marry her.'

'Well, congratulations, André. Does that put you into double figures for fiancées this calendar year?'

'What a cruel question to put to a man in my situation.'

'Karen. Sophie.'

'Well, I hardly –'

'Well, *she* thought you were going to marry her.'

'This Taiwanese midget.'

'Don't forget the Malay princess,' Charles said. 'Me boom-boom. Me marry big tuan.'

'And the girl from the jewellery shop in Singapore.'

'Oh God, I'd forgotten her,' André said. 'Olympia Wong, her name was. Is, I mean.'

'Anyway, Charles, to sum up as best I can, everyone on Tung Lung is now a millionaire, except me. What about you?'

'I am not about to become a millionaire. I have much better news than that.' He made this admission on his most orotund tone, normally used only at moments of great importance, such as a suggested adjournment to Ah-Chuen's or that the dice be brought into play.

'Come on, Charles.'

'Have I everybody's attention?'

'Yes.'

'Sure?'

'Certain.'

'All right. Listen to this. *I have been struck by the thunderbolt of love.*'

'Oh,' Alan said.

'Is that all?' André asked.

'Certainly it is all. It is in fact everything.'

There continued to be an eerie solemnity about him. He was poised somewhere between facetiousness and transcendent joy. After a pause, one that Charles clearly relished, Alan said: 'Well. Go on.'

'Have I not said enough?'

'Come on, Charles, the details. Back in Wanchai with your lady of the night?'

'All right. I shall be serious. I have met a girl. I have, as I say, been struck by the thunderbolt of love. It appears that this was a reciprocal business. I have proposed marriage. I have been accepted. We intend to marry as soon as possible.'

'Well,' said André. 'Tell us all about her. Is she beautiful?'

'Naturally.'

'Does she fuck?'

'André, you intrude on sacred mysteries.'

'You mean she doesn't.'

'I don't think you understand, André. This is love. As in, I love her and she loves me. Can you imagine such a thing? I have just spent the most perfect – no, the *only* perfect week of my life. I have been on holiday, driving round the New Territories in a Land Rover looking at birds, making love, and planning how to change my life for ever.'

'Well,' Alan said. 'Congratulations. Now tell us everything.'

'Her name is Chloe. I met her, of all the extraordinary things, at my father's house. She was, in fact, a Nice Girl. She is the daughter of the Professor of Zoology at the Chinese University. He's a gweilo, English, bilingual in Cantonese. Chinese wife. Two daughters, Chloe is the younger. Just returned to Hong Kong; she's been at university in UK, reading zoology. Came here to think things through. I arrived at the old man's, she was already there, and I fancied her at once, you know. So I thought, I've got *no* chance here. I'd had a couple on the ferry, but I was still pretty much sober, so hardly at my most sparkling.'

'How did you ever get to speak to her, then?'

'Got to speak with her old man. Turned out he's a bit of a birder, rather a whiz on the subject. Asked me what we've got on Tung Lung. Told him about the Bonelli's eagle. And she just sort of came into the conversation, saying she'd love to see the Bonelli's. So being a bloody fool I said, well, you can't, they've finished nesting and they've buggered off. Though I didn't say buggered.'

'Very wise.'

'Not that she'd have minded, or her mum and dad for that matter. It's all bugger this, bugger that and fuck the other at their place. But I'm getting ahead of myself.'

'Bunch of Hong Kong bohos,' André suggested.

Charles considered this. 'Sort of. Not my old man's sort at all. Must have been at his wits' end for a Nice Girl. He's got a beard, you see, corduroy suit. And Chloe's a bit whacky for a Changa, or half-Changa. Jeans and silk shirts, that sort of thing. God, she's beautiful. Did I tell you she was beautiful?'

'She looks like a Changa then?'

'Oh yes. Dark hair, longish, Changa eyes, that sort of neatness, you know? But something not quite right. Not quite Chinese. You keep looking back to see what's different about her.'

'So what happened?'

'Well, we were placed next to each other at the meal. Started to talk, and just kept going. All about Hong Kong and nature and stuff, where best to go. Birds and animals and trips we'd like to make. And she said maybe we should make a trip together one time, and I said, nothing I'd like better in the whole fucking world. I did say fucking that time. And she just said, well, that's settled then. Anyway, I ended up going back with her family for supper. They've got a wonderful place out in the New Territories, an old Chinese house, with a garden, plenty of mature trees in it. Sort of thing that's mostly been knocked down now. And everyone went to bed after a while, but Chloe and I sat up. In the garden on the terrace, listening for owls.'

'I must try that,' André said. 'My God, you're beautiful. Let's sit up and listen for owls.'

'No mockery, André. And we did hear owls too; we heard a couple of collared Scops, young birds, probably. Then we kissed rather a lot, and then we went to bed together. About dawn she tiptoed off down the corridor. I rang work next morning and asked for permission to take the week off. I was owed quite a bit of leave, and they'd been pestering me to take it, so there was no problem. And oddly enough, they said something else. I'm to have a promotion. They want me to work in the New Territories.'

'Good God.'

'As manager, of all things. But take some leave, they said, but make sure you come in on Friday and we'll talk about this new job. Which was today, of course. And yes, it's all sorted now. I have to take up the appointment in a couple of weeks. Rather a lot of money, as it happens.'

'Charles, this information about your professional life is all very fascinating, but we want more details about this girl of yours.'

'Fair enough. There is, after all, nothing else in the world I want to talk about. She borrowed this Land Rover off her parents, and we went out every day. Sleeping back at the family house. Evening of the first day, Chloe told her parents we were going to get married and would it disturb the routine of the household if we were to sleep together.'

'Golly. What was the response to that little bombshell?'

'Well, in a way, that was the most amazing thing about it all. Great delight, you see. You know – as if they really liked me.'

'Perhaps they do.'

'I've never been in a family before. It's rather nice. Two eggs this morning, Charles? Yes please, lovely. And what are you and Chloe up to today? Well, we thought we'd go up the Lam Tsuen valley to look for passerines in the feng shui woods there, and then look for a nice quiet spot where we can take all our clothes off. Though I didn't say the last bit, though I expect they guessed. And the week ended, four days really, five if you count Sunday, and it was bloody lovely. It really was the Time of my Life.'

'When do we meet her?'

'Oh, when the Bonelli's come back, if not before. But look, chaps, I'm going to be leaving Tung Lung. I'm moving in with the family, and then we'll get a place of our own. Need to be in the New Territories for work now. Sad to be leaving you chaps. But – well, everything changes, doesn't it?'

'We'll miss you, Charles.'

'I'll miss you. But look, André, how do you feel about doing a circumnavigation tomorrow? For old times' sake?'

'My dear, I'd love to. But I've got to go into town. Really can't get out of it. Business appointment. How about Sunday?'

'Sunday I shall be gone. Moving out, you see. As I said. Got to do it right away. Still, Alan and I shall have a few beers, yes?'

'Of course. But I've got to go into town too, get *HK Biz* off to the printers. Be back, mid to late afternoon. So we'll have a beer then, yes? But really, Charles, I can't believe you're going. The place will be like a morgue without you. All the same, I'm really happy for you.'

'You're happy? You're happy? What about me? A week ago I was a cunt. Now I have everything. I have absolutely fucking everything.'

PART V
CHRISTMAS AGAIN

Some days it was the first thing he thought of. The instant Alan awoke, the terrible thing would come to him again. But sometimes it did not. Sometimes he would be up, bustling about, drinking coffee, assessing the strength of the current hangover, making plans for the day. And then the thought would come again and that was somehow worse. Sometimes it came directly; a single, dreadful fact. At other times it took a back route. He would be carrying on as normal and would, perhaps, say to himself, oh yes, I wonder if Charles – and *then* it would come.

For Charles was dead. Alan lay thinking of this. He sat up in bed. Better to walk around than to lie about thinking things through. At all costs avoid that. Very carefully, he placed the heels of his hands in his eyes and left them there for a while, before bringing his hands slowly down the length of his face.

The front door banged open and Charles burst in behind it, beaming and booming. 'Happy Christmas, you bastard! Here's a proper breakfast for you, the Bloodiest Mary you have ever tasted in your young life.' Well, he didn't, of course. But he should have done, Alan thought. That is precisely what should be happening now, this very second. Perhaps in his white trousers and white shirt, black silk tie with an absolutely preposterous drink, 50-50 vodka and Tabasco, an absolutely preposterous expression on his face. And King and André would be following him down, perhaps also dressed in bizarre finery, because white men go bad in the tropics if they don't dress up for Christmas Day.

'Oh God damn and blast it all to hell,' Alan said aloud. He got up, wrapped his sarong about himself, and washed sleep from his eyes. 'Sorry, world, I shouldn't have said that,' he told the mirror. 'What I meant to say was Happy Christmas. Happy Christmas everybody. God bless us every one. Why do we live here, God fuck it?'

He set to making himself coffee.

Charles had died a few weeks earlier, in fact, the day after he had spoken on the ferry of Chloe and the thunderbolt of love. Alan and André discussed it in some detail as they travelled in on the eight thirty, on the morning after the great protestation of love. Once in town, André went off to do whatever André was doing, and Alan went to hand *HK Biz* to the printer. He had spent the morning wrapping up the issue, both figuratively and literally, before giving it to the printer whose abilities, not by coincidence, were to be so roundly praised in a future issue.

These things always take longer than you can see any reason for. Alan had hoped against hope for the one twenty but in the end, he caught the four thirty, looking forward to a rather belated start to the promised drinking session with Charles.

He had stepped off the ferry with a bright and breezy step – why not? It was a bright and breezy day, the warm dry weather of autumn being, some said, the best that Hong Kong can offer. Meaning, no doubt the most like an English summer. The wind whipped little whitecaps in the Tung Lung Channel, but it was nothing to which the most fastidious could object.

He walked along the harbourside, looking for Charles and failing to find him. He would be at Ah-Chuen's, then: a bottle of cold beer before him, another, beside it, unopened, waiting.

But he was not. Well, perhaps he was at the top of the 176 steps mixing a killer cocktail. Or maybe he had bought champagne. There was, after all, a good deal to celebrate.

Ah-Chuen appeared from his shop and stood before him, smirking happily. 'Josun, Ah-Chuen.'

'Fu' o'.' They grinned at each other. 'You want beer?'

'I suppose so.' Ah-Chuen tossed him a can from the fridge. Alan caught it, and opened it in a little spurt of excitement. 'You know where is Charles?'

'Chuz? In bo'.' Ah-Chuen gestured broadly at the sea.

Alan looked at the harbour. André's boat was not there. Fair enough, then, he had gone for a sail. 'André with him?'

'No.'

'King? Karen?'

'No. Ony Chuz.'

'Christ, the silly sod,' Alan said mildly. 'Hope he doesn't drown himself. Gone long?' He tapped at his watch. 'Charles. Gone long?'

'One hour. Maybe two.'

Alan sat down and looked at the sea, whitecapped. There was no brave rainbow sail in sight. But Charles was a very competent sailor. André always said so. He drank some more beer.

'He trank,' Ah-Chuen said.

'Eh?'

'Chuz. He ve'y trank today. Ve'y happy. Ve'y trank.'

'Silly sod,' Alan said again. 'Oh well. I expect he'll be back soon.'

But he wasn't. The boat was found the following day by the Cheung Chau ferry. It had capsized, the sail lying along the surface, one yellow hull riding clear of the water. The weather had changed, and it was a duckpond of a day. The ferry had alerted the coastguard, and they had gone to investigate. They had righted the boat, and then they found Charles. He was attached to the trapeze by the long wire that led to the top of the mast. He was hopelessly entangled. And of course, long dead.

There was an inquest, and a misadventure verdict. He had not been wearing a buoyancy aid. There was no other firm conclusion. It was thought possible he had struck his head a light blow on capsizing, though no mark was found on him. Alan read all this in the report in the *Hong Kong Times*. Charles, it was suggested, might have become entangled in the line when disaster struck. It was a freak accident; he was very unlucky. There was a small amount of alcohol in his system, but not enough to affect his sailing abilities. So either Ah-Chuen was wrong or there was some kind of cover-up.

They had all gone to the funeral – Alan, André, King and Jim. Alan borrowed from Charles's flat the black tie Charles had worn on the day of the Bloody Marys. It was a dreary do at the Anglican Cathedral. They were introduced to Charles's father, who seemed vague to the point of senility.

'Said to be the most deceptive front in Hong Kong,' King said after they had all shaken hands and exchanged awkward condolences. 'An old friend and a great man.'

On the coffin was a small bunch of wild and semi-wild flowers, the kind that grew beside the 176 steps, and all over Hong Kong, wherever there was a gap in the concrete. King whispered to Alan they were from Chloe. It was then that things got a bit much.

Afterwards, the Tung Lung contingent, though invited by Charles's father to partake of the baked meats, went instead to Wanchai, which, they felt, was far more appropriate to Charles's memory than his father's house. They moved from bar to bar and drank themselves stupid. Alan wondered if on their travels they met Charles's first fiancée. Maybe if I had got the one twenty, Alan thought to himself, again and again, or even the two fifty. If I had been more efficient, or less conscientious. Met Charles before he had set sail. Hello, you bastard, coming for a sail? Certainly not, you must be crazy, let's stay on Tung Lung and drink beer. What a very excellent plan, it shall be as you say. And so they drank the afternoon away and never once went near the sea.

Alan poured water onto brown powder and added milk. He went out into his concrete garden, feeling a little, but only a little, underdressed, for it was a bright, sunny day with a perfectly acceptable bite in the wind. The sky was pale, almost an English blue, and there seemed not a drop of humidity in the air. Down on the valley floor, he could see a farmer at work in the chessboard fields, for Christmas was a day like another for the choy sum. The sea was lightly wrinkled, no whitecaps today. He could see one of the triple-decker ferries and beyond, its destination, Cheung Chau.

It was ten o'clock. Soon the next ferry would arrive. Was it a Sunday timetable today? Of course it was, Sundays and public holidays. Ten thirty, then. Perhaps André would be on it. Perhaps

King would be. Jim would not, because he was spending the Christmas break with friends on Hong Kong Island: 'Al, I really hate to leave you on your own, come with me, decent crowd, they'll love you, we're just having a barbie and a few beers.'

But Alan had refused, though grateful for the offer. He had said he wanted to be by himself: though he was partly lying. Really, he was hoping for the sudden dramatic return of King, or André, or, indeed, both. André had been gone about ten days, setting off with attaché case and garment bag.

'Where to this time?'

'Just slipping over to Macau for a few days.'

'Business or pleasure?'

'My dear, you should know me too well to make hard and fast distinctions like that.'

'Do you know any beautiful Macanese girls?'

'Funny you should mention that. There is a blackjack dealer in one of the casinos who might remember me. But no, I have a few contacts to look up.'

'Chinese medicine?'

'Are you in the market for a bowl of tiger's penis soup? Only five grand a bowl to you.'

'Are you serious?'

'Not entirely, no. I'll tell you more when I get back. So long, old thing.'

A few days after this, King had vanished. No advance warning about a little trip; he just vanished. Alan had learnt this when, feeling a need for solids, he had climbed the stairs to borrow an egg and found the place deserted. Alan had emptied his mailbox a couple of days later, when it was full, but that was all he could do.

Well, perhaps King was already heading homeward, riding the ten thirty in triumph. And perhaps not. No point in setting yourself up for a disappointment Alan told himself sternly. Be independent. Self-sufficient. Like last Christmas: yes. A good, brave thought. Walk over the spine of the island, down to the village on the far side, and feast on seafood and beer. A perfect day for it. Perhaps he would see a Bonelli's eagle.

While sudden absences were part of André's pattern of existence, King's disappearance was more troubling. King gave stability to island life. What complex convolution of business could have called him from his beloved island on such a day? Perhaps the next ferry would bring the answer.

Alan stood, and looked at the quadrant of sea visible from his garden. He waved his arms about a little to keep warm. Yes, there was the ferry. More or less on time. Well, it would determine the course of his day, that was for sure. He wondered for a moment about going to meet it, but at once banished the thought. Let fate come in its own good time, in whatever form it chose.

Instead, he went back into the flat and dressed: jeans, a new black sweat shirt he had bought from a barrow in Causeway Bay for the sum of ten dollars. Streetwise in Hong Kong, was he not? He put the kettle on. It held enough water for more than one cup, but that did not count as tempting fate, did it?

He was right not to be on the jetty. It would soon be thronged with thousands of Chinese adolescents all armed with deadly toasting forks.

There was a mass arrival at Ng's: it seemed that this was a day for the gathering of the clans: adults, children, grannies, a great tribe of them, all dressed in perfect crispness and talking in great excitement. There was joy in the air. Mark Ng gave him a cordial good morning, Chai a stately Josun.

No one else. Lunch on the far side of the island today, he told himself firmly. What a good idea.

But then another figure. Moving at the end of the terrace. Unquestionably female, and equally unquestionably, non-Chinese. In fact, though Alan was not sure why, unquestionably English. She was something to do with André, no doubt. But was she? She was wearing, he saw, a rucksack. A backpacker. Contempt stirred within him: he had nothing to do with the lost wandering skinflints of Asia, the would-be intrepid throngs who huddled together in every capital from fear of the land they were visiting.

She looked as out of place on Tung Lung as a bird of paradise in a flock of starlings: an odd thought, Alan told himself at once, because she was dressed in black. But unquestionably exotic, for Tung Lung. In fact, altogether ridiculous: an absurd anomaly in the tranquillity of island life. She had dark hair, worn rather long, with a single lock dyed chestnut. She was a little stocky; a perfectionist, and certainly André, might have thought her overweight. But only by comparison with bird-boned Chinese. The fact was, Alan thought, that there was not a straight line in her body. Her face was broad, eyes melodramatically outlined in black. And she walking up to him. Alan's eyes were drawn at once to her nose. It bore on its left extremity a jewel. It would do, Alan thought.

'Hello,' she said. Even from so brief an utterance it was clear she was English, middle-class with a faint overlay of imitation cockney, and not terribly sure of herself at that precise moment.

'Hello.' Surely her eyes were not purple. No one had purple eyes.

'I'm looking for John Kingston.'

'He wasn't on the ferry then?'

'Well, obviously he wasn't.'

The voice was unambiguously hostile. Alan replied in the same tone. 'Look, he lives here, this is his house, I'm his tenant, he lives in the flat upstairs.'

'Yes I know that. A few years since I was last here, and I couldn't remember at first which was his gaff. I just wondered if he was down here with you.'

Impatience filled him. The frank hostility and the black-ringed eyes made him angry and uneasy. Surely it would not be hard to get rid of her. 'No. He's not upstairs, either – go and check if you want. I don't know where he is. I haven't seen him for about a week.'

Her face fell. Alan had clearly knocked her hopes to the ground and danced on them in hobnailed boots. 'Oh,' she said.

Alan was a little awed by his own triumph. 'Look, I'm awfully sorry to bring you what is obviously bad news. Can I help you? Do you want to use the phone or anything?'

'Oh God,' she said, infinitely weary. 'Oh God, I hope he's not done something silly again.'

Alan's first thought was that she was talking about suicide, for death was much on his mind. Then he was aware that the use of the word 'again' tended to put that theory out of court. He still found the utterance bizarre. Silly? King was many things, but surely never silly. Clearly she had met King, but equally clearly she hardly knew him.

'Have you got a key?' she asked.

'A key?'

'To his flat, of course.'

Alan looked at her rather shiftily. 'I haven't, actually.'

She gave a sudden brief laugh, as if gathering the ironies about herself. 'I'm awfully sorry, you don't have any idea who I am, do you?'

'Well no, obviously not.'

'I'm Jass.'

'Jass?' Alan was unable to keep disbelief from his voice.

'Jacinta Kingston. Daughter of John Kingston.'

He was at once filled with a kind of despair. There would be no getting rid of her now. And God, a female version of Byron: could things get worse? A right little bitch, Charles had said, and he the most charitable of men. 'Oh. I see. I see it all now.'

'Oh good.'

'You don't look like your photo. What happened to the pig-tails?' Alan said this in a spirit of unambiguous malice. She just gave him a look. 'I'm Alan Fairs,' he countered.

'Oh good,' she said again, not without bitterness. 'Well, good morning, Alan Fairs.' She extended a hand to him. It was smaller than he expected, and had rather a lot of rings on it. The clasp was surprisingly businesslike.

'Good morning – er, Jacinta?'

'I know, silly name. Friends call me Jass, mostly.'

'Jass?'

'Or Jassie.'

There was a pause. Alan could see no escape from it, though he certainly tried. He had better ask her in. Perhaps she would ask him to punch her in the stomach. That was a cheering thought. 'Er well, would you like a cup of coffee?' He did not even try to say her name. There were, after all, limits.

'Yes please. Very much.'

'Or a beer?'

'Oh God, it's easy to see I'm back among Hong Kong whites, isn't it?'

'For Christ's sake, I'm only being civil.'

'Don't yell at me. I know about Hong Kong, and I know about Hong Kong piss-carts, too. Yes please, coffee would be excellent.'

'Well, good. I'll make it. Come in, if you want. There's plenty more to criticise inside.'

She smiled at that; Alan wasn't quite sure if he had wanted her to smile. 'Thanks.'

The kitchen was full of steam, for the kettle had been boiling merrily throughout the conversation, but there was still a good deal of water left. Alan made two cups of coffee wondering what to do next. He seemed to be rather stuck with her. At least for the moment.

'All right if I put my pack down here?'

'Sure. Unless you want to do any hiking.'

'Hey, aren't those my cushions?'

'Your dad lent them to me.'

'Bloody decent of him.'

'Take them bloody well back, if you want.'

'Is that your entire library?'

'More or less.'

'Don't you read anything except James Bond books?'

'Don't even read them much. I've got them pretty well by heart.'

'Are you joking?'

'Test me if you like.' He fetched milk from the fridge and added it to the coffee.

She read aloud: ' "Bond had never cared for Orleans." '

'Oh, that's when he's chasing Goldfinger across France. Sugar?'

'Good God. Yes, three.'

They returned to the garden of concrete. 'So what are you doing here, er . . . ?' He couldn't make his tongue say Jassie.

'I've come out to see my dad for Christmas.'

'Oh yes. I'd forgotten that aspect of the day. Happy Christmas.'

'Thanks a lot. And the same to you.'

'Yeah, well.'

'Dad gave me money last time he was back home. Said it was to buy a ticket to Hong Kong, so I could come out for Christmas.

'Oh yes. I thought you pinched the money and ran off with it.'

'Who said that?'

'Your little brother.'

'My little brother, yes. You obviously have a great deal of affinity with my little brother.'

'Haven't you?'

'No. I didn't pinch the money. I added to it. I worked, and got some more money, and bought a round-the-world ticket. Came here after spending a few months in India.'

'On your own?'

'Off and on.'

Alan let that go. 'I see.'

'And so I ended up here on Christmas Day, just as I'd planned all along. And it's all gone bloody wrong.' Suddenly there was a sense of tears pricking the air, invisible, unshed.

'No, Jassie, it's gone all right,' Alan said, with sudden immense decision. 'I was going to walk over the island and have lunch on the other side, on my own, and then walk back. Would you like to come with me? My treat. In every sense.' Alan listened to himself, appalled. It was as if a devil were speaking through his mouth. It was as if he were actually enjoying the hostilities of this conversation. The invitation had been uttered much in the way that no one can resist biting on a bad tooth.

She turned and looked at him. Her eyes were not actually purple after all. Yes they were. 'Thank you, Alan. I'd like that very much.'

'Happy Christmas, Jassie.'
'Happy Christmas.'

They stopped at the highest point of the island crossing and sat for a while. From there, they could see both sides of the island, Cheung Chau and the open sea to one side, the Tung Lung Channel and Hong Kong on the other. She had climbed without palpable effort, in her long black velvet skirt and ridiculous boots that could have taken her up Everest.

'You live in a wonderful place,' she said.

'I know.'

'And you spend your life sitting around in the village drinking beer with my dad and reading James Bond.'

'There's good stuff in James Bond.'

'It's all complete tosh.'

And so Alan quoted Bond to her, for he had, as he said, got the books pretty much by heart. Bond, brooding over his latest killing as he sipped a double bourbon: 'Life had gone out of his body so quickly, so utterly, that Bond had almost seen it come out of his mouth as it does, in the shape of a bird, in Haitian primitives . . . the thing that had gone out of the stinking Mexican bandit was greater than all Mexico.'

At the far side of the island, they had feasted; feasted royally on beer and the fruits of the sea. And they talked.

She spoke a good deal of her father, his wildness, his irresponsibility – 'let's be honest, Alan, his perfect madness. Just another boozy Hong Kong fantasist.

'After he had his first set of disasters here, way back, he went to Australia. It was easier then. That's where he met Mum, and I was born soon after. Then he went back to Hong Kong, and Mum and I came too, though not at once, I don't think. And then Byron was born, and we lived in Hong Kong for about ten years. Till I was about fourteen. Then we all went to England. Dad more or less had to leave. He couldn't settle in England, though, and came back to Hong Kong, and Mum despaired of him. I'm awfully fond of the old bugger – can't help but be, he means so well, but, well, you can't take him seriously, can you?'

And Alan, who had taken King with perfect seriousness for a year, agreed easily.

'Basically, you see, he's mad. I sometimes think people go mad unless they're in the right place. It worries me because I spent most of my life in Hong Kong, but I don't feel it's anything to do with me at all. At the same time, I'm not really English. And I hardly remember Australia at all.'

And Alan had talked about his own dislocation, his own sense of place. And he told her about Charles, of course. 'I don't suppose Charles and King and I would have been friends anywhere else in the world. Certainly not in UK. Perhaps not even on Hong Kong. But out here on Tung Lung, we became – not quite a family. More like a team. But it was a magic period of my life.'

'What's so magical about drinking and talking? Expats do it over the world. I've seen it in Hong Kong all my life.'

'On Tung Lung, it's been special.'

'Self-destruction is always special.'

'I'm not self-destructive.'

'What about everybody else?'

Alan felt wounded to the heart, wanted to cause pain in his turn. 'Your dad has taught me –'

'Dad and his cronies. I know. I've seen it before, remember. Always Dad and his cronies, always drinking and talking. Every time I see it, it always reminds me of my mum talking about the Aboriginals in Australia. Nothing to do but sit down and drink themselves to death, because their civilisation has gone.'

'My civilisation's gone?'

'No. Aboriginals live in the wrong time. You only live in the wrong place.'

It was said to wound, but Alan had a weird feeling that no harm was intended. To justify himself, he talked of his work, journalism and paid editorial.

'What an unbelievable waste of time.'

'So what have you done to put the world straight? Travelling from country to country as you've been doing, what is the great point in that?'

'I'm going to Australia. That's the idea. Perhaps to settle there. I have an Australian passport, you see. Mum insisted on that. I might have a place there, I don't know. Australia is still inventing itself, so they say. I'd like to try. I'd like to *see*.'

And on and on. She had gone to India with a boyfriend, had travelled round together. It had been good. But he 'went off with a hippified bimbo in Goa'.

'The fool.' Alan hadn't intended this piece of vague gallantry. A devil, a gallant one, was speaking through his lips. But she smiled: rather more, he thought, than the remark was worth.

Alan looked at her: the overstated black-lined eyes that were, or perhaps were not, purple; the nose-jewel in the form of a dolphin. What the hell was she trying to be?

At last there came a point when they had to leave the restaurant or cross the island in darkness. So they moved, and once in motion, became hilarious. As they approached the highest point once again, laughing and gasping and protesting that they would never make it, Alan reached out a hand and in jocular fashion hauled her to the summit.

Then they sat, side by side, and they looked across the generous flat spaces of the South China Sea, the darkening sky, the first lights of Tung Lung village shining below them. And Alan though of death and of the thunderbolt, and Jassie asked: 'Why the sigh, Alan?'

'It just wasn't fair, was it?' he said. 'That's what I can't stand about it all. It just wasn't bloody well fair.'

She sighed in her turn. 'Let's go home,' she said.

'Home?'

They followed the path down in fading light. A light air tugged at them, chilling but somehow cheering. They reached the small beach, and stood for a while, looking out. On the sea, the lights of passing ships.

'Like toys,' she said.

'Maybe.'

'Yes, all like toys, this is bloody Toytown, after all.'

'Oh, for fuck's sake, Jassie, stop insulting my home.'

'Noddy in Toytown.'

He seized her shoulders, goaded to sudden anger. Kissed her with a kiss of fury. And was kissed back. Did something leave his mouth, or her mouth, in that instant, leave in the form of a bird? And was that thing greater than all Hong Kong? In the form of a Bonelli's eagle, perhaps.

'I love your dolphin,' he said.

'My mother thinks I had it done to spite her.'

'Did you?'

'Maybe. But I had always wanted a nose-jewel, and the dolphin stole my heart away.'

'And mine.'

He kissed the dolphin and the nose. Then a party of Hong Kong youths crossed the beach, their several ghetto blasters booming competitively, and Alan and Jassie resumed more decorous positions. And talked of course.

'It's all changed, you see. With Charles. But I don't know *how* it's changed. I love it here. I was all set to stay for ever and to be a Hong Kong Belonger and so on. But I don't know now.' Alan had not thought such thoughts before.

'It's the same with me. I thought I was cutting loose but all the while I was just coming out to the place I grew up in, to see my dad for Christmas. And the bugger isn't here.'

'I am,' Alan said.

The ghetto blasters were fading away, and another bout of grappling took them over. Eventually, they stood, giggling again, and brushing sand off each other, a process that threatened to start the whole cycle off again. But instead, they managed to walk to the village. Alan suggested they eat food before climbing the 176 steps. 'I have nothing to offer you upstairs.' So they went to Ah-Chuen's.

'Melly C'immus.'

'Merry Christmas, Ah-Chuen.'

And it was still warm enough to sit out by the harbour, so

they drank beer, though not very much, not by Tung Lung standards, at any rate. They shared a plate of Singapore noodles, and then another one, a little later.

Perhaps the second plate was to postpone something. For a quietness stole over them. Not quite a sadness, but a faint slipping away of whatever it was that had lit the day up. Alan felt a cold, quiet fury rise inside him, but it was fury directed only at himself. He saw now that he had blown it. He had been given half a chance, that day, to change – well, everything, really. He had held it in the palm of his hand and had let it go. Fool to have let it go: fool even to have started. For the first time in the day, conversation slowed.

'Alan?'

'Yes?'

'I don't really know how to explain. You see, I think, the thing is –'

He placed his hands on both her soft shoulders. 'Doesn't matter.'

'You're terribly sweet.'

Alan was possessed by a terrible coldness at this. 'I have often been told that terrible sweetness is my best quality. Come. Let's be away.' But it was not the terrible sweetness that accompanied his lame courtship of Sophie, not the same thing at all.

At the top of the stairs, back in the flat, he made jasmine tea, of all things, feeling that beer would be inappropriate. They drank it sitting on the cushions, at right angles to each other. Not touching. A shame, Alan thought, remembering, that they were not both naked. That would have simplified matters.

They argued about the cushions. 'No, no, I insist.'

'I am not depriving you of your bed. I feel bad enough –'

'Nothing to feel bad about.'

'I just feel so –'

'It simply doesn't matter, Jassie.'

'Lost.'

Alan sighed. He was to be deprived even of the comfort of disliking her. He leant over and, careful to make his moves seem merely affectionate, kissed. A tear escaped the possible purple of her eye.

'I wish you would stop being so nice to me.'

'I'll be horrible in the morning. We'll regroup then. Boxing Day, remember. No work. Day of ritual licence.'

They manoeuvred politely around the rituals of the bathroom. Alan took a shower first, emerging in his sarong, wondering if the sight would stir Jassie into wild ecstasies of passion. But he did not press the point, merely blowing a kiss to where she sat, unhappily, on the cushions and on her now unrolled sleeping bag.

He lay in bed for a while thinking of her. He heard her walking about the flat, and then the splash of the shower. No, she had blown it too, had she not? She too had held the moment, lost it. She too had retreated from the abyss. There was, of course, no lock on the bathroom door. He thought about bursting in to surprise her, though not with any intention of actually doing so. It was just a pleasant thought. Then after a pause, he heard her clattering about in the kitchen. She must be making coffee. Foolish girl. He thought he would never get to sleep himself, but he was wrong.

She was wearing a large T-shirt. The neck had slipped a little, revealing a soft, round shoulder. There was a mole on the shoulder. Her face had been cleansed of make-up, the bold black lines gone, and she looked absurdly young. Her hair had been brushed and brushed. Only the dolphin, leaping from the wing of her nose, spoke of adventure. She was sitting on the side of his bed, looking down at him. He wondered for how long she had been doing this.

'Hello,' she said.

'Hello.'

'I think I've changed my mind.'

As if in a dream, Alan smiled. And he was right. There was

not, he was soon pleased to have confirmed, a straight line in her. Not anywhere.

That night Alan dreamt of a dolphin. He watched it leap and plunge and roll; he watched it jump high into the air and return to the water splashless, spinning and curvetting for the joy of it, and he knew that the dolphin was Charles. And he awoke and he told the dream to Jassie and she asked if he were the dolphin too. So the day began. They made love, they shouted at each other, they roared. They had friendly arguments that always escalated, always climaxed with more love. It was awful. It seemed that everything was allowed now. The most hurtful things could be said, the most shameful things confessed. It was indeed a day of ritual licence: a day stolen out of time.

They dressed at last as night was falling and the long naked day was ending, and they descended the 176 steps for a meal at Ng's. Ng, the favour long since called in, gave his usual cold nod as he watched them from his high desk. No ritual licence for him, only the clicking of his abacus, as if calling Hong Kong to order.

At length they climbed the stairs again, and entered the flat, too spent to make love again, but they did anyway. And afterwards, they lay, as lovers do, Alan on his back and Jassie on his arm, both looking at the dark ceiling and planning how their lives should be for ever different. Such conversations need a place, and so they spoke of Australia. It was the place to be, she said. Alan explained that he knew two Australian journalists from his days on local papers, and both had returned, one to Sydney and one, he thought, to Melbourne, or maybe Perth. Both said to look him up: it was a start, wasn't it? Scientists say that God dwells in the details; perhaps, Alan thought, that was also true of love.

But what of staying there? Surely they didn't let you just turn up and work, did they? 'Remember I've got an Australian passport.'

'That's a good start, anyway. But I haven't.'

'There are ways round that. You could marry an Australian, for example.'

This small remark grew and grew in the silence until it filled every corner of the room. 'Why not?' he said.

'We'll talk about it in the morning.'

But they did not. Instead, they had a titanic shouting match. Alan had thought that Boxing Day was excessive; this went beyond anything he had ever known. He could not believe it was himself that he could hear, howling and bellowing, as if this, too, were part of the dream.

Jassie was going to Hong Kong. She was going to find her father, stay with an old schoolfriend. She wanted to think things over.

'Alan, I've had enough trouble in my life from one Hong Kong piss-artist. Please understand that I might have second thoughts about tangling myself up with another.'

And she had gone.

You know Alan Fairs? Well, you know what I mean, then. Classic Hong Kong type. I mean, a really good solid Hong Kong man. Above all else, a survivor, you know?

The panoply of Hong Kong commerce stretched out before him; the ramparts and castellations of Central behind him, the eternal boat-thronged harbour before him. Alan sat on Blake Pier and considered his future and the great partnership that lay in front of him.

Everything was fixed now. Strange: the terrible, wild events of the last few days had not unsettled him at all. Quite the reverse. Not even that desperate meeting with Bill. No, nor the midnight encounter with André that seemed to turn all reality upside down. And the madness with Jassie, the mad making of plans: these did not fill him with restlessness. Not any longer.

No. Quite the reverse. He was reconfirmed: a Hong Kong

man. The great lunch with Jim seemed to have settled all questions. Good operator, Fairs. When he says he'll deliver, he'll deliver. It was a just a small, one-title operation when he and his partner, James, took it over. But they know the markets, you see. And rock solid, nothing fly-by-night about their operation. That's what made it the institution it is today. Oh sure, Fairs is the best editor in town, everybody says so. Good to freelances, too – he used to be one, himself, way back. Hundreds of other publications have tried to poach him, but he got where he is by sticking to it.

Alan sipped at his drink, as he sat there in the café at the end of Blake Pier. It was disgusting: it was coffee. But it was right to drink it. No, he was not going to be one of those sad Hong Kong figures with his corner seat at the bar and the never-empty glass before him. That much was decided; Bill had decided him. There would be no more madness in his life: not like the past year, like the past few days. Madness had gone, with Charles, with King, with André; and, thank God, with Jassie. That was no doubt an important part of the Hong Kong learning process: and he was beyond that stage now.

Oh yes, old Fairs has things very well sorted out. *HK Biz* does awfully well, of course, and then there was *HK Computing*. Fairs keeps a fatherly eye on it, as editor-in-chief. Talking of fatherly eyes, what does he do domestically? Is he one of those weekend-in-Bangkok types? Oh no, not old Fairs. Married his secretary, oh, years ago. Standard Hong Kong marriage. Very nice Chinese girl; I think there's a couple of kids. He's very well set up, is Fairs. Everything's going for him.

That reminded him. It was surely six months since he had been to Hong Kong and got his passport blessed. Time to do it again. Six more years and he would be a Belonger. Vote in municipal elections. But it wasn't the voting that mattered. It was the belonging.

Poor old Jassie. That was a crazy kid. Where was she? No telling. And all he could do was to send her good vibes. She would certainly need them now, with the news about King. He wagged his head wisely over his coffee. Lord, but he was well out of that. Taken leave of his senses for two days. Which was all very well for two days. But no. Part of the real world now. And a more important partnership lay ahead. Not one that would change his life: one that would reconfirm it.

It had been towards work that he turned almost the instant that Jassie left. He had thought briefly about beer, but with Jassie's last gibe still ringing in his head, he went instead to the telephone. Turn to work, to hide from reality, or from dreams. To find his level of Hong Kong sanity once again.

He had gone into Hong Kong on the day of Jassie's departure, catching the noon ferry. If he had some wild fancy of finding her meeting it, or of meeting her in full repentance, he was able to control it.

At *HK Biz* he found Reg uncharacteristically distant and pre-occupied. Alan assumed that his mind was filled with impossibly minute Thai women accepting his embraces with Buddhist resignation. He had not been to Bangkok since Charles's death, but he was off again for the New Year. This did not coincide with the completion of an issue this time, but there was much to be done to get the following issue to the printers before the Chinese New Year break that followed hard upon.

'Hey, Reg. You've forgotten to scheme in the Regional Round-up.'

'Oh God, no wonder the mag looks a bit thin.'

'Not like you, Reg.'

'Sorry, Alan. Lot on my mind at the moment. Business decisions and so on.'

'What's up, Reg? You going bankrupt? Am I out of a job?'

'No it's all looking pretty good, actually. But I'll let you know in a couple of days, if everything gets sorted out.'

And that was as much as he gave away.

And perhaps there was a way of tracing her, if only he could think of it. Or perhaps she would be back at his flat when he returned – sorry, Alan. I think I may have changed my mind. Yes, all right, and maybe she wouldn't. Though maybe King or André would be back, and the great Tung Lung cycle could begin again. And maybe they wouldn't, and maybe Jim would be spending the evening in town, and thinking things through. He really did not care for the idea of a full evening alone.

So he rang Bill at the *Hong Kong Times* and they arranged to meet that evening. Country Club at about eight? There was a fractional and distinctly odd pause before Bill agreed. Perhaps Simpson was passing by the subs' desk. Wally was on a day off, he said, so it would be just him. Fair enough, see you at eight, Bill. How to fill in the time between finishing at *HK Biz* and meeting Bill? He rang Belinda: she would be delighted to meet him for a drink.

They met at the Fragrant Harbour, not at André's favourite rooftop bar with the cheongsam-wearing ladies, but at the bar in the lobby, a far more businesslike establishment. Or 'outlet' as you had to call them when writing in *Asian Hotelier*. It was one of the great Hong Kong places for a working drink.

'So have you heard that Fragrant Harbour are opening a new hotel in Singapore?'

'No, really?' What was the name of the girl André had known in Singapore? No really, impossible to remember.

'It's to be called Lion City Hotel, too dreary, and they want me to go to the opening. It's in two weeks and I really can't.'

'Belinda, are you making me an indecent proposal?'

'I expect it will be heaven and I'll regret for ever not going, but there's a bash at the Repulse Bay Hotel and I really am not going to miss that. So will you go to Singapore for me?'

'Why don't we both go to Singapore, Belinda? It's a place that might weave the spell that our relationship lacks.'

'Our relationship is perfect as it is, Alan. I hope nothing ever sullies it.'

She was indeed a delightful person to work for; and Alan was more than delighted with the idea of a little trip at last. Yes, Fairs, always popping off somewhere or other, knows the region like the back of his hand. Angel? No that was the Taiwanese midget.

He said his farewell to Belinda with a cheek-kiss and then, having time in hand, went to a more sordid drinking establishment to fill in. There was no one he knew; he sat, sipping San Mig and watching a pair of pear-shaped gentlemen playing yah-tze at the end of the bar. It seemed an eternity since he had last rolled the dice. He thought of King, and of his daughter. And of his own lucky escape. A holiday romance with pretensions to be something else.

He finished his beer at his leisure, in fact, in growing content. He then swooped the length of King's Road in a taxi, getting dropped off at the corner. He walked towards the *Hong Kong Times* building. Lord, how life had given him a good roll of the dice when he had been fired. He remembered the crippling boredom as he worked at Johnny Ram's behest; the despair of his walk to Central the night the blow, the immaculately disguised blessing, had fallen.

Bill had not arrived, but the old man at the Country Club recognised Alan. 'Hello.'

'Hello.'

'Hello.' What was Cantonese for how are you? Was it *Nei ho ma*? Or was that what's your name? He mimed for a table and two chairs, and asked, this time in adequate Cantonese, for two cans of San Mig. He was furnished with all he asked for, and a roll of lavatory paper as well.

He pulled the ringpull, dispatched it into the gutter, sipped. Solids, yes, good idea. He asked in English for peanuts.

'Aaa?'

'Peanuts?'

'Aaa!' The old man, his face a traditional Chinese painting ('The Enlightenment of Lao-tzu'), held up a packet of peanuts.

'Hoho! M'goy lei!'

'M'sai!'

And there was Bill walking towards him. 'If you're hoping to get your job back you've got no fucking chance.'

'Hello, Bill. Here's a beer.'

'Oh, er, thanks, er, actually –' he turned to the store-keeper. 'Yat goon olok m'goy.'

Olok? Bill accepted with thanks a can of Coca-Cola. He opened it, said cheers, and drank from it.

'You all right, Bill?'

'Well, actually –'

'Antibiotics!' Alan said. 'Mystery virus. Picked up a nail in Wanchai, dirty bastard. It's all right, your secret's safe with me.'

Bill looked at the floor, at the can, and then sought Alan's eye. And uttered, not without effort, the traditional sentence, one he had clearly practised a good deal, but which he still could not say quite right.

'I'm an alcoholic, Alan.'

There was nothing for it but to hear the details. For Bill, sobriety lay in the details. Afterwards, much of it became jumbled up in Alan's mind, the mixture of pride at past excesses, self-awareness at this and other examples of 'characteristic addict behaviour', his uncanny ability to maintain professional standards in order to remain employed and therefore to pay for his drink. That too, apparently, was typical addict behaviour. The amounts that he used to drink. How much he needed before going to work. The bottle in the desk, of course. The binges. The DTs, and his assault by a legion of parrots.

One detail stayed in Alan's mind. 'I remember,' Bill said, 'putting my jacket on in the morning to go to work. And finding the pockets full of vomit.'

'It wouldn't stay in,' Alan said.

'Don't be fucking silly, of course it wouldn't. I mean *dried* vomit. I put my hands in my pockets and I felt dried vomit.'

'How did it get there?'

'How the fuck should I know?'

'I mean did you throw up into each of your jacket pockets in turn?'

'Something like that, I suppose. I'm a tidy person – you know that from my work. And I suppose I just thought that this was a nice, neat and tidy way of disposing of the problem.'

'I see.'

'Look, Alan, I must be getting back.'

'Let 'em get on with it. Have another Coke.'

'I'd love to, Alan, but I can't. I'm chief-subbing tonight, Johnny's night off. I'm Johnny's deputy, now. I got promoted.'

'Do they know? At the *Times*?'

'Yes, Simpson was great about it, actually. But I must go.'

They shook hands, more formally than usual. And Alan wished him luck and congratulations. 'I'm so glad you put these problems behind you.'

'There are a few things I still find difficult, Alan.'

'Such as?'

'Getting up in the morning. Putting my clothes on. And so on.'

It was astonishing how often he saw Charles. Not so often on the ferry, but among the crowds of Central or in the hurrying throngs of Wanchai. For a fraction of a second he would catch a glimpse of him, generally from the rear, a figure about to turn to him that very second, hello you bastard, why aren't you buying me a beer, come I know a very sordid little bar not a million miles from here. But almost at once it would be apparent that the figure was nothing like Charles at all. Funny. He did not have the same experience with King or with André, and he was seriously expecting to see them at any moment. Jassie would no doubt have said that he really was seeing Charles in that splinter of time.

Well, he wouldn't be seeing her that night, would he? He was getting close to the ferry pier now. He had planned to go to a bar after leaving the Country Club, but that was somehow not possible after his meeting with Bill. Instead he had walked, repeating his hike of the night of the dreadful sacking, the night the blow or blessing had fallen. And in the same way, he was eaten up with worry about his past, his present, his future, his mind filled with bleak self-examinations, terrors barely kept at bay by the rhythm of his walk. I've had enough trouble in my life from one Hong Kong piss-artist. Please understand that I might have second thoughts.

He saw Charles very briefly among a group of revellers in Lockhart Road, and then again in the passengers leaving the Star Ferry. Walking kept troubles at bay. He arrived at the Outlying Islands ferry pier a little after half-past ten, and climbed on board the waiting boat. He walked to his, Charles's, favourite place at the very back. He sat there for a while and then placed the heels of his hands in his eyes. At once, unbidden, a face appeared before him. Eyes tough, tender, and possibly purple. Funny. He had tried, off and on, to conjure her face before him all day. No, he told himself very firmly. She will not be there. Not be sitting naked on the cushions. My, what a time you've been, sorry about this morning.

He was well out of it, was he not? Two days was enough. The engine roared and bore him backwards into the harbour. And then the boat swung around and set sail for Tung Lung.

'G'dye, digger. You pissed again?'

Alan took his hands from his eyes. Jim was wearing one of his more restrained suits, this one a kind of mushroom soup colour, with a yellow shirt unbuttoned to the bottom of the sternum. 'Evening, Jim. All well?'

'Really fucking excellent, as it happens. Really really really excellent. Here's a beer. Drink it.'

'I won't, actually, Jim.' He felt weak pride flow through him as he said this.

'Christ, call the helicopter, major emergency.' Jim ripped the top off the can and drank from it himself.

'So how's businesses, Jim?'

'What have you heard?' The question was darting, suspicious, quite unlike his usual manner.

'Heard?'

'Why are you asking me about business?'

'I ask everybody about business. Standard Hong Kong manners.'

'Aw, Christ yes, I'm an arsehole. Sorry sorry sorry. Been

involved in some rather delicate negotiations; don't want 'em public just yet.'

Alan thought this was nothing less than nonsense. Jim sliding away on another of his millionaire fantasies. 'Sure.'

'Might affect you rather closely, you see.'

Why was it that the vain could not be trusted even with their own secrets? 'What is happening, Jim? You going to evict me from my flat and get me sacked from all my magazines?'

'What the fuck have you heard, God damn it?' Jim was quite alarming in this sudden rising of anger.

'Jim, calm down. I've heard nothing. That was a joke. I quite often make jokes, remember?'

'Look, I'm sorry, Al. Bit on edge. Come and have lunch with me tomorrow. We'll talk it through then.'

'Is it good news or bad news?'

'It's the best news. The best. Do you know something, Al? We're going to mica fackunmillion.'

'I can hardly wait.'

The ferry turned past Green Island and out into the Tung Lung Channel. The boat heaved about a little as Jim talked of the drunken japeries and elaborate feasting of his Christmas. The ferry arrived and they climbed the 176 stairs companionably.

'I wonder if there'll be any sign of our neighbours,' Alan said.

'What makes you say that?' Jim asked.

'Just wondering where they might have got to.'

'You mean you haven't heard anything?'

'No. Have you?'

'Not exactly, no.'

I'm imagining things, Alan thought. My nerves are on edge. I haven't had enough to drink. They walked in silence along the terrace at the top.

'You coming in for a beer, Al?'

'I won't thanks, Jim. Got a lot on tomorrow.'

'Fair enough. But hey, looks like you got company anyway.'

It did. Lights shone from his windows and the front door was open. I must start using the key, Alan thought. It would be easier on my heart. 'Will you come in?' he asked. 'Since I seem to have company?' It took an effort to offer this standard politeness.

'Er no, I'll leave it, thanks, Al. See you tomorrow.'

'The French place, sure. Good night, Jim.'

They parted at their side-by-side doors in the concrete garden. Alan, heart pounding like an Olympic sprinter awaiting the result of a photo finish, called out, 'Hello?'

No one in sight, clad or unclad.

A voice called from, of all places, the cupboard, the one which lay under the stairs that led to King's flat. 'Hello, my dear.'

Curiosity and disappointment fought for the mastery.

André emerged from the cupboard. He was wearing jeans and his Harlequins jersey; his hair shining and curled from recent showering. But his eyes were almost cosmically tired, as if he had been to the end of the universe and back, sunken and red-rimmed from the stresses of faster-than-light travel. He looked a dozen years older; perhaps he had been spinning round the earth in the wrong direction. 'My dear old thing, how are you keeping?' There was plenty of the old dash about his manner, but for once, the effort showed.

'André, are you all right?' He had never asked such a question before; never, it seemed, had needed to.

'Up to a point, my dear. Better than I have been, anyway.'

'Well, welcome home, anyway. Have you got a beer? By the way, what on earth are you doing in the cupboard?'

'Haven't got round to stealing a beer yet. Fact is, I've been trying to steal something else.'

Alan went to the fridge, took two beers, put one back, and gave the other to André. 'Shall we sit down?' he suggested, feeling a strange formality about these proceedings.

'I was looking for a suitcase I could steal,' André said.

'But, André, you always have so many suitcases of your own.'

'Alan, my dear, I will tell you the tale. But if you could lend me a suitcase you would be saving my life.'

'Help yourself. Since it's a matter of life and death. There's a big holdall under my bed, use it for carrying laundry into town.' Alan sat down on the cushions; André went into the bedroom and returned with the bag, tossed it lightly onto the floor and then sat himself down on the cushions and drank more beer. 'Thanks, my dear.' It was prettily said.

'Where have you been, André? Judging from the state of you, it must have been one of your better trips.'

André laughed briefly. 'Fair comment. Yes, one of my better trips. Fact is, I've been in prison.'

Alan would have spilled his beer had he been drinking any. The thought was impossible. But the fact was that such fabled places as Siam and Cathay were far more the stuff of everyday life. 'André, you poor thing, what's happened? Have you escaped?'

André laughed. 'Something like that, yes.'

'Well, tell me all.' Alan felt a sudden fear, rather a base one, that he was going to be asked to perform some difficult, dangerous and illegal task to facilitate André's escape from justice. Worse, that he would go along with it from feeble companionability.

'Perhaps not quite all,' André said, recovering something of his bantering poise.

'Let me guess then. Something to do with those three bags you left at the Fragrant Harbour Hotel.'

'Those bags? Christ, I forgot you knew about them.'

'Only risked bloody life and liberty for them,' Alan said, rather miffed that his role in Alan's affairs had been lightly forgotten.

'Anyway, nothing to do with them. Or I might have been in serious trouble.'

'You mean you're not in serious trouble?'

This time André laughed outright. He stretched out his legs and placed his heels, in their tennis shoes, on Alan's low table. 'Well, it could have been an awful lot worse. I think I'm going to be all right, you see. What happened was that someone informed on me. Got a bit cross that a gweilo was making so much money. Bastard. I had arrived back in Hong Kong on the Macau ferry in time for Christmas, but I got stopped by Customs.'

'They found your demon deodorant?'

'Jesus, the things you know. No, they didn't, thank Christ.

Found some other stuff. Rather funny, it was, in retrospect, because I was carrying it, and it contained some faintly important stuff. One of them shook it and squirted a bit on his hand, even tried to unscrew it, but twisted it the wrong way. I really was most awfully lucky. In a way. They found enough stuff to hold me on, but really, it was count-your-blessings time. I was up before the beak on Christmas Eve, remanded in custody over Christmas, up before the beak again today, and this time I got bail.'

'Congratulations. If that's the right thing to say.'

'Oh it is. Because I'll not stand still. The charge they're holding me on – that's nothing, two or three months at most, more likely a fine. But they'll try and get something else on me. I know they've been tipped off and I know they haven't found what they expected to find. That was clear from the interrogation. And they'll look all the harder now.'

'The Fragrant Harbour bags?'

'They just might have something to do with it. Best I don't tell you exactly what. In fact, you know too much already. I've been insanely indiscreet. Lord, I wasn't cut out for this business. What do they want with all these laws? Have you got any more beer?'

Alan fetched him one, managed not to take one for himself, savouring another moment of self-delight. 'So what's next, André?' he asked, resuming his place on the cushions.

'Catching a plane tomorrow, best you don't know where. To regroup. After, I don't know. Might try Saudi. Have to think it through. Main thing is to get out of Hong Kong.'

'Is that allowed?' Alan asked.

'Of course it's not allowed, you bloody fool!' André laughed with sudden real delight. For the first time since Alan had found him in the cupboard, he seemed relaxed.

'All right, sorry, silly question. But honestly, André, how will you manage? Did they confiscate your passport? Won't you be on the stop-list at the airport? And what about bail – won't you lose that?'

'Correct on all three counts. But there are ways, you know.'

'Oh, come on, André. Not a lot of point in being mysterious now, is there?'

'Fair point. Well, the bail was put up by a friend of mine, who will lose the money, but will gain instead the contents of three suitcases. Which are no longer to be found at the Fragrant Harbour Hotel. I have a ticket for Bangkok already. Remember Pearl? Perhaps you never met her, but anyway she works in a travel agency and she fixed it for me.'

'And what clever stuff have you done about passports and so forth?'

'Fact is, I've got another one. Not in the name of André Standing, either. Got a bank account in the new name too. Shame there's not more money in it, but some, anyway.'

'Will it work?'

'It's worked before.'

There was a pause. 'André, you are cleverer than I thought. More crooked than I thought, too.'

André laughed. 'Thanks for your confidence, my dear. Oh, and that reminds me, I have another tale to tell. I met a friend of ours in prison, who was also on remand.'

'Who, for God's sake?'

'Isn't it obvious?'

'André, my mind has taken quite enough punishment over the last couple of days. Couldn't begin to guess. Charles's father?'

'Nice try. No, King.'

'*What?*' This was like a slap in the face, one that dazed and left the wits scrambled.

'King.'

'I don't understand.'

'John Kingston is in prison. Bumped into him in the exercise yard, as it happened. Managed to get a quick word. He's in bad trouble.'

'What for, for Christ's sake?'

'Debt, I think.'

'André, you can't go to prison for debt any more, can you? That's eighteenth century, debtors' prison and so forth. André, that can't be right.'

'Can't you? Well, what is it called if you write huge cheques you have no intention of paying?'

'I'd have thought you'd have known about that.'

'My dear, I always intend to pay.'

'Is it fraud? Or fraudulent dealings or something?'

'Law is not really my subject, old thing. But to use technical language, he really is *in excretum profundissimum*. As we used to say at school.'

Alan left a pause before saying: 'Poor King.' And thinking, poor Jassie, but he did not wish to discuss Jassie. And no way of telling her. 'I don't suppose King has a spare passport lying about.'

André placed his fingertips together in front of his face, giving himself the air of a schoolmaster. 'The trouble with King is that he has always tried to kid himself that he is honest. And in that endeavour, if in no other, he succeeded.'

'Not a mistake you have ever made, then, André?'

'When I was in the cadet force at school they taught me never to hold on to a fixed position too long; because a fixed position can become a trap.'

'I've just had rather a thought, André. Do you have any idea where this leaves the flat? Who do we pay rent to? Do we have security of tenure, or what?'

'Not exactly my most pressing problem right now, my dear.'

André tossed back the rest of his beer with rather a flourish. 'Look, I must get on. Pack, get an hour or so of sleep. I'm on the six fifty tomorrow, then straight to Kai Tak. Raise a glass to me at nine o'clock, because, God willing, I shall be away. So – so long, my dear. It's been great, you know. Tung Lung and all that. I'll miss you a lot. You'll understand if I don't leave a forwarding address. But I expect we'll bump into each other sometime.'

'Perhaps,' Alan said, doubtfully.

'Oh, sure to. Certain. We're both the same, you and I. Travellers. Moving on. We'll meet up in some transit lounge, or in some seedy bar in some country or other. And we'll start up all over again.'

'I suppose you're right. Well – I'll look forward to it.' They were both standing up now. André gracefully picked up Alan's holdall in his left hand, and extended his right.

'Good luck, André.'

'You too. Au revoir, my dear.'

Blake Pier coffee was foul; almost as foul as the red wine that Jim had bought for him at lunch-time. That had tasted of old lead pencils. Jim had addressed the sommelier as digger, which had gone down rather well, and had told him: 'Choose us a poky little claret, at about a hundred bucks a hit, right?' Alan had taken but a single glass. But the talk rather went to his head.

He had begun the day by getting up early and hammering out in quick time six hundred words for *Business PanAsia*. The previous morning Colin had had a gap that needed filling on his 'people section'; he had called Alan at *HK Biz* asking if he had any ideas. Alan had said yes without considering the matter, promising delivery the following morning. In the end, he reworked one of the interviews he had done for the *HK Biz* printing feature. That would be four hundred bucks: at ten o'clock he spun it from his typewriter, and made ready for the ferry.

He opened the door and stepped into the garden: yes, it was cold. Hong Kong winter was setting in. V-necked pullover, long-sleeved and navy, not ideal with the old purple herringbone, but it would have to do. Tie: would the purple one go? Better take the blue one. He rolled it briskly between his fingers and thrust it into his jacket pocket. Ten minutes to ferry time: got the copy? Yes, it was in his bag. He left, closing but not locking the door behind him. Though come to think of it, there was nobody left in his life to enter uninvited.

He walked along the harbourside as the boat began to unload its passengers. A blue streak caught the tail of his left eye: surely a kingfisher. A microsecond's thought of asking Charles if it could really have been such a bird. Though hadn't Charles talked about kingfishers one night? Yes, he had talked about halcyon days, because kingfishers had the scientific name of Halcyon.

On the ferry he asked for yat boy gafay, mo tong-aaa?, and received a Styrofoam beaker of coffee. Corrected his typing errors as the deck stirred beneath his feet. A professional, you see. Then a minibus to Causeway Bay, a man at home in his city. Gai how yow lok, he called, and the vehicle stopped at his word.

No one at reception at *Business PanAsia,* so he walked straight in. He exchanged greetings with Colin, and then watched as Colin read the copy. 'Excellent, Alan. It's all there, isn't it?'

'Of course.'

'Anything in mind for the next ish?'

'Going to Singapore in a week or so, might have some stuff for the people section from the hotel trade. Anything else I can do for you out there?'

Colin regarded the desk lamp with an air of wisdom. 'Know anything about quartz technology, Alan?'

'Course I bloody don't. I expect I could find out, though.'

'Yeah. I expect you could, too. Got a couple of people I'd like you to interview, just opened in Singapore. Interesting.'

'Yes.'

'I'll get it finalised and give you a call,' he said, meaning, he would get Dean's approval before committing himself. They shook hands, and Alan left.

This time as he passed through reception, there was someone there. 'Hello, Sophie.'

Sophie smiled slowly, and apparently lovingly. 'Alan.'

'You're looking more lovely than ever.'

'Oh, Alan.'

'Haven't seen you for ages. Has Tung Lung lost its magic for you?'

She lowered her eyes. 'Oh, Alan. You mustn't tease me. About . . . you know. Tung Lung.'

'But I love teasing you, Sophie.'

She giggled, rather intimately. 'But, Alan, you must not.' She rested her hand under her chin, in a slightly contorted way, so that the back of her fingers faced towards him.

'Give me one good reason why I should stop, Sophie.'

She giggled, and covered her mouth with her hand, really rather stagily. 'Alan.'

'Alan what?'

She giggled again, keeping her lips very close together, and lowered her voice. 'Alan, I am engaged to be married. See my ring, how pretty!'

'Oh, Sophie, how frightfully dense I am. Who is the lucky man? Tell me so I can fight a duel with him.'

'Have you not heard?'

'Not a thing.'

'Alan, I am going to marry Dean.'

'Oh, Sophie, well done. Congratulations, I hope you'll be very happy.'

'Thank you, Alan.' She smiled, lowering her eyes in sudden acute self-delight; eyes that had bewitched a publisher; eyes that had wept for André's wickedness. Alan took his leave with more elaborate courtesies. Well, he thought. It proves at least that there is life after André.

He took a taxi to the Great Orient, and then walked to the bank of phones in the lobby. He made three calls, one of which involved the taking of rather complex notes on the importation of motor vehicles. Strange, he thought. He could just spin that dial six times, and be talking to Jassie. What were the odds against hitting it by perfect intuitive chance? But he didn't try it. He was, you see, learning wisdom.

He retired instead to the gents, where he pulled his tie, blue and knitted, from his pocket, and knotted it carefully.

And Alan went to the French restaurant, pretentiously and unimaginatively (or, according to André, highly imaginatively) called Le Gourmet. 'Table for James?'

'Certainly, monsieur.'

Monsieur, indeed. The maitre d' was as French as Confucius.

Alan was shown to a table: Jim leapt to his feet to greet him. 'G'day, sweetheart.'

'G'day, monsieur,' Alan said.

'Gin and tonic? Martini?'

'I'll just have something with the meal, thanks, Jim. Got to work this afternoon.'

Jim took this in his stride, not asking any explanation for abstinence, instead ordering mineral water. He was in his mushroom soup suit again, this time with a white shirt, though he had the knack of making even white seem an outrageous colour. The tie, appropriately enough, bore the picture of a Campbell's soup tin.

The restaurant offered a choice of meals from what they called the Executive Menu. Alan and Jim chose from this, and discussed business as they ate. It was almost, Alan thought, as if they had been real executives, he a client being buttered up. For there was no doubt about it, Jim was out to soothe and charm, and this was disconcerting, though Jim did it so well that Alan had only the mildest misgivings by the time they ordered coffee.

'Want a sticky with it?'

'No thanks, Jim.'

The coffee arrived. Alan took his black, to get rid of the taste of the old lead pencils. Jim spooned sugar into his cup and stirred with a decisive little clanking noise. 'OK, sweetheart. I expect you are saying to yourself, well, this is all very nice, but why is my old friend Jim entertaining me at such vast expense?'

'I assumed you were planning to seduce me.'

Jim laughed, paused, and then laughed again. 'Yeah. Damn right. But this isn't an indecent proposal, a little quickie, coupla days and forget it. No, this is the real thing, digger. Life-long partnership and all that.'

'For richer for poorer?'

'Fuck poorer, sweetheart. Mica fackunmillion.'

'I'm all ears.'

' 'Kay. Well, you know Reg, obviously. And how he keeps talking about retiring.'

'Not to me he doesn't.'

'Not exactly retire, more like taking a back seat. He's got a great little product here, but the best thing about it is the mailing list. So the first thing to do is get this computer magazine started, catch the wave, right? Everyone in Hong Kong will be computerising over the next five years, and there's no computer mag.'

'I still don't believe computers will catch on.'

'They will, and Hong Kong will be on the cutting edge. We got the right mind-set here.'

'What does Reg think?'

'All in favour, because I'm buying into the company as a partner – equal partner, right?'

'Oh,' Alan said. This did not seem to be possible. 'Is this lunch a nice way of telling me to piss off?'

'Christ, Al, I don't work like that. When I tell you to piss off, you'll know all about it. No, I want you to work for the company full time, editor-in-chief. Get some smart kids, one to work as your assistant on *HK Biz*, another to run the computing mag under your supervision. And I'll do the rest. Sell space, I'm the best at that. So are you on board?'

'Well, I'll need to know about how much and so forth.'

'Al, trust me. We'll put a great package together. I want you on board and I'm prepared to talk stock options.'

What the hell were stock options? Alan knew what the idea meant in general terms, but that was as far as it went.

'And there'll be plenty of travel. I want you moving about the region.'

'I can't say it doesn't sound interesting. But –'

'And what do you say to rent-free accommodation?'

'Not much of a temptation, that one. I don't want to move away from Tung Lung.'

'That's what I mean, sweetheart. I'll throw in your current accommodation with the rest of the deal.'

Alan looked at Jim across the table. He picked up his coffee cup, and sipped air from it. 'And just how will you manage that, Jim?'

Jim was absolutely fizzing with hidden delight. 'Because, Al, I just happen to be your bloody landlord. Isn't that whizzo?'

'Are you serious?'

'Bloody Kingston lost the lease. He hasn't paid anything to old man Ng for about a century. I negotiated a new lease with Ng yesterday. In fact, I'm going to take over the top floor, 'cause I need more space.'

'You know King is in prison?'

'Of course I bloody do. It's been the talk of the village. Ng is the main reason Kingston got banged up; he's taken the old man for thousands, and Ng got fed up with it. So Ng and I had a little talk and got it all sorted out. Ain't that wild?'

A waiter came and filled their cups, which gave Alan a moment for thought. For there were a lot of gaps in the story. 'Jim, how do you mean, it's the talk of the village? How did you negotiate with Ng? Have you suddenly become bilingual in Cantonese?'

'Yeah, you could put it that way. You know Karen Song?'

'I introduced you.'

'So you did. Well, I owe you a lot of thanks for that. She and I are running steady now; that's why I need more accommodation. I mean, is she a smart chick or what? Loves to deal. She'll be selling space for me, too – dealing with Chinese clients, gweilos, too. And she knows this village all right, did the stuff with me and Ng.'

Alan thought briefly of the night of projectile vomiting, of her slim body, her rages, her orgies of reconciliation with the vanished André, his own brief moment of not-quite-love. 'Do I congratulate you?'

'Oh, you bet. Couldn't be better. Asked her to marry me, matter of fact. I'm keen to start up straight away, but she said no hurry, maybe in a year. We'll make it. I've got good feelings.'

'Great, Jim.'

'There are some times when the luck all starts running your way. The trick is to recognise that. And to ride it all the fucking distance.'

They parted company at the hotel entrance, Jim having paid with a lordly flourish of the credit card. Alan walked with him as far as the taxi rank, and they shook hands with great warmth.

'I'll think about all you said, Jim.'

'Yeah well, don't think. Act.'

Jim stepped into the cab, and it cruised to the street entrance. The window wound down and Jim thrust his face out. 'We're a match made in heaven!'

And Alan laughed and waved in acknowledgement.

And so he had walked to Blake Pier, having just missed the two fifty, and had sat drinking coffee. And thinking, rather than acting. Though not really thinking, either.

Soon be time to go for the four thirty.

He thought of himself again, of good old Fairs, the great Hong Kong editor, master of paid editorial. Really, you know the craziness of the last couple of days should have left him full of uncertainties. But it had not. And the mad business with Jassie, that should have left him filled with restlessness. But it had not. No, he felt certain: restful; settled.

You need these strange happenings in order to feel reconfirmed. He could face the future with a new confidence. He was a Belonger now, was he not?

The ferry was a triple-decker with a sundeck, and what's more it cost five dollars. Crowds of gweilos, perhaps a hundred or more, mingled with the Chinese commuters and schoolchildren. Where had they all come from? Where would they all go, when the end came?

The driver had met them at the airport as promised: a smiling, smartly dressed Chinese man bearing a sign that said 'Hi Al!' They were escorted to a shining white BMW, and the driver, a traditional Hong Kong swooper, but with more grace than most, swooped them through the harbour tunnel, past the Fragrant Harbour and along the new elevated waterfront road to the ferry pier.

They had timed their arrival with good fortune, for a ferry was scheduled to leave soon. But with an hourly service, missing a ferry hardly mattered any more. The boat pulled away from the pier, and Alan surveyed the cityscape. Between Blake Pier and the Macau Ferry Pier, scene of André's last and disastrous return to Hong Kong – or had he subsequently returned under his alias? – Alan counted twenty-three waterfront towers that had been built since his time. The place was unrecognisable: he would have known it anywhere. Many of the towers shone like fairy palaces in the bright winter sunlight, clad from head to foot in mirror. One gleamed gold like Mr Ng's tooth. Blake Pier itself was no more: land reclamation had swallowed it up as Hong Kong Island marched inexorably towards the mainland.

For the future that Alan had outlined for himself on Blake Pier in the dizzy aftermath of Jim's great lunch at the Great Orient had never been called into being. Because she had come back, and the great certainty that had filled him was dashed away in an instant and replaced by a thousand wild doubts: but the doubts were stronger than any certainty.

Jim told him he was mad, and he agreed proudly. So he and Jassie travelled in an arc through Thailand, Malaysia, Singapore and Indonesia, rowing bitterly, shouting incontinently, reconciling orgiastically. They made love and plans and eventually reached Sydney. A short while later, the urge to travel still strong in them, they visited New Zealand, and something in the quiet green hills undid them.

Alan found work in journalism; Jassie, recalling her horsy girlhood, picked up a temporary job in a livery yard. She was rapidly promoted head girl, and found the beginning of a new fulfilment. Loyally, Alan learnt to ride, without ever being much good. But he fell in love with the business of stable management, and later, he found in himself the knack of starting young horses. Horses brought out in him reserves of calmness that he did not know he possessed. After a few years, they opened a livery yard together, Jassie as riding teacher, himself as yard manager.

And they married, and had two daughters, who both spoke with New Zealand accents, and they continued with life's great adventure of trying to pay the bills each month.

Jassie made an annual visit to Hong Kong to see her father, but Alan never wanted to go, and could not afford to either. King had been released from jail without his case ever going to court; presumably some deal had been fixed. And strange to tell, King had worked more closely than ever with Ng after his release, though on what terms it was hard to tell. King always talked about the arrangement as if it were a partnership still, on the occasions when he and Alan spoke on the phone. Alan suspected that he had a more menial role; perhaps it suited Ng's vanity to have a kind of gweilo secretary to run errands for him.

King moved into a small flat on the main street of the village, and was mostly looked after by Chai, though Jim and Karen kept an eye on him. And after Ng had died, four or five years previously, Mark, Ng's number one son, had kept King on as a kind of old retainer. King made regular promises to visit his grandchildren in New Zealand, but never did. He was never quite the same, Jassie said, after his Christmas in jail. Even he stopped believing in himself, she said sadly.

The Tung Lung ferry pier had been extended out into the South China Sea to take the triple-deckers, and it bore an ugly roofed pavilion for sheltering waiting passengers. From the boat, you could see nothing but buildings. They waited aboard, allowing the crowd to disperse before stepping ashore. A Chinese boy, teenaged, stood before them bearing a sign, this one saying 'G'day Digger!' He took their bags from them, and then shoved his way ahead through the loiterers and the late ferry-catchers.

Alan and Jassie followed more closely. The banyan tree had gone. Ah-Chuen's café was a sizeable restaurant, many tables and chairs spread out on land reclaimed from the harbour. There was no sign of Ah-Chuen himself. Three large signs advertised three different hotels. Beside the South China Bank building stood an establishment that claimed to be an Irish pub, called Finnegan's Wake. The main street was lined with restaurants and cafés, and had a bar about halfway along, bearing a huge sign that read 'Mad Dogs'. The street tables contained many people, among them perhaps a dozen all-gweilo groups. No head was raised in curious inspection of arriving strangers.

They climbed the 176 steps, slowly and with a couple of rests, they being out of training for such exertions. The gate to Ng's palazzo, and its pug-nosed door-guarding lions, was the same. But beside it, Alan's concrete garden was a thing transformed: a green bower, with a thousand plants leaping exuberantly from a thousand containers.

Alan looked down at the valley, where the chessboard fields had been, where the beautiful Priscilla had once covered the ground in liquid excrement, where now the houses stood, houses he had helped to build with his words. But he could still lift up his eyes to the pointy hills and the South China Sea to the right. Did the Bonelli's eagle still nest there?

A pretty Chinese woman, in her twenties perhaps, welcomed them into the house, showed them to a bedroom, offered them refreshment, brought them a tray of tea and biscuits. Their room was on the middle floor, part of what had once been André's flat, though quite unrecognisable. Alan had first turn at the en suite shower, and laughed in surprise at the powerful jet of water that needled his back. He then lay dozing on the bed while Jassie showered, and then she joined him and they made love, because there was a faint sense of honeymoon about the trip, and because the presence of death makes such a thing almost obligatory. They dozed, and heard the rise and fall of Chinese voices, and later, the voices of children.

They got up soon after that, because Jim had told them that he would be back on the six o'clock ferry. They found Karen already home, having caught the five o'clock to see the children. She looked older and less slim, though not much of either. Her hair was cut in a careful casual flop onto her shoulders; she was wearing a black business suit, with a skirt, and with a soft white shirt beneath it. She looked what she no doubt was: a woman of confidence and not a little power.

She greeted them with great warmth, and they all traded news. Her voice still had traces of cockney, and also faint touches of Australia in the vowels. She showed them around the house, which was stunning, with picture windows, plants, and clean, uncluttered surfaces. She explained how she ran the establishment with a fleet of poor relations. They discussed each other's children and their schooling; she and Jim had two daughters and a son, the youngest. 'Jim is training him to be a hooligan,' she said. 'He is doing a bladdy good job.' Alan had wondered, on the plane, about stealing a moment with her alone, perhaps covering her hand with his own, and asking: 'Has it worked out for you, Karen? Are you happy, Karen?' But she was clearly a lady fulfilled and self-certain and had no need of tenderness, certainly not from him.

She talked a little about the funeral service, and suggested that she and Jassie read a Chinese poem together, she reading the original and Jassie an English translation. Jassie read the poem and cried and said the thing was wonderfully apt, but quite impossible. Alan offered to read it, and was accepted.

Jim returned, loud and grinning, and behaving as if nothing could have given him greater delight than this gathering. They shared a meal, cooked by one of the poor relations, Chinese food, naturally, and excellent. Beer and tea were served with the food. Alan had feared a sticky evening, since they had all lost the habit of each other's company, but Jim was able to make everything a delight. He had gifts that way.

He talked them through the arrangements for the funeral, or rather the cremation, the following day, and a small gathering afterwards. He asked about guests: Jassie explained that her mother would not, after all, be coming: 'I'm sad, Jacinta, of course, but frankly, I gave up mourning for him twenty years ago.' Byron claimed he was going to arrive any minute, but was not seriously expected. He was working as a security guard at London airport, X-raying people's hand-baggage.

Alan and Jim sat up for a while after Jassie and Karen had gone to bed. Jim drank Scotch. Alan drank his third, wild behaviour, beer of the day. 'You've done well, Jim. I'm pleased for you.'

'Could have all been yours, sweetheart. Half of it, anyway.'

'I told you computers would never catch on here.'

Jim laughed out loud. He and Reg had expanded *HK Biz*, and *HK Computing* had been an inevitable success. Karen took an increasingly executive role in the business. After a few years, Reg had retired, considerably richer than he had expected. He'd returned to England with his wife; Alan wondered what he did without his weekend trips to Bangkok. But perhaps it had dropped off. The company now ran Chinese language versions of both its titles, and employed a squadron of journalists and space-sellers, both gweilo and Chinese.

'You'd be a rich man if you'd stayed.'

'Tell me, Jim – have you really made a fackunmillion?'

'Sure, sweetheart. Course, it's all tied up in the business. Did you doubt me for a second?'

'Never, Jim. Will they let you keep it?'

'The Chinese? What, do you think the Chinese are going to take over Hong Kong or something? Nah. Hong Kong's going to take over China.'

'You're not worried?'

'Course I'm worried. I'm also committed.'

The cremation was a grim affair, as these things are supposed to be. There were few mourners apart from themselves. Mark Ng turned out, as escort for Chai, who looked notably ancient now, but still erect and serene. There was also an old, rather bulky gweilo who looked a little like King Lear on the heath.

Alan read his poem without tears, a triumph of self-mastery, Karen's voice firm beside him, reading slightly halting Mandarin.

> Gingerly walked the hare,
> But the pheasant got caught in the trap.
> At the beginning of my life
> The times were not yet troublous.
> In my latter days
> I have met great sorrows.
> Would that I might sleep and wake no more!

After the body had been committed to its funeral pyre, a kind of nightmare microwave, they walked out into the air. Winter sunshine cheered them: encouraged them to set aside thoughts of mortality, and of the passing of people and places and time.

'Sad business,' said King Lear. He shot at Alan a glance of disconcerting keenness. 'Know you. Met before.'

'Alan Fairs. John Kingston was my father-in-law.'

'Friend of Charles's.'

'Yes, that's right.'

He offered Alan a hand. 'Peter Browne.'

Charles's father. Alan took the hand. 'Good to see you.'

'Always meet at funerals.'

'Yes.'

'Tung Lung.'

'I lived there for a while, yes. In Charles's time.'

'Rum place. Bad thing.'

'I liked it when I was there. But perhaps you are right.'

'Know what Charles said?'

'No.'

'Told Charles to leave Tung Lung. Going bad.'

There was a disquieting silence. So Alan said: 'And what did Charles say?'

'Said, "I've been searching all my life for an island. Where the hell do you think I can find another?"'

Rogue Lion Safaris

Simon Barnes

'A delightful story . . . an exceptionally good first novel'
Mail on Sunday

Armed with his late father's trilby and a degree in zoology, Dan Lynch heads for Africa and work as a safari guide. The somewhat primitive Lion Camp is run in an endearingly eccentric fashion by George Sorensen, who is a world authority on lions and a legendary figure in the South Mchindeni National Park.

Sharing George's passion for the bush, Dan fits easily into the ramshackle style of Lion Safaris, where getting close to big game, preferably on foot, is regarded as more important than providing creature comforts. It is a policy that can lead to moments of extravagant beauty and heartstopping fear.

However, things are changing in the Park. George may be a brilliant zoologist but he is no businessman, and Lion Camp is threatened by lack of visitors, competition from a slick neighbouring operation and corrupt local politicians. While Dan is falling in love with the country (not to mention the unattainable freckled beauty Caroline Sandford) George is in danger of losing everything.

A beautiful evocation of place, a warmly observant love story, a suspenseful battle against the odds, *Rogue Lion Safaris* marks the debut of an outstanding new voice in fiction.

'Barnes has created a new category of adventure story, doing for safaris what Dick Francis has done for horse-racing, but better written'
The Times

'It has the feel and smell of the bush'
The Spectator

ISBN 0 00 649849 3

The Last Blues Dance

Ferdinand Dennis

Warm, humorous, poignant, *The Last Blues Dance* is a novel about coming to terms with love and loss, belonging and exile.

Boswell Anderson, a reformed gambler and rake, is proprietor of the run-down Caribbean Sunset Café in Hackney, far from his native Jamaica. When his friend, Stone Mason, invites him to a big poker game and the chance to win – or lose – enough money to change his life, Boswell finds the world coming into much sharper focus. In days gone by, the café was famous for its bacchanalian blues dances. Now, its former habitués have all returned to the Caribbean, or dream of doing so. Against this wistful, elegiac background, Boswell must come to terms with his past as well as sorting out the problems of the present, not only for himself, but also for the younger generation of his family.

The Last Blues Dance is a wonderfully engaging novel that weaves together the lives of a rich cast of characters, creating a sense of both community and individuality, tenderness and suspense.

'Dennis writes with abandoned, poetic relish and a contagious affection; he is a writer to watch'   *Sunday Telegraph*

'The skill the author brings to his portrayal of character is matched by the vivid realism with which he depicts place'
The Times

ISBN 0 00 649783 7

Divorcing Jack

Colin Bateman

'Richly paranoid and very funny' *Sunday Times*

Dan Starkey is a young journalist in Belfast, who shar‹
his wife Patricia a prodigious appetite for drinking and
ing. Then Dan meets Margaret, a beautiful student, and
begin to get out of hand.

Terrifyingly, Margaret is murdered and Patricia kidn
Dan has no idea why, but before long he too is a target, r
as fast as he can in a race against time to solve the n
and to save his marriage.

'A joy from start to finish . . . Witty, fast-paced and thr
with menace, *Divorcing Jack* reads like *The Thirty-Nir*
rewritten for the '90s by Roddy Doyle'   *Ti*

fireandwater
The book lover's website

www.fireandwater.com

The latest news from the book world

Interviews with leading authors

Win great prizes every week

Join in lively discussions

Read exclusive sample chapters

Catalogue & ordering service

www.fireandwater.com
Brought to you by HarperCollins*Publishers*